Praise for Rita A. Gordon

"Rita Gordon crafts masterful tales full of depth, romance and passion that always leave you desperate for more!"

— J.L. Seegars, USA Today Best-Selling Author

"Rita Gordon has proven to be a natural in the contemporary romance genre."

— Johanna McCloy, Editor, *Six Car Lengths Behind an Elephant* and *Dare to Be Fabulous*

30 Days in Belfast

***Publishers Weekly* Indie Spotlight February 2023 (Romance & Relationships)**

"An addictive, rollicking tale of friendship, love, and lust."

— *Kirkus Reviews*

"Gordon's debut offers readers a winning combination of intrigue and romance, revealed slowly through the lens of opulent travel and luxurious living."

— *BookLife Reviews*

"I loved the relationships between the characters, the storyline was heartwarming and after a while, I couldn't put it down. Would definitely recommend!"

— *LoveReading, Indie Books We Love (starred review)*

"...It's the best book I've read, period."

— Sana Aubuliel, author of *Letters to The Person I Was*

"A[n] easy, beautiful, knowledgeable read!"

— *Goodreads Reviewer (five-star review)*

Taming a King

LoveReading, November 2024 Indie Books We Love (Favorites)

"Taming a King is an eminently readable bodyguard romance for fans of the trope."

— LoveReading, Indie Books We Love (starred review)

Seven Days in Seattle

BookLife's Best of 2024 Romance

"Swoon-worthy romance indulges fantasies of wealth and seduction in Seattle."

— BookLife by Publisher's Weekly

"Readers will connect with the realistic banter whose humor and subtlety is worthy of a Hollywood script."

— BookLife Reviews, Editor's Pick

"In Seven Days in Seattle, Rita Gordon weaves a swoon-worthy story that kept me riveted until the end."

— Kenya Goree-Bell, bestselling author of The Blood Legacy Series

"...intriguing story with a complex protagonist that flouts convention."

— Kirkus Reviews

"Seven Days in Seattle is a riveting fusion of passion, sightseeing, and coincidence with twists and turns every reader will wish to experience firsthand. To Rita A. Gordon: more, more, more, please!"

— Jacqueline Luckett, author of Passing Love and Searching for Tina Turner

"Rita Gordon has proven to be a natural in the contemporary romance genre. Beyond the hot and steamy romance, Gordon also takes you on a trip to Seattle (like a little travelogue) and beautifully weaves in references to African American literature, history, music, and art."

— Johanna McCloy, Editor, Six Car Lengths Behind an Elephant and Dare to Be Fabulous

The Days with Rain

"The relationship between Rain and Parker was so deeply nuanced, packed with layers of frustration, annoyance, heartbreak, and sadness. When a book can evoke such a range of emotions, I know it's a winner."
— BookKraves, *Goodreads Reviewer (five-star review)*

The Fall of Us

"If you crave a billionaire romance that will leave you smiling from ear to ear, this is your book."
— A. Noelle Smith, author of *Shadows and Sunshine*

Other Titles by Rita A. Gordon

Standalones

30 Days in Belfast
Taming a King

Let It Rain Series

Seven Days in Seattle
The Days with Rain
The Fall of Us

Inspirational

The Book of Love

Troy

"Love makes your soul crawl out from its hiding place."
– Zora Neale Hurston

Troy

A Novel

RITA A. GORDON

12:56 a.m.
California, USA

Contents

Dedication

This is dedicated to my big sister. Peace out!

Author's Note

The character Troy Armstrong has been with me since the very beginning of my writing journey, making his unforgettable debut in the novel *30 Days in Belfast* as the unshakable protector of Rose Ross. A man of few words, his quiet strength left a lasting impression that inspired *Taming a King*, another bodyguard romance filled with suspense and heart-stopping moments.

Now, it's time for Troy to take center stage. Set two years after *30 Days in Belfast*, this story explores the man behind the stoic façade—someone whose life has always revolved around protecting others. Then came Dr. Kennedy Green, a woman who, in addition to confronting a challenging past, is pursuing the mysteries of life itself. Their story features a collision of caution and curiosity in the quest for truth. However, in their dangerous world, both characters discover that what they truly need is each other.

I hope you become as captivated by Troy and Kennedy as I was. Let their journey draw you in—you won't want to let go.

As with all my books, this one comes with a trigger warning. Please be aware that some passages in this work allude to and describe acts of gun and other violence both on and off the page, including death. As with everything I write, my intent is to *do no harm*. With that in mind, I advise you to consider your health and well-being before diving into this love story.

Prologue

Mystery of Life

"No one is so brave that he is not disturbed by something unexpected."
– Julius Caesar

Kennedy

Five years ago

"And in other news tonight, the family of famed biophysicist Dr. Winston Rutledge is looking to locals in London, England to help in the search to locate him."

The glass in my hand trembles as I stare at the TV screen, the words scrolling across the bottom like a cruel taunt. *Missing. Last seen in Oxford. Experimental AI work in evolutionary biochemistry.*

My best friend Sasha's voice cuts through the fog of disbelief settling over me. "Holy shit, Kennedy," she gasps, her hand frozen halfway to her mouth, still clutching the pizza she's been eating. "Isn't that your former professor? The one who said you'd win a Nobel Prize someday?"

My heart twists sharply, a pang of dread anchoring itself deep in my chest. "Yeah, that's him," I whisper, my throat suddenly dry. The sound of his name—*Dr. Winston Rutledge*—echoes in my mind, pulling with it memories of late-night discussions in the lab, his booming laughter as he scribbled on the chalkboard, and his endless enthusiasm when he spoke about unlocking the secrets of life.

I set my glass down with a clumsy thud, afraid my shaking fingers might betray me. "He was in the UK?" I ask, though I've already heard the answer in the news anchor's clipped tone.

"Yeah, something about a lecture at Oxford," Sasha replies, her voice tinged with worry. "The news said he vanished after leaving the venue Monday night."

I sink into the couch, my knees giving way under the weight of it all. How could this happen? Dr. Rutledge wasn't just a genius, he was the genesis behind my career.

The anchor continues, their polished tone at odds with the growing unease in my gut. "Doctor Rutledge's family urges anyone with information about his whereabouts to come forward. Authorities are particularly interested in the hours immediately following the lecture."

I grip the edge of the coffee table, my nails digging into the wood. *Immediately following the lecture.* The words claw at my thoughts. I can picture him, standing at the podium in his tweed jacket, adjusting his glasses as he fields questions with his usual dry wit. Did someone follow him? Was he targeted?

"I don't understand," I say aloud, more to myself than to Sasha. "He's brilliant, but his work isn't...dangerous. Is it?"

Sasha's brow furrows. "Didn't you once say his research could change the world? Maybe someone else thought so too—someone who didn't want to share."

The thought hits me like a slap. Could his groundbreaking work in evolutionary science have painted a target on his back?

A cold chill runs down my spine as I recall his final lecture to my class, his words now hauntingly prophetic. *"Knowledge is a gift, Kennedy, but it's also a burden. Never forget that."*

I clench my fists, my pulse pounding in my ears. "Something's not right about this," I murmur. "Dr. Rutledge wouldn't just disappear. Not willingly."

Sasha's hand lands gently on my arm. "What are you saying?"

I meet her gaze, determination hardening in my chest. "I'm saying I need to find out what really happened to him. If he's in trouble, I owe it to him to figure out why."

And as the anchor moves on to the next story, I know one thing for sure: this isn't just a mystery. It's a warning. Whatever happened to Dr. Rutledge might not be over.

And I'm not sure I want to know what—or who—is behind it.

CHAPTER I

The Assignment

"Efforts and courage are not enough without purpose and direction."
– John F. Kennedy

Troy

THE NIGHT IS STILL. Too still.

I feel it before I see him—the shift in the air, the faintest flicker of movement that doesn't belong. My pulse doesn't spike. My breath stays even. This isn't adrenaline. This is calculation. Training. Instinct honed over years of watching men like him take their final steps.

I track the assassin's approach from the shadows, watching how he moves, how he breathes, how he hesitates for just a fraction too long. A pro wouldn't hesitate. That's his first mistake. His second is stepping into my crosshairs.

This isn't personal. It never is. It's a job, just like all the others, and I don't pull the trigger unless I'm sure the target deserves it.

And this man? He does.

I lift my gun, align the sights. Exhale slow.

The weight of the trigger is familiar beneath my finger. The math of it—trajectory, velocity, impact—is already solved before I make the decision.

It takes nine months to create life but only a millisecond to end it.

Bang.

The blast of my gun ends the circle of life long before his body hits the ground.

I blink, lower my weapon, then take a deep breath. *He doesn't even know he's gone.* They never do. By the time the caliber tore through his head, shattering the bone and creating a pressure wake as it went, it turned everything surrounding it into mush, killing him. I've always wondered how long the soul takes to leave the body. I suppose if I were really curious, I could ask Siri.

"Tiger, call the cleaners," I signal to Lucien, my top strike team member, through my earpiece. The nickname "Tiger" suits him perfectly, as he possesses extraordinary agility and strength. I once saw him tackle a man, grab him by the legs, and swing him like a bat to knock down five others. They never saw it coming.

As for me, I'm fast with a gun. That's not to say I can't kill a man with my bare hands—because I can. But I prefer not to break my skin. I like things swift and clean—get in, get the mark, get out. The only trace I was here was a single bullet between their eyes and the mess it left behind.

I return my gun to its holster and rub my thumb across my knuckles. *No, it takes too long to heal these things,* I tell myself as I head back inside. It's almost daybreak. In a few hours, my client, Bill Buckner, will wake up and head to court to testify against the man who murdered his wife. Bill won't know that someone came here tonight to silence him—not until after the trial. There's no point telling him now. I eliminated the threat. If he knew, fear might shake his resolve. Right now, all that matters is he stands in that courtroom and speaks the truth.

I usually don't get involved in protection services outside of my regular clients. However, when the mayor learned that a prominent business own-er in his city had gone rogue and put a hit out on Bill Buckner, another well-known businessman, he became concerned. The mayor wanted to ensure that this criminal faced serious consequences and went to jail for a long time. When he found out that Bill had hired a security guard, the mayor grew anxious. He wanted someone reliable to ensure that Bill would appear in court to testify and help bring the perpetrator to justice. In desperation, the mayor reached out to my client for a referral, which is how I ended up in this situation.

Fortunately for him, I'm available to take on the assignment. My current client, Rose Ross, is on her honeymoon under the watchful eye of her husband, my peer, and one of Europe's most revered personal security professionals, Niall King. Between him and me, she's among the most protected private citizens in the world. At the top of that list is her father, Rick Ross, chairman of the board of Ross Enterprises, the largest company in the world.

Several hours later, Bill Buckner testifies. The jury returns from deliberation with a guilty verdict, and the defendant is convicted on all charges. With the threat eliminated, I deliver Bill home safely, leaving him back in the hands of his rent-a-cop security team. Another high-stakes job is under my belt.

Afterward, my team and I gather at Lucien's place—an impressive five-thousand-square-foot bachelor pad in a downtown high-rise overlooking San Francisco. We take turns hosting get-togethers once a month. A tradition we established over ten years ago, long before they joined my strike security team.

"To another successful win," Lucien says, holding a glass of sparkling cider.

I raise my glass of water. "Another win."

Daxton raises his glass and says, "Another one." We all sip our drinks, none of which contain alcohol. We take our bodies like our jobs seriously. "However, I am disappointed I didn't get to cut anyone open," he adds.

With his smooth baby-face appearance, curly sun-streaked brown hair compliments of mixed parentage, and custom-tailored suits, anyone seeing Daxton Day would think he's joking. He looks more like a young congressman than a knifeman. We know better. I gave him the handle "Doc" because of his surgical-like knife skills, which is his weapon of preference. It makes sense, being a former military surgeon. After he got out, he traded a scalpel for a knife. Doc can cut you open and remove your heart in seconds while you watch it beat in his hand as you bleed out. *Yeah, the man has skill.*

"Contain yourself, Doc."

"I'm good. What's next on the agenda?"

"A couple of clients contacted me for a special assignment. I need to pick up Rose when she and Niall return from holiday, so I'll be preoccupied with them. Lucien, I'll assign you and Doc to lead the next client operation."

"What about Mack?"

Mack, short for Mackenzie, earned the nickname "Bear" for his impressive strength and imposing stature. At six-eight, he's three inches taller than me. A former military special forces member and secret service officer, Mack is an essential part of my team.

"He's still on assignment with June Ross. Now that Aedan has formally retired from security fieldwork to focus on his company and care for his growing family, I've assigned Mack as their US lead," I tell them.

Aedan King, Chairman of King Enterprise and older brother of Niall, finally settled down two years ago by marrying the love of his life. When I assigned June's security detail to him, it was clear they were like oil and water. They say opposites attract, and even I could see that something would spark between them that day. Although I don't get involved with clients, Aedan and his brother have managed to find love in their own lives through their work. It shows that when your soulmate comes along, you will stop at nothing to be with them and, in their case, to protect them at all costs. I'll turn thirty-eight this year and still don't know what that feels like. If my person is out there, I have yet to meet them.

"Man, I was shocked when I heard that Aedan was stepping away from the field. His work was legendary," Lucien says in admiration. "But it makes sense—he seems happy. Wife, two kids, a company that ranks number one year after year in the European markets." He sips his drink, walks over to me, and pats me on the shoulder. "Man, you're at the top of your game. Next thing I know, you'll be announcing you're settling down with a wife and starting a family."

When he laughs, Doc almost spits his drink, then says, "Right. The man of steel takes a wife. Sounds like a cheesy daytime movie."

Lucien adds. "Or a steamy romance novel. I read one of those...*once*."

"Get the fuck outta here," Doc chides.

"Seriously, it belonged to my client. We were on one of those long transatlantic flights. Reading that shit had me hard." He pinches his chin. "Hum, maybe that's why she gave you the handle 'man of steel.' What are you not telling us, Troy?"

Man of steel. Rose gave me that handle. I'm sure she had any number of reasons for it. It's not like I wear a cape. Still, I did take a bullet for her a few years back. That shit stung. As for settling down—it's not in the cards. "Anyway. We can stop with the jokes. I don't do clients. And settling down is not happening any time soon, guys." I take a deep breath. "I doubt the woman exists that can pull me out of the danger zone." Truth is, one woman came close. But I don't say that part aloud.

"You just haven't met the right one. Then again, it appears none of us have," Lucien says.

My phone buzzes. It's Niall King. Good. I can get away from this conversation. I'd rather stick to discussing global security than getting women. I step into another room to take the call.

"Troy," I answer.

"Mate. Rose and I are heading back."

"Everything is locked in for your return."

"There's one more thing."

"I'm listening."

"Can you meet Rose at the office to set up a new employee with a device? I'm sending over the files as we speak."

"Another engineering executive?"

"Scientist."

I press my lips together and nod. "No problem. The product can be ready quickly."

"She a newbie—this will be her first foray with security."

"I got this."

"Thanks, mate."

Niall taps his screen. My phone pings, signaling that the file came through. I open it to find a picture of a young woman with her hair in braids hanging over her bare shoulders and wearing a simple sundress. With a youthful face and carefree pose, she could barely pass for a college freshman much less a famed scientist. Beneath the picture is a name and a bio: Doctor Green, biophysicist, professor, AI researcher, and a host of other impressive titles, providing insight that despite the old photo, this woman is no college freshman.

"Who's after her?"

Rose enters the screen, peering over Niall's shoulder. "No one at the moment, and I hope it stays that way. I'm recruiting her to take over a project to accelerate my work. I want only the best for the biotechnology research and development wing of RE I'm building. She is the best." She punctuates her words with pride. "I'm on a deadline to deliver the first iteration of a product for board review by year-end. The longer it takes, the greater the opportunity for those with nefarious intent to discover what we're working on."

Rose's typical approach involves finding the best and brightest women to join her team. However, this inadvertently puts them in danger due to the increased attention associated with groundbreaking technology developed by the company. As a result, her key employees shift from relative obscurity to becoming overnight sensations. The outcome is not intentional but a consequence of working for the most recognizable company in the world.

"It's not like you to be unsure you can meet your own deadline."

She comes from behind Niall. He moves the phone away, and she reappears, sitting on his lap.

They share a knowing glance before he says, "Rose is pregnant. I'm not putting my wife or our child at risk. We're dialing back on public-facing activities as she gets closer to her due date."

"That's right," Rose says. "I'll focus on RE until I go on leave, and then June will take over as acting CEO until my return. I'm keying up Doctor Green to take over and run the secret project we labeled Project Grace."

Project Grace. If it's even slightly similar to the AI technology Rose developed two years ago that disrupted the industry, Dr. Green could be in trouble.

"Congratulations are in order."

"Thanks."

"You good mate?"

"I got this."

Chapter 2

What Would You Do?

"Man selects only for his own good: Nature only for that of the being which she tends."
– Charles Darwin, *The Origin of Species*

Kennedy

Focus. You only have a few minutes left. I keep telling myself to forget about my ex, Ford, who called ten minutes before I stepped in front of an audience of my peers to say he moved back to San Francisco. Forget about him. I've done it for eighteen months and four days. I can ignore his existence for a few more minutes. *Fuck.*

I take a deep breath and continue my presentation, pretending I'm not perturbed by the news—acting like my mind isn't reeling with thoughts about what awaits me at home.

"Currently, we can use building blocks such as cellular membranes and synthetic DNA to make living organisms. However, as I mentioned earlier, the challenge is reaching chemical equilibrium, at which point the cell can no longer grow. So far, no technological advancement has successfully achieved the modular assembly of artificial cells while maintaining the non-equilibrium status of each component reaction. With my research, I believe I'm on track to develop technology that will do exactly this," I say, as murmurs sweep through the crowd in reaction to this news.

Peering over the audience of distinguished academics and peers in biophysics from around the world, I reflect on the effort it took to get here. The hours spent studying and researching—the life I didn't live because I was so focused on the origins of life instead of truly living my life. Yet, if I stay committed, I will achieve something that exists only in the minds of sci-fi writers or on the big screens of fantasy movies. I can do this, but I need funding and resources to continue my research. Traveling globally, lecturing, and working as a professor has brought me prestige. However, it doesn't give me the time to continue my work without interruption. Having Ford Taylor drop back into my life won't, either.

I glance at my watch. Perfect, I'm on time. Wrapping up my keynote, I leave my audience with one final thought: "In conclusion, what would you do if we could recreate life from scratch at an accelerated rate? Thank you to the Institute of Advanced Life for hosting me, and thank you all for listening. Goodnight," I say, stepping away from the podium.

Several attendees approach the stage and gather around me. Some seek answers to complex academic questions arising from their research; some wish to expand on their theories related to my keynote, while a small subset of people fangirl over me.

This is the moment at events when people typically take selfies. However, this audience won't have that opportunity; the only evidence they can share on social media will be pictures of their entry tickets, programs, and exterior shots of the building. Attendees are required to forfeit their phones before entering. I don't use social media and don't allow anyone to take pictures of me. In advance, attendees receive information about emergency contact procedures, and a team is dedicated solely to managing incoming calls from them. In an emergency, a staff member serves as the first point of contact. Throughout my years of lecturing, emergencies have occurred only twice.

As the crowd begins to disperse, I head toward the back exit.

"Doctor Green, great job on your keynote."

I stop and turn toward the familiar voice. "Nate?"

"You look lovely."

"Thank you. I'm surprised to see you here. You must know this presentation by heart by now. Are you in New York on business?"

"I'm here for your keynote," he says, shocking me.

A former graduate student of mine, Nate Bradshaw has a brilliant mind. However, his enthusiasm for attending my lectures seems unusual. Traveling all the way from California to New York to hear me speak on a topic he's already heard before resembles the behavior of a fan of a multi-platinum pop star more than that of a biophysicist. This is the third time he's done this.

"That's nice of you, but I invite you to consider exploring the work of my colleagues who are building on my research. That'll provide you a broader sense of what can be done in evolutionary biochemistry."

"I'll take that under consideration."

"Great. Well, thank you for coming. If you'll excuse me, I was just about to leave," I say, stepping past him.

"Uh, Doctor Green."

"You have another question?"

"I was wondering if you were free for dinner tonight."

"Nate, we talked about this. I'm not interested."

It's common for students to develop crushes on their teachers. Several of my former students, both men and women, have asked me out. I respond to all of them in the same way: "No. I'm not interested, and I don't date students or colleagues." The age-old notion of the allure of being with your professor, whether due to admiration for their intellect or the attraction tied to power dynamics, is indeed real.

"I'm no longer a student if that's the issue."

"I'm not interested. Now, if you'll please excuse me."

"But Doctor Green—"

"Do I need to have security escort you out?"

"No. I didn't mean to offend you. Have a good evening, Doctor," he says, then leaves. So do I.

When I finally reach the lobby, a building staff member escorts me to the vehicle waiting to take me to my hotel. I arrive in a matter of minutes.

Stepping inside, I drop everything in the living room and order room service: a Wagyu beef burger, garlic fries, and sparkling wine. All my years in academia haven't improved my poor eating habits. After dinner, I organize my things for tomorrow's flight and settle in for the night. Today was one of my last presentations for a few months. That's the best part about being a professor, guest lecturer, and research consultant—I can pretty much create my own schedule. Unfortunately, the nerd in me tends to use this time to continue my research. I check my email: more requests have come in to be a keynote speaker this fall and into next year.

One message seems interesting. I expand on the email from my friend Rose Ross, the CEO of Ross Enterprises. Although we haven't met in person yet, we've been following each other's work for the past few years and talk at least once a quarter via video—mostly about AI technology. She's a legendary technologist and the brilliant mind behind AI algorithms that require less processing power, which has earned her company billions and propelled her into the international spotlight. I read the email.

"Kenni, I hope the lecture circuit is going well and that everyone is as impressed with you as I am. This is why I'm reaching out. There's finally an opportunity for us to collaborate. I've started drafting a proposal for a new project that I would like you to lead. It's within your area of expertise, so having you on board could speed up our progress. If we can demonstrate early results, the board will allocate funds to establish a biotechnology R&D entity for Ross Enterprises. I would love to have you involved in this exciting venture. Please call me when you return to town so we can discuss it. Best, Rose."

And just as the laws of attraction suggest, I might have manifested funding for my research.

CHAPTER 3

What Are the Chances?

"Courage is the power to let go of the familiar."
– Raymond Lindquist

Kennedy

WHEN I ARRIVE AT the restaurant, Ford is already here, which is unusual for him. When we were a couple, he rarely stuck to the schedule, even though he knew I had a thing about being on time. Ford is many things: cute, clean-cut, and charismatic, but considerate isn't one of them. The cerebral side of me didn't realize until he left that being a caring person is at the top of my list of must-have qualities in a man, in case I ever date again. I sigh, taking a moment to absorb my surroundings. I try to forget old feelings and remind myself to handle this lunch like a transaction rather than a treat. His being here early...his very presence, suggests he wants something. I'm here to find out what.

I weave through the maze of tables. Ford stands as soon as he sees me. He looks great in his gray slacks and white dress shirt—not that I expected otherwise. He's a handsome man, exuding all the Charles Michael Davis vibes, flashing a sexy smile as if he didn't turn my world upside down when he left. He did. But, unlike before, I'm immune to his smile. As I approach, I awkwardly pat his arm, more like a gesture of comfort than a greeting to a former lover. He leans in and kisses my cheek, sending notes of sandalwood wafting between us, reminding me of who we used to be to each other.

"Hey, Kennedy, you are looking fine as ever. Here, have a seat." He pulls out a chair and gestures for me to sit. "Thanks for meeting me."

"Ford—," I begin but am interrupted.

"Before you say anything, I apologize for the random call. I didn't realize you were heading into a presentation when I reached out the other night."

You didn't let me get a word in edgewise like now, I want to speak up, but instead, I say, "We're not together anymore. You wouldn't know my schedule."

"I was anxious to get to you before you discovered I was back in town by accidentally running into me or something."

"It's a big city. What are my chances of running into you unless you move back into your old building?"

Before leaving, Ford lived in a residential high-rise in downtown San Francisco, just a few blocks from my place. He ended his lease when he moved to Seattle for a new job—*the opportunity of a lifetime,* as he described it back then. One that didn't include me in his life, long-distance or otherwise. We went from seeing each other daily to a monthly check-in call. By the fourth month, that turned into random text messages that lasted only a bit longer. Until two days ago, I hadn't heard from him in over a year.

Ford waves his hand to signal our server. The server promptly approaches, setting two glasses of water and a basket of bread with garlic butter on the table before taking our lunch order. I order carbonara and a cabernet sauvignon, while Ford chooses ossobuco and a beer.

When the server leaves, I raise an eyebrow, waiting for Ford to explain why he's here. "Actually, my chances of running into you are pretty high. I'm just a block away. There were no vacancies in my old building."

I break a piece of bread, spread it with butter, then pop it into my mouth. I'm not sure what to make of this new information. The man I spent three years in a relationship with, the one I believed could be "the one," who then turned around and broke up with me to take a job out of state, is back. Not just back—back in my neighborhood. Back in my life.

"Why?"

"I suppose it's a popular building."

"No. Why are you here? Why are *we* here? What do you want from me, Ford? I'm not trying to be flippant. I'm trying to understand the situation. When you left, you made it clear that you didn't want to continue our relationship. 'I need to get my life together and focus on my career,' you told me. What's changed?"

Ford opens his mouth to speak but hesitates when the server returns with our drinks. He says, "Your food will be out shortly. Is there anything else I can get you in the meantime?"

"No, thank you," I reply. Once the server leaves, I lock eyes with Ford. "You were about to say something," I prompt.

Staring at him, waiting for his response, I remember the day he chose his career over me. We made spaghetti for dinner that night, which wasn't unusual; we often cooked together when our hectic schedules gave us the chance. After he left, I must have analyzed that night a thousand times in my mind during those first few months. If I had paid attention, the signs were there. He was quieter than usual, and his movements while making the meatballs were slow and deliberate, as if he was overly focused on getting everything right. It wasn't the meatballs he was trying to perfect; it was his speech—the verbal equivalent of a Dear John letter.

"Remember the VP promotion I was trying for?" he asked.

"Yeah, you were supposed to hear back soon."

"I didn't get it. They promoted Shelby."

I remember how let down I felt for him. "Ah, Ford, I'm sorry to hear that. You worked so hard for it. I'm sure they didn't make the decision lightly. Your company is in high growth mode. There will probably be another opening soon."

"It's okay. I accepted another role."

"*Outside the marketing department?*"

"*No. In Seattle with another company,*" *he announced, leaving me speech-less. Seattle? He had never mentioned considering positions out of state. I stared at him in disbelief, certain he could read the shock on my face. Then he added.* "*I know this is news to you. I wasn't sure about considering the role until the promotion fell through. I really want to take my career to the next level. This is my opportunity.*"

I, of all people, understand ambition—trying to forge a path for myself as a Black woman in a patriarchal society. However, I also recognize the importance of considering those closest to us and the impact our actions have on them. If I were in his position, I would have approached this differently. But I'm not him; I have to face the consequences.

In response, the supportive side of me said, "*I'm disappointed you didn't share that you were exploring options elsewhere, but congratulations! Seattle is lovely. My students Seth and Lisa moved there after graduation to work for Gene Tech, which has a significant presence in the area. Gene Tech also tried to recruit me when I graduated. I can introduce you—at least to Seth—so you know someone out there.*" *I didn't mention that I almost failed Lisa for trying to cheat on an exam; she always seemed suspect.* "*What's the timeline for starting the new role? Will you be able to work remotely?*"

"*That's the thing: all the officers work onsite in the corporate offices in Seattle, and I need to be there in four weeks.*"

That's when the virtual shoes, glasses, and everything—including the kitchen sink—dropped.

"*Are you saying you want to do this long-distance?*" *I pointed between him and me.*

He got up, walked to the refrigerator, and picked up a water bottle. He leaned back against the counter and said, "*No. I'm doing this alone. I need to get my act together and focus on my career.*"

At that moment, my mind was blown. I closed my eyes for a few seconds to gather my thoughts before opening them and my mouth to speak.

"Hold on a moment. Let me restate what I believe you said; feel free to correct me if I'm wrong. I heard you say that this relationship is over, effective today. You're moving to Seattle. That's the end of it."

"Not quite that blunt."

"What did I miss, Ford? I'm a biophysicist and I only work with factual data. You said that you're due in Seattle in four weeks...alone. No live-in girlfriend, no long-distance girlfriend. Did I miss something?"

"No."

"I thought I meant more to you than that."

"You—"

I raised my hand in a stop gesture. I felt drained, disappointed, and done listening to Ford rewrite my life. "Since we're no longer a couple, it's best if you leave...now," I told him, and he left.

That was almost two years ago. Did I let him explain himself better after I calmed down? Yes. After five days of binge-watching *The Last Kingdom*, an empty vodka bottle, one red velvet cake, and a trash bin full of takeout remnants, I was ready to listen to Ford instead of punching him in the throat. Did it help? Not at all. I curl my fingers, thinking about it. There's no way to soften "I don't want to be with you anymore" in a way that makes me feel better. I thought I loved him. Letting him go left a gaping hole. But for what? Over the past year, I've come to realize we never truly loved each other. If we had, we would have fought tooth and nail to stay together. When we broke up, I would have been devastated. Instead, I was just disappointed. Still...it didn't lessen the pain of losing him.

"I made a mistake."

"Can you be more specific? Did you make a mistake taking the job? Leaving? Or breaking up with me? Which is it?"

"All the above." And there it is—still no definitive commitment to *us*.

The waiter returns with our meals. This time, Ford hurriedly dismisses him. Once the waiter is gone, I twirl my pasta on my fork and then shovel the forkful into my mouth. I adore pasta. Who am I kidding? I cherish every calorie-laden meal I can get my lips around.

I stare at Ford, hesitant to delve deeper into the past than we already have. I don't want to disrupt my life...again. I swallow the bitterness lingering from his departure, refusing to let old feelings resurface.

"Tell me about your job," I say, shifting the focus away from our failed relationship.

During our meal, Ford fills me in on his life without me. He left the Seattle company and made a lateral move, taking a new position with a high-tech startup in San Francisco. He hopes this new company will be a better cultural fit. He admits that his former company reached out to him six months ago to discuss a return in a newly opened VP role. Not one to say, "I told you so," I try to listen without judgment.

"Well, I hope this new role is everything you expected." I sip my drink

"What about you? How's your research going?"

"It's going well. I'm making progress. I might be able to secure funding to help speed up my work."

"That's great. I'm glad to review your latest published findings and use my connections to have someone write an article about you for *The Post* or *The Times*."

I let a small smile slip, but only for a moment. This is the marketing side of Ford, doing what he does best. I can't allow myself to see it as anything more than it is. This is where I made mistakes in the past. The charm he exudes when he discusses my work as if he's genuinely interested makes me feel good, but beyond his words—there's nothing. It's not me he's interested in; it's the problem he enjoys solving, completely detached from me. I don't even think he's aware of what he's doing—or maybe he is, and I've been a fool all along.

"Thank you, but no. The work I'm doing isn't something I want to discuss beyond the research community right now." I wipe my mouth with my napkin and set it on the table. "Ford, thank you for lunch. I need to head out."

"Kennedy, I wasn't kidding when I said I made a mistake. I'd really like to see you again. Maybe we could go out for dinner."

"No, that's not possible."

"Are you seeing someone? Is that the issue?"

"No, I'm not seeing anyone, and honestly, that's not my focus right now. As for us, we had our chance; it didn't work." I stand and slip my purse strap over my shoulder. "Listen, Ford. It was nice to see you again. I'm genuinely happy for you. Truly. Thank you again for lunch. Have a great week," I say, then leave.

Standing outside the restaurant, I'm surrounded by the sounds of the bustling city. People walk or drive, continuing with their days just like any other. But for me, for a moment, time stops, and I can no longer suppress the emotions that washed over me upon seeing him again. Our former life floods my mind with a stream of vivid memories. I still remember how strong his arms felt around me, the weight of his body above me in bed. The sound of his desire for me still echoes in my ear. The warmth of his breath, his scent—everything lingers. Even though I don't want to, I remember it all. As tears well up in my eyes, I quickly walk down the street and turn the corner.

Fuck you, Ford Taylor. Why did you have to come back?

Chapter 4

The One

"Important encounters are planned by the souls long before the bodies see each other."
– Paulo Coelho

Troy

A lot goes into keeping my body running like a machine. Eat right. Work out. Hydrate. Meditate. My day starts early. From four to five, I work out at my home gym, where I fit in fifty minutes of weightlifting and ten minutes of stretching. Sometimes, I meet up with one of the guys to spar. Other times, I run five miles in thirty minutes. I use the extra time to catch up with family, like today.

I put my brother Marcus on speakerphone while I get ready. He's carrying on about Mom and Dad. Our parents have lived in Palm Springs since they retired from their multi-billion-dollar container manufacturing business.

"All I'm saying is if you have some time off this summer, consider spending it at Mom and Dad's. I plan to head out there, too," he says.

I fasten my holster, retrieve my gun, and check it before sliding it into the holster. "I'll let you know if I have an extended break in my schedule. Ever since Rose became CEO, I've been flying constantly. However, her husband is thinking about taking charge of her security, which is what I would do in his situation."

"You need to find a woman first."

And there it is…talk of settling down. It makes me wonder where I'd be today if things had turned out differently…if *she* had been someone else. I push that thought back into the junk drawer, alongside broken pencils, bread bag clips, and ten-year-old ketchup packets.

"Now you sound like Mom. I'm not saying I want to be in his shoes; I'm just relaying the facts of the matter. Besides, you're one to talk. Are the women still wandering around the hospital ward, giggling and whispering when you walk by? 'He can check my heart anytime. Doctor, I need mouth-to-mouth resuscitation,'" I mimic the suggestive remarks I heard the last time I visited my brother at work, surprising him while in the area. As chief of surgery, he rarely takes time off for himself. Then again, we are our parents' children—workaholics.

"Just think about it."

"Sure. But you know how the conversation goes. When are you two going to settle down and start a family?" I echo what my mom said the last time I saw her. It's the same thing she always says. When my parents were my age, they already had us. My dad said he always wanted sons and was blessed with two. They expect us to do the same. It's a reasonable expectation for Marcus, but not for me—not a man chasing bullets. And certainly not a man who learns from past mistakes.

"What do you expect? They want grandchildren to spoil."

"You're oldest—get to it."

"Right. When I find the one, I will. They have an anniversary coming up. At least be there for that."

"I'll keep that in mind. I gotta get ready to hit the road."

"Same. I have surgery in a few hours. Keep me posted on your schedule. Later."

"Will do," I say, ending the call.

My brother is right, as always. We should be there together to celebrate our parents' forty-fifth anniversary. We're a close family, but it's becoming increasingly rare for us to spend time together, especially as Marcus and I become more immersed in our careers. As I develop more technical devices to enhance physical security, the demands on my time have grown significantly. I now run a multi-million-dollar operation with products used by some of the world's elites.

However, I'm not in it for the money; there has always been plenty of that around. Marcus and I received access to our trust fund at twenty-one, but I've barely touched mine. I don't really have a reason to, and like Marcus, I haven't found "the one." To be honest, I stopped trying ten years ago. I get a natural high from my life and I'm not sure anything can replace that.

I push all that out of my mind, get in my car, and meet the team at Rose and Niall's place. I take the lead vehicle that escorts them to her downtown office. At the office, the duo separates and goes to their individual offices because Niall, along with his brother, runs King Enterprise.

I make my rounds, meeting with various members of the building security team. Everything is running smoothly, showing that I've built a great team over the years. After my rounds, I host a virtual meeting with several engineers from my nationwide team who work remotely. They've helped me bring several security products to market, including a hack-proof wireless headset and a high-end tracker jewelry.

Rose spots me through her glass-walled office and waves me in.

"Troy, please be nice to my friend when you meet her. I really need her on this project, so please don't scare her off," she says, stretching out the words *please*.

This is a constant battle I face in my role with Rose. She shifts between wanting me to be her friend and recognizing that I'm her protector. It's hard for her to reconcile that I'm not Raven, June, Jake, or any other person she can casually talk to whenever she feels like. My primary responsibility is to focus on every detail of her life that could threaten her safety. Because of this, I don't comply with her whims and wants. I can't coddle her hurt feelings or temper the blow of bad news. There is no softness in my work or downtime with her. My job is to protect, not pamper. That's partially why she nicknamed me "Man of Steel." There's a certain hardness about me when she watches me work—my stance, my expression, my energy, it all says, "fuck around and find out."

My eyes shift from taking in my surroundings to Rose. "It's not my job nor in your best interest for me to ever appear meek."

She narrows her eyes at me. "Thirty minutes. That's all I'm asking. If you could just tone down the Man of Steel act and be Troy, the human, for just half an hour. *Please.* She'll be here soon."

Her eyes lock onto something or someone beyond the wall of windows facing the hall. I follow her gaze to a tall, honey-colored goddess with a head full of dark brown curls that bounce as she walks on long, lean legs that disappear into a fitted skirt, showcasing a body that has curves in all the perfect places for holding. Watching her, something washes over me. I don't know her, but it feels like we've met before. *How is that possible?*

When she notices me, I'm greeted with a burgundy-colored, tight-lipped smile that says, "I'm about to set your world afire." *Fuck.* I check myself because, in my line of work, women with beauty and brains like her are dangerous. The kind of danger I don't need.

CHAPTER 5

Introducing Mr. Armstrong

"No one can possibly know what is about to happen: it is happening, each time, for the first time, for the only time."
– James Baldwin

Kennedy

THIRTY MINUTES. ROSE PROMISED I'd only be here long enough to get a device, receive a debriefing, and be on my way. However, when she mentioned the added security measures, I began to reconsider my relationship with her. Initially, I thought this wealthy woman needed professional help, the kind I'm not qualified to provide. Then she explained the kidnapping attempt on her that occurred a few years ago, as well as a subsequent attempt on her cousin. It became clear why these precautions are necessary.

In science, everything has a threshold, and exceeding that threshold triggers a different reaction. This principle applies to security measures as well. As the newest team member, I meet the criteria: I'm part of the senior staff leading critical technological development and rank among the top in my specialty in the country. Rose even assigned personal protection to escort specific individuals to and from work. That's where I draw the line.

I step out of the elevator into a fully enclosed, well-lit reception area adorned on three sides with modern wood paneling—a lavish change from the sterile gray walls found on campus. At first glance, this windowless space seems to be the only room on the floor.

"Hi, Doctor Green. Mrs. Ross is expecting you." The receptionist presses a button on her computer screen, and one of the wooden panels, serving as a door, slides open to reveal a bright office floor bordered on one side by frosted glass.

A member of the security team opens the frosted glass door as I walk into the main suite of offices reserved for the Ross and King families and their executive admins. The conference room is directly ahead, but my destination is to the right of the conference room—Rose's office. Along the way, I pass the offices of individuals I've come to recognize by name due to their proximity to her, including her cousin Jake, the CFO. Next to his office is Rick Ross, her father and the chairman of the board, while across the aisle are the offices of June, Aedan, and Niall.

I turn to my right and see Rose sitting at her desk. Standing beside her, by the wall of windows overlooking the city, is a tall, striking figure with beautiful ebony skin. I hesitate briefly as his captivating umber-colored eyes lock onto mine. A small smile plays at the corners of his perfectly shaped chocolate lips, which seem tempting to try. I note the fleeting expression as it washes over his face, disappearing just as quickly. Taking a deep breath, I open the glass door.

Rose glances at her watch, fully aware of what it will show. It always displays the same message: I'm right on time. It's in my DNA. "Rose, it's great to finally meet in person."

She stands, rounds her desk, and hugs me.

"Kenni. The pleasure is all mine. Oh my God, you are a genius. I just read your latest report. We need to lock your brain in a safe...pronto," she emphasizes the last word with her best accent, which she sometimes does. I think she secretly uses me to practice her multilingual skills. Even if I tried, I couldn't match the number of languages she speaks.

"¿Es eso lo que estamos haciendo hoy en día?"

She pretends to be thinking. "No. But if you keep working as if you're getting ideas from another planet—"

"It's not that way."

"Trust me. It's that way. That's why we're taking precautions."

Two years ago, when Rose took charge of the company and rebranded it with its current name, she also launched a groundbreaking new AI product into the market. It was groundbreaking not only because of the product itself but also because she achieved it with just a fraction of the processing power usually required. Word spread before product development was completed, and there was an attempt on her life in Belfast.

When she learned I was working on AI in biophysics, she called. However, she wasn't the first. Companies in China and the UK reached out, but none had the advanced technology necessary to produce results with the processing power that Ross Enterprises could offer. Now I'm here.

"Troy." Rose turns to the man behind her, who embodies the essence of tall, dark, and handsome. "This is Dr. Kennedy Green."

I extend my hand. When his large hand envelops mine, I feel a synapse like the electrical signals that cells transmit between us. It's a concept I always discuss in my lectures, but until today, I had never actually experienced it. "Troy, it's nice to meet you. The flicker in your eyes suggests you weren't expecting me."

Rose narrows her eyes at him as if they're communicating telepathically. "Troy, what is she talking about?"

Unflappable—that's how Rose once described Troy. Yet something caused him to break character briefly.

"Dr. Green, it's a pleasure to meet you. Mrs. Ross said I'd be seeing Dr. Ken Green." The deep timbre of his Barry White voice resonates through my core. This man...this living, beautiful individual has my complete attention.

"I'm an academic and a scientist. Using my nickname helps to circumvent some of the bias that is common in my field."

"Understandable. I have your file, but your picture..."

"Hasn't been updated since undergrad. That's intentional. I'm not in this for the fame."

"Also, understandable."

"Well, Mr....."

"Troy."

"Do you have a last name, *Troy*?"

"I usually just go by Troy."

"That wasn't my question."

"Armstrong."

I lock eyes with him and nod. "Well-suited for a man like you."

Rose purses her lips, hiding a smile. "Troy, did I mention that Kenni is particular about everything?" She's right. After years of dealing with students and male peers who believed they were my superiors, I say exactly what's on my mind—they do, too.

"It comes with the job," I add.

Rose waves for me to sit. "We should proceed with the matter of security."

"Let's," I confirm, walking over to the round table near the wall of windows and taking a seat. Rose sits on the edge of her desk. Her eyes bounce between Troy and me. "You have something for me, Mr. Armstrong," I say.

"You can call me Troy."

"I'll stick to formalities for now, if that's okay with you. It's nothing personal." Troy nods. I gesture for him to sit. He closes the distance with a single stride of his long legs but doesn't take a seat. Instead, he reaches into his suit pocket, pulls out two bracelets, and lays them on the table.

"Do you prefer platinum or eighteen-carat gold?"

"Mr. Armstrong, is it your intention to intimidate me? I promise I'm no threat to you." I pause before saying, "My father would say, 'You're not going to get any taller by standing up.' Please, have a seat."

I glance past him at Rose. She opens her mouth to say something, but I subtly shake my head. I don't need her to rein in her bodyguard. I need him to show his humanity. She smirks.

"Mr. Armstrong," I insist. Troy pulls out the chair and takes a seat. I smile, then meet his gaze as I say, "Thank you. If I were your woman, which of these would you give me?" *There's that flicker again.*

"I would prefer if you wore platinum."

Logically, I would, too. It's purer, stronger, and more durable, not to mention more expensive. But I don't need to state the obvious.

"Then that's what I'll wear. Tell me about this," I pick up the hammered platinum bracelet. "It's small. Are you sure this will fit me? It seems like you were expecting a child. I suppose I'm a surprise on several fronts." I set it on the table and slide it over to him.

He doesn't respond to my joke. Instead, he says, "I designed it just for you." He pulls a phone from his pocket, types something in, and the bracelet opens. "Your wrist, please."

I reach my arm across the table. He lifts it slightly, places the bracelet on me, and fastens it. I feign indifference to the warmth of his touch and the subtle scent of spiced musk and leather lingering in the air between us. "Wow. It fits."

"A device inside will let me pinpoint your exact location down to the inch. You won't be able to take it off by yourself."

I glance past him at Rose.

"Troy, Niall, Aedan, and I can remove it. Troy created the technology in these bracelets. My father altered the security protocol so that the wearer cannot remove the bracelets independently. Apparently, Dad didn't like that June and I have a history of taking them off."

"It's for your safety," Troy interjects. "They're waterproof. I designed it to fit your wrist perfectly, making it virtually unnoticeable as you go about your day. It also has embedded AI technology."

Rose grips her wrist where the bracelet is. "That's where I come in. I got tired of calling and checking in when I had unscheduled events and stops to make. I programmed it to sync your calendar with the satellite location and pick up signals nearby. The algorithm will gradually learn your behavior."

"It builds on the features that are available on our phones," I say.

"Exponentially."

"So, if I leave early to go to the grocery store, it won't raise any alarms. But if I never arrive home and don't have a flight scheduled or…"

"Something else is planned—yes, it will notify the security team about a potential issue."

"Like if someone tried to kidnap me."

"That's right. It'll detect the nearest device and gather information about the person, car, or any other data it collects. The team can analyze the data in less than a minute and decide on the next course of action."

"This is so thin. Is there a battery in it? Do I have to come in to get it replaced?"

"There's no battery. Your movement generates the power needed to sustain the internal mechanism that keeps it running," Troy says, extending his hand to me. I place my hand in his, and he shakes it as though greeting me. "Simple movements like this are all it takes." He holds my hand for a few seconds longer than necessary, then lets it go. His touch feels noticeably absent when I withdraw my hand.

"Sounds like you thought of everything."

"Nothing is foolproof," Troy adds.

"Don't worry, Mr. Armstrong. I'm not like my colleagues, who detest wearing the device. You and I are on the same page because I prefer not to be followed by people like you. Not that there's anything wrong with you specifically." I raise my arm. "This is the compromise."

"Dr. Green, there is a serious threat of foreign governments uncovering your connection to Ross Enterprises and Project Grace. People would go to great lengths to gain access to the work being done here. If you succeed, they will resort to extreme measures to reach you."

"Troy," Rose warns.

"Dr. Green needs a complete understanding of the potential security risks associated with her work."

"It's okay," I reassure Rose. "It's no different from the precautions taken in a chemical lab. Mr. Armstrong is subtly trying to alert me that my life could be at risk."

"Stick to the protocol and you should be fine," Rose assures me.

She and Troy exchange another knowing glance, the kind that comes from spending years together, instinctively understanding how each of them will react to certain situations.

"I received the list of people you frequently associate with."

"You mean my family, friends, and colleagues? I doubt anything out of the ordinary came up."

"Nothing that would raise security concerns," Rose confirms.

Troy leans back in his seat. "Is there anyone you think we should add to the list?"

"Like who, Mr. Armstrong?"

"Like someone you met recently at the bar."

"Are you inquiring whether I'm seeing someone? Is this for business or personal reasons, Mr. Armstrong? Regardless, my answer is no."

Rose does that thing again as she purses her lips. "I believe Troy is trying to ask if anything unusual occurred recently that might give you pause."

"One of my former students showed up at my recent keynote in New York. He asked me out."

Leaning forward Troy asks, "Why would that seem unusual?"

"He knows the keynote by heart. He flew from California to New York just to see me, even though I had previously rebuffed him. He has a brilliant mind. His behavior could be benign, but... there's always a chance."

"Are you saying that you think there's a thin line between his brilliance and something else?"

"I do. It's a real thing. I've witnessed it before. When I was in high school, I noticed similar behavior from a former student who graduated but returned to campus. Everyone knew about him; he was legendary for his brilliance. He spoke thirty languages, including Latin." My eyes shift to Rose. "No offense."

"None taken."

"He began attending random classes again. As you can imagine, he was viewed as an adult trespassing on school property. Eventually, the police got involved and he was arrested."

"I'll monitor the former student of yours."

"Then you'll need his name. Nate Bradshaw."

CHAPTER 6

Life is Lifing

"Apparently there is nothing that cannot happen today."
– Mark Twain

Kennedy

PUSHING BACK MY CHAIR, I press my fingers to my eyes and rub them, hoping that will bring clarity to my life. The clink of my bracelet against my watch prompts me to check the time. I've been at this for hours, though it feels like only moments. That's how it goes when I'm immersed in my work. I stand and shift my focus to the city view beyond the office windows, taking a break from reviewing hours of predictive analysis. It's summer in the city and it's lovely.

Two months ago, when Rose first approached me about leading Project Grace, I never imagined how satisfying it would be to develop technology that aligns with my research without having to seek grants for funding. I'm living my dream because I'm part of a company like Ross Enterprises, known for its technological advancements and equipped with the resources to support this work internally.

My phone vibrates on the desk. I hesitate to check it, fearing it might be Ford. He has called or texted me at least once a week for the past few months, wanting to know if I'll have dinner with him. Each time, I give him the same answer... no. It's not an outright no. I tell him I've been working late to meet a deadline. If I can show positive results, we can present them to the board to greenlight an official biotechnology wing of RE. It's the truth, but he remains persistent.

I pick up my phone. Thank God it's my friend Sasha. I've been trying to reach her.

"Hey, girl, you back?" I ask. She's on the road more than I am. Apparently, medical geneticists are in high demand.

"I'm here for three days, then I hit the road again. Are we on for tomorrow?"

"Yeah. But I need a favor."

"Shoot."

"One of my colleagues brought two of your books. They're dying to get your autograph," I say, emphasizing the word dying.

Sasha laughs. "Okay. I'll sign them this weekend when I see you."

"Cool. I'll drop by campus on my way home to pick them up. Oh, am I playing bartender, or are you?"

"I'm handing the shaker to you. Hands down, you make the best concoctions. I'll bring the food."

"Twist my arm." I laugh. I live for this stuff. "I've been playing around with spicy drinks."

"Oooh, hot stuff. I'm here for it."

"All right, see ya tomorrow," I say, ending the call.

Sasha is the perfect best friend. We've experienced both good and bad times together: from graduating to commiserating and everything in between—it's her and I. When Ford left, she was there for me. This weekend, we plan to hang out, relax, have some drinks, and catch up on life. That's what best friends do when they miss each other for a month due to our busy schedules.

I manage to squeeze in a few more hours of work before heading to my office on campus. When I arrive, it's dark and the place is nearly empty. I walk down the hall and turn the corner, noticing a few office lights still on. There's a faint rustling sound, and I pause to identify its source. It could be anything on a large campus like this. I keep walking and find the culprit—a flyer tacked to a bulletin board that has lost its grip. I pick it up and reattach it. It has a QR code to scan to connect with someone searching for a roommate. I proceed to my office and collect the two books, each weighing about two pounds. Sasha had a lot to say about genetic mutation. I shove the books into my tote and head back outside. My mind drifts to my list of things to do: buy drink ingredients, devise a new twist on a vodka cocktail, document the algorithm that keeps popping into my head.

Outside, the crisp air brushes against my cheek. I grip my tote a little tighter, as if it will shield me from the chill. The lot is as sparse as the building, with only a few cars scattered around, likely belonging to students taking advantage of the library's quiet to escape small apartments and noisy roommates. I quickly walk to my car. The only sound besides the hum of the floodlights is the click-clacking of my heels on the pavement. I'm acutely aware of my surroundings. They say women should keep their keys between their fingers to use as a weapon, but that's impractical when you only have a key fob. Still, it could be effective for giving someone a bloody nose. Instead, I have a blinged-out taser. My biophysicist side rationalizes that if cells have a constant flow of electrons powering them—in essence, giving us life—I can also deliver an electrical shock to immobilize someone composed of billions of electrical currents.

It's frustrating that women have to constantly be alert to their surroundings. That's why I always park next to the parking island, which is equipped with floodlights illuminating my car. I walk around the vehicle to the passenger side to unload the two tomes. As I step up onto the curb, it's hard to judge my distance from it, and my ankle gives way. The way the books fly from my arms when I try to break my fall by landing on my hands and knees would be comical if it weren't for the excruciating pain.

"Shit. Shit. Shit. Ugh, God. Ouch," I scream. Kneeling on all fours, I shift my weight to my right knee. Pulling my left leg forward, I plant my foot on the ground and force my weight forward to stand. Upright,

I straighten my right leg and try to put pressure on my foot. "Fuuuuck." I can't do it—it hurts too much. I lean back against the car for support, glancing around for my tote and keys. They're nowhere in sight because I know exactly where they are...under the car. Closing my eyes, I let out my anguish and annoyance in a guttural scream.

"Dr. Green. Are you okay? What happened?"

Nate.

My eyes snap open. Nate stands in front of me, extending a hand to help.

"I fell. I think my key is under the car."

He glances down at my bent knee. "You're hurt." I nod. "Can you walk?"

"No," I force the word out with a wince.

"Okay, give me a sec." Nate kneels and retrieves my belongings from beneath the vehicle. He opens the passenger door. "Sit here a moment. I need to call an ambulance." He places my belongings on the car floor beside me. He has a pained expression, which I'm certain reflects mine, and I wonder if he's an empath.

"No, I just need to go home."

"Dr. Green, your ankle is swollen. You should get it examined."

As much as I want to argue with him, I don't. I can barely see straight because of the pain. He takes out his phone and calls for an ambulance. I listen as he describes our location and the situation.

"They'll be here in five minutes."

CHAPTER 7

Standing Guard

"When I let go of what I am, I become what I might be. When I let go of what I have, I receive what I need."
– Lao Tzu

Troy

I'M DRIVING TO MY downtown penthouse apartment after leaving Niall and Rose with the evening shift crew. My dashboard lights up with a message: "Doctor Green en route to the ER at UCSF." All I can see is red. *What happened to this woman?* I keep asking myself as countless scenarios run through my mind.

It's been two months since I issued Kennedy her tracker and I haven't seen her since. From the moment I met her, I felt an instant connection. What was meant to be a simple security introduction with a new executive turned into a core memory that I replay in my mind every night. When she headed toward the office door, it was as if the sun had come out to warm my soul. And when I shook her hand, I recognized her touch from another lifetime when we shared space in each other's lives. Then she left, disappearing behind the lobby door; her absence felt as though a part of me went with her. I've never experienced the absence of a woman I just met so deeply. A man in my position, whose life is always at risk, shouldn't feel this way.

Upon arriving at the hospital, I learn that Kennedy has been taken to a private room and her emergency contact has been notified. I take the elevator to the fourth floor and navigate the bright, beige corridor until I reach her room. A young man sits in the guest lobby near her door, wringing his hands. I recognize him from my security brief.

I walk up to him and say, "Mister Bradshaw."

"Do I know you?" He stands but has to step back to meet my gaze. He must be five-ten at best.

"No. But I understand you called the ambulance for Dr. Green. Thank you."

"Who are you?"

"Troy."

"I don't recognize the name, but the physician is still inside with Dr. Green. I think she broke her ankle."

"She'll be well taken care of. However, I doubt she's in a position for visitors. You must have things to do. You can leave now; I'll stay here to watch her."

"I was going to make sure she got home safely."

"Everything's taken care of. Thanks," I say, staring down at him. He hesitates, but then leaves.

Soon after, the doctor exits the room.

"Dr. Collins. How is she?"

"Have we met?"

"I'm Troy Armstrong."

"Mr. Armstrong, I've been expecting you. I see the resemblance to your brother."

"It's in the genes."

"Dr. Green sustained a stable distal fibula non-displaced fracture."

"Will she require surgery?"

"No, I ordered an orthopedic boot for her. They'll put it on her before she leaves. If she follows my instructions, she should only need to wear it for four weeks, at which point I recommend she return for a follow-up exam."

"Is she awake?"

"She was in a lot of pain when she arrived. She told me that if I didn't give her medication immediately, she'd create a nanobot to go directly to my brain and rewire it so that I'd do her bidding for life." He smiles, lips pressed together. "The medication has taken effect. She's resting now."

A wave of relief washes over me. I smirk, confident that Doctor Kennedy Green will be just fine.

"Thanks for treating her."

He pats me on the shoulder. "It's uncanny how much you resemble him."

When he leaves, I step into the room, locking the door behind me. The air is a blend of sterility infused with hints of lavender and honey. Her eyes are closed, and she could easily be an angel resting after a day of saving the world: calm and content. I want to reach out, cup her face, and caress her cheek with my thumb to confirm that she's real. The upper part of the electric bed is elevated, and her head rests on a pillow, her hair splayed around her like a crown. Standing a few steps from the foot of the bed, with my back against the wall, I watch her. *Can she sense me? Does she know she's safe?* Her arms rest at her sides as her slender fingers curl around the blanket, moving slightly, opening and closing. I wonder what's going through her mind. Is she dreaming? Is she contemplating the meaning of life behind closed eyelids or simply sleeping?

Regardless of what happens, I'll be standing guard, watching over her until her friend arrives.

My heart is racing. I know why. *It's because of her.*

CHAPTER 8

Baby, I'm Back

"Do not dwell in the past, do not dream of the future, concentrate the mind on the present moment."
– Buddha

Kennedy

THIS IS NOT HOW I expected my weekend to begin. My foot is in a boot. My mind feels foggy, and I feel strangely lightheaded, but not in a good way. My arm, draped over Ford's shoulder, bounces to the rhythm of his steps as he carries me out of the elevator and down the hall to my apartment. We didn't talk much in the car. Under the influence of pain meds, it was best for me not to. Given our history, I might have said things I would later regret. However, I did thank him for coming to get me.

When we arrive at my unit, the door is already open.

"Ford," Sasha punctuates his name with irritation. Her eyes closely follow his movements as he carries me through the living room. She's been suspicious of Ford since his return to San Francisco. As have I.

"Sasha. It's good to see you again," he tells her, his voice guarded.

"Put me down already," I say.

"Why is she talking so slow?"

Ford sits me in the occasional chair, pulling the ottoman closer to support my legs.

"She's taking pain medication. I need to go back to the car for her crutches," he says bluntly before disappearing. There was never any love between them, and his breaking up with me ended their chance to reconcile.

She is just as shocked as I am to see Ford today. I'm to blame for not removing him as my emergency contact. I expected to see Nate when I was discharged. Not that having Nate bring me home would be any better; evading him, in general, has been difficult. My chances would drop to zero if he knew where I lived. Ford seems like the lesser of two evils.

I lean back against the seat cushion and say, "When I can think straight, remind me to update my emergency contact."

"So that's how you ended up back in his arms."

"Not by choice. If I weren't on these drugs and could walk, I would have called a ride service."

"You should have called me. I would have come to get you."

"They called Ford as soon as I arrived at the hospital. He mentioned seeing a guy standing in the waiting room when he got there, but the guy was gone when we came out." It's not like Nate would walk away without me forcing him to leave. I wonder what happened.

"Well, you're here now. And with all these meds...," she says, picking up my purse and going through it. "You won't be drinking anything but water for the next few days."

"I gotta pee."

"Okay. Thanks for the PSA."

"No, seriously, I gotta go."

"Do you need your crutches? Ford isn't back yet. I can offer you a cup," she says with a slight smirk.

I roll my eyes which makes me even dizzier. "Funny. I don't know how to use those crutches yet. I'm not sure I can, the way my head feels. I'll just hop."

"I'll take you," Ford says coming in. He leans the crutches on the chair, and before I can protest, he reaches under my legs and back, lifts me, and takes me down the hall.

"Well, this isn't awkward at all," I say as he sets me on my feet near the toilet.

"It doesn't have to be. I used to eat you. Remember?" Leave it to a man to say some shit like that at a moment like this. He lingers, locking eyes with me. His hands grip my elbow while I hold onto his biceps, steadying myself, hating that his presence affects me.

Narrowing my eyes at him, I say, "Do you mind? I'm about to wet my pants."

"I'll be back to check on you," he says, then leaves, closing the bathroom door behind him.

"What the hell is happening? This can't be my life. If there is a divine, I'm gonna need you to intercede," I say to the marble-tiled walls.

Thoughts swirl in my head like neutrons. What is this I'm feeling? The medicine? Embarrassment? Exhaustion? What the hell is happening to me? I'm on the verge of the most significant scientific breakthrough the world has ever seen, and I can't even walk my behind to the bathroom to pee. My ex and best friend, who hate each other, are waiting down the hall to help me. I'm thirty-three and have yet to experience true love. *What am I doing?* I should be somewhere sunny and warm, like a private beach in Lanai, lying beneath a god of a man being loved on. A tear rolls down my cheek. I swipe it away with my knuckle. Yeah, good one, Kenni. You're not on a tryst; you're on the toilet amid an existential crisis. *Lovely.*

Ford comes back to collect me as promised. When he sets me back on the chair this time, Sasha hovers close by.

"I ordered dinner," she says. Then she turns to Ford. "Thanks for your help. I think Ken will be fine for tonight. I'll be here until she gets back on her feet."

"You can't carry her. I'll stay until she gets used to these." He moves the crutches from where they're leaning against the chair to the wall.

Ford and Sasha stare at each other, then their gaze shifts to me. The tension in the air is thick with unspoken feelings. *Damn. What should I do?* They both make valid points.

"Okay, you two. I appreciate the love. Sasha is right. It'll take me a few days to get back on my feet, especially since these drugs make me drowsy. Ford, I might need your help tonight and tomorrow, but I don't think you need to stay overnight. You're only a block away."

"I'm staying. How do you think you'll manage getting in and out of bed?"

"Hop."

"While high?"

I sigh. "I guess it's a good thing I have two guest rooms," I say, giving in.

Sasha heads to the kitchen to plate the meal she had delivered. When she returns, she moves the occasional table closer so it's within reach. I take a pill she set out and wash it down with water. "There's more in the kitchen," she says, directing her comment to Ford as she places the plated pizza on the table.

Leaning against the wall with his arms folded, Ford pushes himself off. "Sasha, I'm just here to help Kennedy. I haven't done anything to you, so you can ease up on the cynicism. It's not going to help her heal any faster."

Oh hell. Sasha power-walks past me toward Ford. Her hand is raised and her finger is barely an inch from his nose when she screams. "I have every reason to suspect you. You acted like you were in love with my girl, then switched it up and left, saying that you needed to take care of yourself. Why are you here? Did things not go the way you planned in Seattle?"

"That's not how it is."

"Then how is it? Did you go out there for a piece of meat and find out it was spoiled? So, you come back here trying to make amends. What's different, Ford? Explain it to me like I'm five because I can't grasp your logic, even with a PhD, like my girl here. The math doesn't add up." She rises on her toes and leans her face towards his. "Based on your casual account of events, I consider everything you do suspect."

"Sasha, it's okay," I say, but she doesn't back down from Ford.

"You know what? You're not worth it. Just know I have my eyes on you," she says, turning her back to him as she walks toward me. She mouths the words "I'm sorry" to quell any notion that she'll allow the conversation to spiral out of control more than it already has. This confrontation has likely been building in her mind for a while. If this had happened a year ago, it would have been more explosive.

"What occurred in the past is between Kennedy and me."

Shit. Why can't he keep his mouth shut?

"That's where you're wrong. What happened involves those of us who were here to pick up the pieces after you pulled that bullshit disappearing act on Ken. You owe her, me, and her family a damn explanation. No amount of smooth talking or saying, 'Baby, I'm back,' is going to get you back into her good graces. This isn't a *Lifetime* movie, Ford. It's real life."

"I'm going to the kitchen and eat. Kennedy, just let me know when you need me."

Ford was never one to confront conflict, which is why he didn't tell me until the last minute that he was breaking up with me and moving to Seattle. He walks past Sasha, crosses the room, and heads to the kitchen. Sasha slumps down on the couch.

"I'm going to put a knife on your nightstand and keep one with me. If I hear one peep out of him tonight, I'm going to carve his ass up like a pumpkin," she says, making a slicing motion with her hand.

I laugh. It's amusing, but it's not. "Thanks, girl. I know you've got my back. Don't worry, I can handle Ford." The question is, can I forget my past feelings? Can I finally move on once and for all?

I close my eyes, feeling the effects of the medicine as it cancels the noise in my head like headphones, helping me return to the calm I felt lying in the hospital bed. I dreamt he was there. I see him now. *Troy.*

CHAPTER 9

And in Other News

"Just when you think you've seen it all - see more."
– A. H. Scott

Kennedy

TWO DAYS OF FORD and Sasha clashing while I play referee under one roof has spurred me to stop the meds, endure the pain, and learn to navigate my apartment with crutches. After several demonstrations, Ford admitted that I could manage on my own. Though being carried around by him and smelling his scent was familiar—I needed to distance myself from him. To continue breaking away from the past. No matter how good it felt, I refused to get lured into a life with him. Not this time. He abandoned me, and I know from my science that leopards don't change their spots.

That's been my motivation for the past few days: to master these crutches. Also, Sasha had to fly out for work and I didn't want to be stuck at home alone with...him. They're the two closest people to me besides my parents. I didn't dare tell my parents that I was injured. They're leaving on their well-deserved six-week private excursion to trace the history of humanity with Abercrombie & Kent. I wouldn't want to ruin that for them. All they know is I'm a little under the weather, but I'll be fine—at least I will be by the time they return.

If that isn't enough incentive, returning to the office is. The past few days have been depressing as I've gone from a house full of people to

52

just myself. On campus, my day typically included conversations with colleagues and lecture halls filled with students—in addition to conference rooms or ballrooms that hosted thirty to three hundred attendees. In just a week, I've transitioned from that to being alone. The sense of isolation grips me with every intentional move I make.

"I don't want to ask him for help again," I surprise myself by saying aloud. Even though my ankle hurts, I bite the bullet.

Today, I woke up early, got ready for work as best as I could, called a car service, and awkwardly entered the office with an orthopedic boot, crutches, and a leather backpack instead of a tote. *I can handle this.* At the office, I don't have to walk much. One of the executive assistants is always available to bring me coffee or water if I need it. Plus, there are plenty of places nearby that can deliver a hearty lunch. My leg stays elevated on the rolling ottoman provided by the company, so I'm all set.

I glance past my computer screen, letting my eyes drift to the city skyline outside the window. The steady hum of office noises—the clicking of keyboards coming from the assistants' cubicles, the low hum of voices at the coffee machine—feels oddly comforting. Routine.

A knock on the frosted glass door, which is slightly ajar, cuts through the illusion. It's soft, but something about the timing makes my shoulders tense. My executive assistant steps inside, her expression carefully neutral—too neutral.

"Lobby security called," she says. "A gentleman is waiting with a package he wants to deliver."

I blink, my brain catching on the word *gentleman* like it means something more. *It shouldn't.* Still, I immediately think of Ford. "Have him leave it with security. That's the protocol."

"He wants to deliver it to you personally."

That flicker of unease sharpens. I lower my hands to my lap, fingers curling into my palms. "What's his name?"

"He wouldn't provide it."

That's...not normal. "Then they should escort him out."

Her lips press together. "He says you know him. I can pull up the lobby feed."

A chill runs through my spine, slow and deliberate, but my voice comes out steady. "Show me." *If this is Nate again*...I think to myself.

She steps closer, leaning over my desk. Her braids fall over her shoulders as she points to links on my screen, but it's not enough to distract me from the unease tightening in my chest. I click through the links until the lobby camera feed fills the screen.

Here he is. A man stands near the front desk, his posture rigid, like he's waiting for more than just permission to deliver a package. Fair complexion. Sharp features. His face is gaunt, like he's been stretched thin by life—or something worse.

I lean in, searching his face for signs of recognition, but all I feel is a gnawing discomfort in the pit of my stomach. "I've never seen that man before."

My EA taps her phone without missing a beat. "Get rid of him. She doesn't know him."

I should feel relieved. But I don't. I stare at the screen a moment longer, watching Jim at the front desk speak into his radio, his expression unreadable.

"That's strange," I say, more to myself than to her.

She straightens, smoothing her jacket like this is just another day. "It happens sometimes. People claim they're here to see Rick or Rose. They act entitled because they recognize a name or two." She shrugs, but there's tension in her shoulders now. She's trying to play it cool, but she felt it—the strangeness of it all.

"How do I know he won't wait around until I leave?" The question escapes before I can stop it, my voice lower than intended. I think all this security talk has me paranoid.

"When I said, 'get rid of him,' it was Jim's cue to call the police." Her lips press together in a smile but it doesn't reach her eyes. "That guy will be occupied for a while."

Occupied. I don't like that word. I don't like any of this.

"Is there anything else I can get you while I'm here?" she adds, as if offering me tea will smooth over the unsettling edge this has left behind.

I shake my head, forcing a smile I don't feel. "Nothing, thank you. I'll run a few more scenarios, then head home."

She nods, already halfway to the door. "I'll arrange transportation."

"Thanks."

***

Awkwardly, I enter my apartment, set the mail on the console table, and take off one shoe, pairing it with its less-worn mate at the bottom of the entryway closet. Gently, I remove my sweater and backpack and place them in the closet before heading to my bedroom to freshen up.

As I change into my loungewear, I reflect on my career. Being a professor is rewarding, and I still plan to teach special courses on campus, but my work in corporate, where I can make a greater impact, takes precedence. Working for a prestigious company like Ross Enterprises offers more perks than working in a collegiate environment. I have access to a vast array of technology, not to mention a team of engineers available to assist me in developing new programs to meet my needs. This alone will help me meet the upcoming deadline to deliver the project's first iteration before the end of summer, just before Rose goes on leave. I'm dedicated to meeting this deadline. I'm also excited for Rose and Niall; their three-year love story is one for the books.

I grab the mail on my way to the kitchen. I pause before setting it on the counter. Hmm, I don't remember taking a glass out. Everything happening, the man at the office, the stress of limited mobility—it's all getting to me.

My phone buzzes, it's Sasha. "Hey, Sash. You checking up on me?"

"Not this time," her voice sounds rushed. "Have you seen the news lately?"

"I just got home. I was about to make myself some dinner."

"Check this," she says. My phone dings with an email alert. "I just sent you something."

I put the call on the speakerphone, pull up my account, and scan my emails. I read her message. "Is this for real? Are there other articles?"

"The last time I checked, the AP and News Corp have picked up the story. It won't be long before others follow suit."

I reread the newswire.

"Ross Enterprises has appointed Dr. Kennedy Green as the head of biotechnology research and development, according to the company's 8-K filing from last April. Dr. Green is a distinguished biophysicist known for her groundbreaking work in biophysics and is the author of the book This is the Basis of Life. *She was a former student of the late Professor Dr. Winston Rutledge, who was declared 'dead in absentia.' There is speculation that Ross Enterprises may be on the verge of a significant advancement in their field."*

"This is not good. I've been trying to stay low key on this project."

"Do you think there is an ulterior motive behind the original vlog picked up by the media?"

"I doubt it. It's probably just a big social media content creator doing what they do to gain more likes. Their post was probably picked up by mainstream news outlets in search of the next big story, perhaps inadvertently."

"Seems they found it. What happens next?"

"Nothing." I go to the refrigerator and grab a sparkling water bottle. Calling over my shoulder, I say, "Our internal employees are aware that we have multiple projects underway. We hope one of them gets approved for production. If this is approved, we'll create a separate entity focused on further development. The concern is the word getting out to competitors in the UK and China." I take a sip, allowing the fizz to refresh me.

"Then you're not worried?"

"I'm not sure what to think." I scan the article once more. "Wait, it says Dr. Rutledge was declared dead in absentia."

"I saw that."

"I might be losing it, but I remember one of my students, Lisa, discussing the case several years back. She told me the family was holding onto hope that he was alive and that he may have intentionally disappeared to be with another woman."

"Another woman? That seems absurd. Why would she say that to you?"

At the time, I thought it was odd, too. "She always seems suspicious to me—a complete Rutledge fanatic."

I remember her telling me she switched schools to take my class as soon as I became a professor because she knew I studied under him. Her behavior reminds me of Nate.

"You seem to attract these types."

I shake my head, feeling overwhelmed by the strange events that have taken over my life.

"Whatever." I pause a second before saying, "I have a question. Did Ford mention anything about checking in on me this week?"

"You mean he hasn't been blowing up your phone?"

"Well, I have received a few texts. I'm talking about stopping by."

"No, we don't talk. I don't remember him saying anything before I left. Why?"

"Just checking." I don't want to alert her. If it wasn't Ford who left the glass out, it might have been me rushing.

"I'll be back in a couple of weeks. Are you sure you're good?"

"I'll be fine. You should have seen me at work today. I did great getting around."

"You should work from home and gradually allow yourself to heal."

"You sound like a doctor."

"I am a doctor."

"Medical."

"A medical geneticist is a medical doctor."

"You know what I mean. Hang up the phone, girl. I'll see you when you get back."

"I'll check in on you in a few days," she says, and I don't mince words. Sasha is just being her ever-caring self, watching out for me. She's the type of person who gives selflessly.

I'm about to call Ford to ask him about the glass, but the more urgent call I need to make is to June Ross, our COO and second-in-command at my company. When I call, her EA connects me directly.

"Dr. Green, I had hoped you were home resting by now. But I expect this is about the recent AP news report."

I get straight to the point. "It was brought to my attention from a friend. Is RE planning to make a statement?"

"Not in response to the newswire. However, we will issue a press release to announce new key staff members."

"Seems our break from releasing one is over. Do you expect any criticism or backlash?"

"No. It would be different if we were launching something controversial, but the knowledge gained from working with us in your current capacity will be viewed by the mainstream as what it truly is—new product development. They don't know anything confidential. Only those interested in pharmaceuticals or the medical industry will take notice."

"They'll want to know about the advancements we're working on that affect them."

"Exactly. If anything were to leak, then I'd be worried about how widespread the news of your work becomes. A few influential entities might show interest for harmful reasons."

There's rustling on the other end of the call; a young voice says, "Mam," a local Irish expression. Her child shares the same Irish accent as his father, Aedan King, who is also in the room with her. I know that's June's signal to leave the office. I've been in her office on the executive floor a few times when he's come to take her home. Her husband is known for protecting her and their family. I can envision him placing their child on her lap as we speak. Aedan will kiss her cheek and then wait patiently with one hand in his pocket, leaning against the door frame until she wraps up her work and is ready to leave. They have a good life...balance. I wonder if I'll ever have what they have. There was a time when I thought Ford and I would have that. It was wishful thinking.

"Hey, you two. I'll be done in a sec," she says, pulling me back to my house...my situation.

I direct my attention to the call. "Then let's hope the story dies down after a few days."

"If it doesn't, I'd like you to think about the car service arrangement I've set up for you during your recovery, which could be permanent."

"Are you suggesting that I might need a bodyguard?"

"Rose provided you with an overview of the risks."

"She did, but I believed the tracker was all there was."

"Let's see how the week unfolds. In the meantime, I'll have Jean from PR share a preview of the press release with you before it goes out tomorrow. Is there anything else you need?"

"No."

"Dr. Green, I recommend you get some rest. We want you to be fresh for tomorrow, and please adhere to your doctor's orders."

"Will do," I say, ending the call.

So, this is what it's like to be in the spotlight. I clasp my hand around my wrist, twisting the bracelet. I can't imagine living like Rose, always being followed by security, even if he is a hunk. Then there's June, married to Aedan, who put his life on the line for her a few years ago.

Who am I to need protection?

Chapter 10

The Call

"I exist in two places, here and where you are."
– Margaret Atwood

Troy

I sit at my desk, fingers drumming restlessly against the smooth surface, with my laptop open to a draft of my latest project—a biometric security device I've been tinkering with for months. It's good work. Something I should be excited about. Hell, I am excited about it. But right now, my focus is shot.

Rose Ross is back in Belfast with Niall. I just got off a call with him this morning. He assured me they'd stay put for the rest of her pregnancy, so there won't be any more cross-continental travel, which means they won't need my services for the next few months. Niall's got things under control. Rose deserves peace after everything she's been through.

That should be a relief. And it is.

But it also leaves me with time on my hands. Time to think. Time to plan. Time to deal with family.

Marcus has been on my tip about our parents' anniversary and a trip to Palm Springs. I agreed to go—he wouldn't have let me off the hook otherwise—but I'm not exactly excited about it. A week with my parents means one thing: questions about why neither of us has settled down.

Mom will start in right away, probably at dinner. She'll sip her wine, give me *the look*, and say something to the effect of, "You're pushing forty, Troy. When are you going to start thinking about your future?"

Then Dad will chime in with a joke about grandchildren.

Marcus pretends not to care when they give him the same speech, but I know better. He hides behind work, the same as me.

Meanwhile, I'll sit there with a polite smile, knowing I'm not built for a quiet life. Not yet, anyway. Maybe not ever.

I've spent the last two decades keeping people safe. Risking my neck to make sure high-profile clients like Rose Ross can sleep at night. And yeah, maybe there's a thrill to it—staying sharp, staying one step ahead of danger.

But lately...I don't know.

Something's shifting inside me. Maybe it started with Kennedy Green.

The memory of her catches me off guard. That first day at Ross Enterprises, when she walked into the room, all business and focus, barely sparing me a glance. Smart as hell, driven, with just enough fire in her eyes to make me curious. But what really stuck with me was the hospital.

She was asleep when I arrived. Her ankle was a mess, her face illuminated by fluorescent lights like an angel, dark hair spilling across the pillow. I should've left right away, but something kept me there, standing at her bedside like an idiot. Watching her breathe.

Kennedy appeared fragile in that bed. Vulnerable in a way I hadn't expected.

I told myself I was there to make sure she was okay. Just doing my job.

But when her emergency contact showed up—a guy named Ford—I knew it was time to go. I waited nearby until he came into sight. He walked into the room, straight to her bedside, and I slipped out before they noticed me.

Ford. His name didn't appear on the list of people she provided me. But I ran his background as soon as I found out he was on his way—it came back clear. Beyond his profession, I don't know who he is to her. Friend? Colleague? Something more?

Doesn't matter. At least, it shouldn't.

I shake off the thought and glance at my phone, wondering if I should check in with her to make sure she's okay after that fall. It's been a few days since the hospital, and I haven't seen her since. My security team provides me with updates. Still, she's been on my mind more than I care to admit.

Before I can decide, my phone buzzes on the desk. Incoming call.

Daxton.

I pick it up. "Yeah?"

"Troy, we've got a situation."

My chest tightens. "What kind of situation?"

"It's Dr. Green."

CHAPTER 11

One of Those Days

"The greater the difficulty, the more glory in surmounting it. Skillful pilots gain their reputation from storms and tempests."
– Epictetus

Kennedy

WHEN FRIEDRICH NIETZSCHE SAID, "What doesn't kill me, makes me stronger," he was referring to days like this when my ankle is throbbing, my eyes are blurry from staring at the computer screen all day, and I'm starved. Skipping lunch wasn't part of the plan, but I'm trying to make up for lost time by leaving early and going to campus to drop off these two books that Sasha signed. I could have done this days ago if I hadn't broken my ankle the last time I was there. However, I'm taking full advantage of feeling more confident about not using my crutches.

Then, there are all the texts from Ford. The thought of calling him has been gnawing at me since yesterday. I finally muster the courage to contact him about the glass. Surprisingly, he picks up the phone right away.

His voice is low and sultry when he answers. "Hey, Kennedy. It's great to finally hear back from you."

"Hi Ford. Thanks again for helping. I had a question."

"Okay, shoot."

"Did you come into my apartment while I was out?"

"Kennedy, I'm not sure what's going on, but I don't have access to your apartment, nor would I ever try to get into it without your permission. I don't even have any keys. What happened?"

"I don't know. Nothing. It's just..."

"Do you need me to stop by and check something?"

"No. Everything's okay. I think I forgot something."

"You were robbed?"

I laugh nervously. "Nothing like that. It's nothing. It's probably the medication." I lie.

"Listen, I'm just down the street. If you need anything, just let me know. My offer for dinner is still open. If you want to stay in, I can arrange for delivery."

"Ford, I'm not interested in dinner. Everything is fine. I shouldn't have called. I'll let you go now. Thanks again," I say, rushing to end the call before he says anything more.

Leaning back in my chair, I exhale. I wish I could erase all memories of Ford. This is why I can't be around him. He's pushing too hard for a reconciliation, and I can't stand the way hearing his voice forces me to recall unresolved feelings. Our relationship was torn apart so suddenly. One day we were together, and the next...nothing. Now he's back. The scab that formed over the cut has been removed, exposing the wound he left in my life the day he walked out. I know he's not good for me, but seeking closure from a hurt heart is like trying to cure a cold—you can't. I need to work through the symptoms one by one until it's done. Until my heart no longer hurts. Until his name doesn't bring up old memories. Until I'm immune to him. Until my head and heart are in sync. I'm getting there...slowly.

Today has been productive. I successfully replicated the homeostasis property of animated life without collapsing the cell—seven more to go. There's a tap at the door. It's my EA.

"Come in."

"Your car is here."

"Thank you. I'll be on my way down."

It doesn't take me long to finish up and leave the office. However, getting from my desk to the elevator and then to the front door takes longer. If it weren't so sad, it would be funny. Thankfully, I only need to get in the car. My limited mobility makes me vulnerable to crime or whatever else lies ahead.

As I exit the building, the driver stands by the car with the door open, waiting. He takes my belongings, assists me into the vehicle, and then makes his way around to the driver's side.

The ride to campus is uneventful. Traffic is doing what it does best, allowing me to clean out my inbox, which is always a nice win. Among my emails is the final press release I approved this morning, announcing my new role as head of the biotechnology department at Ross Enterprises. I expected my phone to be ringing off the hook with this announcement, but I suppose the impact was softened by the article that came before it. Hopefully, this is the positive scenario that June mentioned.

The car slowly rolls to the curb near the school entrance. A familiar face coming through the double doors catches my attention: *Nate*. Professor Thomas must have informed him that I would be here to drop off the books. When the car stops, the driver rounds to my side, opens the door, and helps me out. He doesn't get a chance to hand me the books or my belongings because Nate rushes to the car to assist.

"I've got this," he says to my driver. "Doctor Green, it's great to see you. How are you doing?"

"Nate, it's nice to see you. I'm managing, as you can tell, but I feel fine, thank you."

"I told Professor Thomas that I would meet you at the car. I can take these to him if you'd like."

"I need to pick up a few items from my office, so I'll drop these off, say hello, and then take care of my stuff."

"I hope you don't mind me helping."

"I appreciate it, thank you," I say as we walk toward the building. While Nate is walking, I'm doing a sort of half version of that. "Aside from me, what brings you to campus? You mentioned earlier that you were working on a contract at that new startup."

"I'm still around. I saw that you're leading a project at Ross Enterprises. I'd love to join your research team if you have any openings."

"We're just getting started. It's a small team for now."

"I would really love to work for you. Please keep me in mind; I promise I won't ask you out. Your friend from the hospital gave off vibes like he might kill me if I tried something like that again."

I stop in front of Professor Thomas' door. "My friend?"

Nate stops and turns to me. "Yeah, the striking tall guy." Nate can't be talking about Ford since they are about the same height. This leaves me wondering what he means by *my friend*. Nate senses my confusion and clarifies, "You know, Troy." When he says Troy's name, my heart skips a beat. *What is this feeling I'm experiencing?*

"Was he in a black suit?"

"Yes. I told him I was waiting for you to be discharged. He said I should go home and that everything had been arranged for you. I hesitated to leave, but the intensity of his stare left me with no choice."

I smile to myself, knowing what he's referring to—the façade Troy wore at the office just before I asked him to sit—unapproachable.

"He doesn't mince words, but I'm sure he thanked you."

"He did."

"We should go in." I nod toward the door as thoughts of that beautiful man swirl in my mind.

Nate knocks on the door, opens it, and I enter. "Professor Thomas, I hope we didn't interrupt you at a bad time."

He stands and walks over to meet Nate and me at the door. He shakes my hand. "Dr. Green, it's good to see you back on your feet. How are you?

Come have a seat." He gestures toward a chair near his desk. Nate hands him the books. He places the books on his desk, but I don't follow.

"I won't be here long. I came to drop off your books and pick up a few things from my office before heading home."

He glances at my boot. "You really should put your feet up," he says.

"Yeah, unfortunately, I'll be in this for a while."

"Are you sure you don't have time to catch up? I read the recent article about you."

"Probably half the staff here has read it. But no, the driver is waiting out front."

"Next time. Thank you so much for getting Dr. Duval to sign these. I owe you big time; you probably wouldn't have fallen if you hadn't been distracted by carrying these." He taps one of the books.

"You don't owe me anything. I was generally distracted. Let's catch up when I'm feeling one hundred percent."

"Deal. Nate, ensure she gets to her car safely."

"I got this."

We say our goodbyes and walk a few doors down to my office. I hand Nate the key and he opens the door. "What in the world?" he exclaims. I push past him.

"What the hell?" I glance around my office, which is a mess. Papers are strewn across the desk. I step further into the room.

Nate grips my elbow, stopping me from going any further. "Don't do that."

"What?"

"Let me call campus security. Someone broke in here."

"For what?" I ask, shocked. Unless someone has a strong interest in the 1869 version of *The Origins of Species*, there's nothing of value in my office.

Nate pulls out his phone and calls the police. While he does that, I text my driver. His response is immediate.

Driver: I need to inform our corporate security team.

Me: I understand.

Damn, what is going on? First, there was the strange water glass situation, the article, and now this. I keep telling myself it's all a coincidence, but my scientific mind says otherwise.

A few minutes go by as Nate and I wait in the hallway for the police to arrive. Nate and I answer several questions about what happened before they enter the room to inspect it. I haven't been to the office since I left almost a week ago. Nate and I continue to wait in the hall. I'm distracted by a loud noise I can't quite identify in the distance outside.

"Why would someone do this to you?" Nate asks.

"I wish I knew the answer to that."

Nate tips his chin up. "Your friend is here," he says, catching me off guard.

"My what?" I turn, following his line of sight to the man approaching me, walking like he has the solution to all my problems. *Troy?*

"Dr. Green, Mr. Bradshaw."

Nate nods in response.

"Mr. Armstrong. I...I didn't expect to see you," I say, surprising myself by stumbling over my words. I'm lost in everything Troy: his scent, his stance, and his Barry White tone. I don't know what this is, but I'm in a haze that's all him.

"Are you okay, Dr. Green?"

I glance down at the boot I'm wearing. "Besides this thing, I was a bit shocked, but I'm good."

I tell Troy I have no idea what happened or who is responsible. He informs me that he'll escort me home after speaking with the police. Troy walks into the office and engages with the officers. I follow his movements, completely captivated by this man. I don't eavesdrop on their conversation since there's nothing I can do to assist them. It's unsettling to think that someone is so interested in me and my work that they would go to such lengths.

"I'll stay here until you leave," Nate says, pulling me out of my daze.

"That won't be necessary. I've already taken up too much of your time."

"I want to make sure you get to your car."

"Okay. Thanks again, Nate... for everything."

"You're my mentor. It's an honor."

I give Nate a half-smile. Troy exits the room and extends his hand for Nate to pass him my leather backpack. How he even knows it's mine is beyond me. Nate hands it over, and Troy slings it over one shoulder before holding out an arm to me.

"Dr. Green, we should head out." Nate offers a tight-lipped smile, and I raise my eyebrows in response. I suppose I'm leaving with the hot bodyguard.

Linking arms with Troy, he leads me outside, intentionally slowing his pace to match mine. When we reach the car, I say goodbye to Nate, and then Troy helps me get into the back seat before joining the driver in the front.

I wait until we're on the freeway to speak. "How did you get here so fast?"

"I flew."

I blink. I catch a glimpse of his eyes in the rearview mirror. It seems too far-fetched that Troy said he flew here to get me. "Flew...what?"

"A helicopter."

The scene outside the car window is a blend of vehicles, pedestrians, and storefronts, none of which clarify the strangeness that has engulfed my life. Certainly not a plane. The rearview mirror serves as my means of communication—I catch his gaze. "A helicopter. Then why are we driving?"

"I wasn't sure how you'd respond or whether you'd go willingly."

I try but fail to mask my smile. *Forget it.* "Mr. Armstrong, I don't know what this says about me, but I feel I'd follow you anywhere."

There it is. The flicker. The one I noticed in Troy's eyes as I walked to Rose's office to get my tracker. As before, it vanishes quickly, leaving me to wonder if there's a feeling tied to it. Does a man like Troy, who once took a bullet for my boss, feel anything?

"Noted."

The way he says "noted" with an undercurrent of foreshadowing leaves me curious about what I'm getting into.

CHAPTER 12

Control

"The first and greatest victory is to conquer yourself."
– Plato

Troy

I'M ALREADY ON MY feet, grabbing my jacket the second Daxton says her name. "What happened?"

"Someone broke into her lab at the university."

Shit.

"She hurt?"

"No, but the police are there. And there's more—someone showed up at Ross Enterprises earlier this week asking for her. Security sent him away, but my guess is it's connected."

"Did they get a name?"

"No, they're working on it."

My jaw clenches. I don't like the sound of this.

"I'm five minutes from you. Get the chopper ready."

Daxton doesn't waste time with questions. "On it."

"And Dax, have the team forward me everything that's transpired up until today."

"Copy that."

As I head for the door, one thought races through my mind: This isn't just a break-in. And I'll be damned if I let anyone hurt her.

It doesn't take us long to reach campus. My heart pounds against my ribs, a relentless drumbeat I can't ignore as I anticipate seeing Kennedy. It's not the adrenaline I'm used to—the kind that sharpens my focus and keeps me alive. This is different. It's raw and unpredictable, and it terrifies me. The loss of control feels like stepping onto thin ice, knowing it could shatter beneath me at any moment. But I can't lose control—not now. Not when she needs me.

My life is built on control. It's how I've survived—planning every step, anticipating every move, staying ten steps ahead, never letting emotions cloud the mission. Protect the client. Maintain distance. Never miss a shot. And above all, never get involved. Those are the rules. Then she came along.

I clench my fists as I stride onto campus, scanning the surroundings out of habit. The air smells of freshly cut grass and coneflowers, but all I can focus on is the thought of her—those piercing eyes, the quiet strength that lingers beneath her composed exterior. She doesn't even realize how much she has upended my world.

She's a client, I remind myself, forcing the words into my mind like a mantra. But even now, as I approach the building, the police cars remind me why I'm here; I know the rules have already been broken.

Entering the building, I walk down the hall. Kennedy is the first thing I see. I breathe a sigh of relief. Even though her back is toward me, I sense she's okay. She's wearing a black-and-white pinstriped shirt dress and a belt that cinches at her waist. My eyes travel the length of her body to the black orthopedic boot strapped to her foot. She leans against the wall, distributing her weight on her foot in the black platform slide, avoiding pressure on her broken ankle. She shouldn't be here. She should be somewhere reclining with her foot elevated, not standing in a hallway at the crime scene. I need to get her out of here.

Her former student, Nate, whom I've been investigating, stands beside her. From everything I know about him, he seems benign—a brilliant fanboy lacking boundaries. Still, a force within me wants to keep him away from her. He notices me. Kennedy turns, we lock eyes, and her smile warms my core. In a few strides, I'm standing beside her, inhaling lavender and honey, surrounded by her aura.

"Dr. Green, Mr. Bradshaw."

Nate nods in response.

"Mr. Armstrong. I...I didn't expect you."

"Are you okay, Dr. Green?"

She inspects her boot, shifting her foot from side to side. "Besides this thing, I was slightly shocked, but I'm good."

"Do you have an idea who did this?"

"None."

"I need to talk with the police. Please remain here. When I'm done, I'll escort you home."

She smiles with pressed lips and nods. I want her smile to thaw my cold steel façade, but I have business to conduct. I need to protect her. I check myself and then step into the office.

"I'm Troy," I announce to the local police.

The two officers pause their activities and turn toward me. "Mr. Armstrong, I'm Officer Scott and this is Officer Dale. We received word that you were coming." He gestures to the papers scattered across the desk. "Nothing seems to be missing. We still have someone on the way to collect forensic evidence. Whoever it was broke into her desk and flipped through a few book pages."

Officer Dale says, "This doesn't appear to be a robbery."

"Officer Dale, this is a campus, not Cartier. They're hunting for information. Send me the forensics as soon as you receive them. Are you done interviewing Dr. Green?"

"Yes."

"Then we'll be on our way. Contact me directly if you need anything."

"What if we need to talk to Dr. Green again?"

"Contact me if you need anything," I say, enunciating every word, then turn and leave.

As I enter the hallway, Kennedy and Nate stop their discussion. Nate fixes me with an intense, assessing gaze, as if he's trying to piece together a puzzle.

"Dr. Green, we should be going," I announce. Then I collect her backpack and hold my arm out, waiting for her.

She doesn't hesitate to take my arm, and when she does, the same rush of electricity passes between us that I experienced the day I met her. She has a breezy ease about her. In the car, she initiates a light and funny conversation that feels oddly...familiar, like we've known each other more than the few hours we've shared over the past few months. I want to laugh when she says she would follow me anywhere. *I feel the same.* But I don't let on to the inner monologue I shouldn't even share with myself.

Kennedy holds my gaze in the rearview mirror and I try to be unaffected. I need to focus. I have a job to do.

"Dr. Green, I need to review a few items with you."

"You sound serious."

"It's protocol. When we arrive at your apartment, please wait for me to open the car door. I will help you out and go with you to your apartment. At your apartment, please wait at the door until I have visually checked each room, and then I will notify you it's safe to come in. Once inside, quickly scan the apartment and tell me if anything is out of place."

"And if there's nothing?"

"That's good. I would have made a mental note during my first scan, so it would be obvious to me in the future if something was off."

"So, You're my bodyguard?"

"Until we find the person that broke into your office. I'll be monitoring your floor until the overnight shift takes over. Then I'll return in the morning to take you to Ross Enterprises."

"Are you serious?" I don't respond. I lock eyes with her in the rearview mirror and let my gaze speak for me. "You are. Holy hell."

The rest of the drive is quiet. I hate that I have to be this way with her. Usually, I'm unfazed when a client doesn't talk to me. It's distracting. My job is to be a protector, not a pal. But with Kennedy, it's different. I'd rather hear her voice—to have her say something clever or ask a random question instead of sitting in silence. *What is it about her?* As the car turns into her neighborhood, I glance in the mirror at her reflection. She feels my gaze and meets it until the vehicle comes to a stop. I step out of the car, collect her belongings, and, as requested, she waits for me to open her door and assist her out.

With her arm locked in mine, we stand in her elevator, staring at the door. "Is this my new routine?" she asks.

"Until we can get a handle on what's happening."

"And if there is a real threat?"

"I neutralize it."

The elevator dings, signaling that we've arrived at her floor. I escort her to her apartment, where she hands me the key. I head inside to conduct my security check while she waits. Her apartment is spacious. Listed online at just over three thousand square feet, it exudes a cozy atmosphere with muted grey walls, gold-accented lamps, and light blue-gray tufted furniture. As I move from room to room, the color scheme remains consistent. Several rooms feature bookshelves filled with books thoughtfully arranged alongside various artifacts and photos. I observe that time is significant to Kennedy, as evidenced by a clock in each room. Everything seems in order, so I let her know everything is clear.

She leans against the door frame, her head tipped up to meet my gaze. She's so beautiful. If this woman were mine, I'd dip my head and kiss her where she stands. "Well, did you find anything?" she asks.

"No, but I need you to verify."

She enters the apartment and I help her carry her belongings to her home office. She seems unfazed by my following her through the different rooms. When we finally reach the kitchen, she says, "Everything is how I left it this morning. However, that wasn't the case yesterday."

"What happened yesterday?" My phone buzzes just as I ask. "One moment, please." I step aside to take the call. It's the RE building security. "Troy here."

"Mr. Armstrong, the person who asked Dr. Green to come down and pick up a package was recorded by our security cameras outside the building."

"Is he still there?"

"No, he seemed to be waiting. Then he left."

"Send me the footage and keep an eye out," I say, then give the security person a list of instructions. I head back to the room where Kennedy is sitting on a bar stool at her kitchen counter. "You mentioned something happened yesterday. What was it?"

"There was a glass on the counter. I don't remember putting it there. I wrote it off as the medication affecting me. But...I don't know, maybe it wasn't me."

"From everything I've witnessed and studied, you're meticulous. Is that the glass on your counter?"

"Yeah, I got sidetracked with work after I came home." She places her hand on the counter.

"Don't touch it. I'll have someone look into it." I type a message into my phone, alerting my team.

"You think someone was here?"

"Dr. Green, if you believe it's out of place...it's out of place. You can't stay here tonight."

"What? Why?"

"The person that came to see you yesterday returned to the office. I checked the time. You come and go like clockwork."

"It's a thing I have."

"Someone picked up on your pattern. They expected you to leave at your usual time. However, you left early today."

"To bring back the books."

"You need to gather some things to take with you. You can't stay here."

Her phone rings. She swipes the screen and takes the call. "Yes, I just arrived. Yes. He's here." I start to leave the room to give her privacy, but she holds up her hand.

"It's Rose. She asked me to put her on speaker," she says, tapping the phone and placing it on the counter. "We're here."

"I have Niall with me," Rose says.

"Rose, Niall," I greet.

"Hi, Troy, Kennedy," Niall greets us.

"Mr. King, sorry you are up at this hour on my behalf. Rose should be resting," Kennedy says.

"I'm fine. This is too important to wait. I'll let Niall explain."

"Rose and I spoke after reviewing the reports concerning recent incidents related to your safety. Troy provided information strikingly similar to the incidents reported several years ago, just days before Professor Rutledge went missing."

"Rutledge? That was years ago. Do you think these are the same people?"

Rose responds, "We can't be sure, but this is too coincidental to ignore. My top priority is your safety. We can pause the project until we sort this out—"

"No, I've dedicated my career to reach this point. I'm in a position to accomplish what everyone believed was impossible. I'm not stopping now."

"Then you'll need to temporarily relocate. Someone has already tried to reach you at the office and the lab. If Troy's investigation finds that they were at your home...you're not safe in the city. Someone is probably watching you."

"Corporate housing or a hotel should suffice," Kennedy says.

"That's the first place they'll look for you," Niall interjects.

"Then we'll figure out another place. We need to consider the fact that you need time to heal."

"I have a deadline for my first deliverable and I plan to meet it. I don't want you to worry about this. You should focus on delivering a healthy child."

"I need to know you're okay."

My gaze shifts to her when I say, "Dr. Green's inability to move puts her at risk no matter where she is in the city."

"What about your penthouse, Troy?" Niall asks.

"Too many variables involved. I own a mountain house, which is a better option."

"No, you don't need to do that. I can stay in the city. What are your thoughts, Niall?" she asks subtly, seeking reassurance.

"There are hundreds of ways, even with security measures in place, for them to access you. This also endangers many lives not connected to Ross Enterprises. Troy's mountain house is the best option."

I'm sure Niall and Rose considered all the scenarios before they called. Niall and his brother Aedan have firsthand experience protecting the women in their lives, and so do I. The advantage was that Rose and June had full mobility, which helped them escape dangerous situations. They've been trained what to do—to expect the unexpected. In Rose's case, they tried but couldn't get to her. No one gets through me.

"Why?" Kennedy asks.

I sense her concern—her eyes search mine for answers. I want to cup her cheek, kiss her, and promise that everything will be fine, but she's not mine. So I don't. I need to maintain control. Instead, I say, "Dr. Green, my house is accessible only by helicopter."

CHAPTER 13

The Mountain

"The world is a stage, and we are merely players."
– William Shakespeare

Kennedy

TROY WALKING TOWARD ME in the campus hallway with all his swagger was a pleasant surprise and welcome relief. I hadn't expected to see him again until Rose returned from her maternity leave. The week before injuring myself, she and Niall had gone back to Belfast to work before her leave began. It's safer than being in the US, and the office is within walking distance of their penthouse. June, who will cover for Rose during her maternity leave in a few months, currently alternates between working in the US and Ireland. With Rose's husband managing her security for the coming months, I never considered what Troy does during his downtime.

I quickly realize that seeing Troy again isn't the biggest surprise. Sitting beside him as he whisks me away in his helicopter to his secluded mountain house feels less like reality and more like the start of a story I never meant to write. The steady thrum of the rotors beats in time with my pulse, not from fear, but from the undeniable thrill of being here with him. The idea of living and working under the same roof as Troy sends a flutter of anticipation through me, a strange kind of excitement I can't fully explain.

But the rush of butterflies is chased by a knot of unease tightening in my chest. I can't ignore the reason I'm here—the shadows creeping closer to my work, the looming deadlines, the fact that danger is no longer hypothetical. I steal a glance at Troy, his jaw set, eyes fixed on the horizon. The headset only adds to his handsome appeal, like he's straight out of a movie, the kind where the girl falls for the man who's sworn to protect her.

However, this isn't fiction. I'm discovering that we have this unspoken connection, this ability to sense each other's presence without a word. I wonder if it's instinctual—something he shares with all his clients—or if what's simmering between us is something different, something that could be just as problematic as the people hunting my research.

He turns to me. "Look out the window to your right. That's where we're going."

Even through my headset, his voice resonates as rich, deep, sexy, calming—like the comfort of a pilot announcing your arrival. I glance down to my right and spot a vast property perched atop a mountain. In the center stands a distinctly modern home made of gray concrete and deep mahogany-stained wood, boasting sharp angles contrasting with an azure-colored pool and other recreational amenities. As Troy maneuvers the helicopter, his house temporarily vanishes from sight until a space that resembles a mall parking lot comes into view, marked not by parking lines, but by a white H. *A helipad.* He flies over it, and we begin our descent.

I take a deep breath as he lands the helicopter with expert precision. He adjusts several dials on the display in front of him. The noise from the helicopter decreases. "Give me a few minutes. I'll take you inside."

He takes off his headset and seatbelt. Afterward, he leans over, enveloping me in his scent as he undoes my seatbelt. Then he carefully removes my headset. The gesture feels intimate. I meet his gaze, savoring the moment. He seems like...*mine. How can this be?*

While I'm basking in the haze of him, he exits the craft and goes around it. When he opens the door, he says, "I'll carry you." I furrow my brows, and he adds, "It's a bit of a distance, and there are a few stairs." I nod reluctantly, allowing him to lift me out of the craft as if I were a feather. I drape an arm around his shoulder.

As he carries me across the helipad and through the lawn, I'm captivated by the breathtaking beauty of his property as his house comes into view. The mountain rises behind his expansive hideaway, resembling more of a modern luxury hotel than a home.

"This is beautiful," I say as he walks up a few broad stone steps leading to a lengthy pathway toward the entrance, which is entirely glass except for the frame. When he approaches the door, it opens automatically. "I didn't expect that."

"I designed the security system to recognize my features."

"And mine?" I ask jokingly as we pass through the foyer into the living room with floor-to-ceiling windows, revealing a spectacular view of the sky and the valley beyond the hillside. He lowers me onto the couch, where my back rests against the armrest and my legs stretch across it.

"Yes."

"I was just joking."

"Dr. Kennedy, according to the data from your tracker, you've been in this boot all day. I'm going to take it off so you can rest for a minute. Are you okay with that?" I nod.

Gently, he removes each black strap, lifting my leg slightly to slide the boot off my foot. "May I?" he asks, indicating my knee-high sock.

"As long as you know what you're getting into." I smile at him, but he remains expressionless, leaving me curious if there's a personality hidden behind his protective façade. Rose always refers to him as her man-of-steel because of his unbreakable, untouchable demeanor. June echoed this sentiment, making me wonder...is he even human?

He holds my calf with one hand and slides my sock off with the other. His hands are large and warm; I imagine them roaming my body. As he examines my ankle, I study our contrasting skin tones—both differing shades of brown. He's so fine...rich, like dark chocolate. He catches me staring at him.

"Your ankle is swollen. Have you been following your doctor's orders?

"Trying."

"If you want to heal, I suggest you follow them. I'll gather your things and show you around the house shortly. Would you like some water or something?"

"Nothing at the moment."

"I'll be back."

"Troy." He turns toward me. "Thank you," I tell him. He purses his lips, then leaves.

Leaning my arm on the back of the couch, I exhale deeply and take in the expansive open-concept room. To my left, there's a dining room featuring a large gray stone table atop a wooden base that can comfortably seat twelve people. Hanging above, at varying heights, is a collection of eight glass spheres attached to gold hardware. I can envision hosting family gatherings here, with breathtaking views beyond the contemporary garden and pool, overlooking an untouched landscape. I close my eyes to dismiss the thought. *This man is not mine.* He's my temporary bodyguard. Even if he were my man, like Ford, I doubt he would sacrifice anything to be with me. Certainly not his career. Once I no longer need this boot, I'll return home, resume my life, and likely have someone else assigned to me until the threat subsides.

The sound of luggage wheels gliding across the stone alerts me that Troy has returned. Though I can't see Troy, the wheels stop, and the rustling of paper signals that he has also brought in our groceries. When he insisted that I come to his mountain house, we gathered a few items from my refrigerator and cupboards that I like to eat and he took me to the market before heading to the airport. He didn't think it was a good idea for me to go inside, so I waited in the car with Troy while the driver went in with the list.

He passes behind me into the adjacent room, which shares the same view. I turn and watch as he sets the bag on the kitchen counter. He puts the items away one by one, and when he's finished, the space is just as immaculate as if he had never been there. I think I've met my match regarding everything having its place. Then he retrieves two glasses from a cabinet, fills them with ice and water, returns to the living room, and hands me a glass.

"The flight can be dehydrating," he says, then sits on the couch opposite me.

"You don't talk much, do you?"

He sips his water before responding. "I let my actions do the talking."

"When I said I'd follow you anywhere, I didn't expect you'd take me up on it." He smiles in response, revealing a hint of his beautiful white teeth. "The way you just lit up the room with that smile suggests I caught you off guard, Mr. Armstrong." I would pay to see that swoon-worthy smile again.

"Do you express all your inner thoughts, Dr. Green?"

Now it's me who's smiling. "Most of them. Seriously, you should smile more often. But only when I'm sitting down; I felt faint for a second."

He shakes his head. "Drink your water. I'll put your things in your bedroom and your computer next to my home office in the library. After that, I'll take you on a tour."

I tilt my head toward my leg. "Are you going to carry me again?"

"I'll return your boot. I suggest you follow a regimen to get that healed properly." Troy drinks the last of his water, gets up, and disappears. In the distance, the soft glide of my luggage wheels disappears with him.

I already know Troy is going to be distracting. The circumstances surrounding my presence here and my impending deadline should be at the forefront of my mind. Instead, I'm thinking about my handsome bodyguard and everything I want him to do to me. Yet, the question lingers...is he even human? Does he feel as I do, as if I've known him my entire life? Can he sense our connection, or is his only concern my protection?

Chapter 14

Sunsets and Her

"Every sunset is an opportunity to reset. Every sunrise begins with new eyes."
– Richie Norton

Troy

She's here…with me. She's safe. This is the mantra I repeat in my head as we leave Kennedy's house with her on my arm, when we are on the road heading to the airport, and while in flight on the way to my mountain home. Mid-flight, I receive a call from Anita, my facial biometrics specialist, informing me that she has identified the person who repeatedly showed up at Ross Enterprises insisting on seeing Kennedy.

"Copy that. Send me everything you have," I tell her over my headphones.

I glance briefly at Kennedy, who is mesmerized by the view of San Francisco shrinking in the distance, oblivious to the conversation that just occurred. Now that we've uncovered one link in the chain, we can begin to dismantle it. It will take time, but it's a start. There is a clear hierarchy in these matters. The most notable individual, the strange visitor, is often disposable. The lead perpetrator chooses someone without suspicion—no prior criminal record, not even a speeding ticket or a jaywalking citation—a blank slate with no cause for concern. In exchange, they gain a false sense of security, assumed immunity, and an untraceable bundle of cash with more

86

on the way once the job is complete—all empty promises. The one who wants access to her is still out there. I will find them.

After I arrive home, settling in Kennedy takes less than thirty minutes. In the brief time she's been here, her playful nature has surprisingly impacted me. I find it hard to keep from smiling at some of her antics.

"I don't want to walk, but you could give me a piggyback ride," she said just before our tour. As I considered the idea, she quickly added, "I'm kidding, Mr. Armstrong. I'm perfectly capable of walking in this monstrosity."

She doesn't know I would have given her a ride...if she had insisted. Maybe she does. I take a deep breath and gather my thoughts. I'm in trouble when it comes to her. At this moment, I would do whatever she asks. *Heaven help me.*

Standing at the stove, I turn off the heat under the rice pot. I step back and crack the oven door to check on the salmon...*just a few more minutes.* That's all it'll take before dinner is ready. Before she comes back from her room, where she's unpacking. Before I put on my mask and pretend to be unaffected by her every move. I sense her presence before I see her as I plate the rice and roasted vegetables.

"Smells good in here."

"Perfect timing," I say as she confirms I can set my watch by her. I've only seen it in a few people, mainly those I work with. We have to be this way. A half a second can mean the difference between life and death.

I slip on a pair of oven mitts, take the salmon out of the oven, and place it on the stove. I return the mitts to the counter and turn to face Kennedy. She is stunning, leaning against the wall like when I found her in the hallway outside her trashed office earlier today. She's changed from her shirt dress into a black off-shoulder cotton dress that hangs to the top of her boots. Even with all the drama swirling around her life, she appears relaxed.

She holds my gaze, and I need to say something to prevent getting lost in her spell. "Feel free to sit in the dining room and I'll bring out dinner."

She pushes away from the wall and gradually makes her way to the table.

"Sit on the other side," I call out. "I have something to show you." She obliges.

I plate our meal, fill two glasses with sparkling water, add other accompaniments to a tray, and carry it to the table. She observes my movements as I take items from the tray and set them on the table.

I sit. "Would you like anything else?"

She shakes her head. "I'm good for now. This is much better than my usual burger or pizza."

"Please tell me that's not what you've been eating this past week."

"It's not the only thing I've eaten. I had some ribs and mac and cheese—though it was delivered. Today is Thursday; I'd usually be at my favorite restaurant—so it's not all bad."

"Anything green?" She cuts a piece of the roasted broccoli and holds her fork up. "Now, Dr. Green, you should know better."

"You can call me Kennedy since I'll be staying with you for the next few weeks."

I smile inside at the thought but don't let it show. "Kennedy, you know—"

"Don't say it."

"Do you know why I asked you to sit there?"

"No, but every seat in your home provides a prime view of something lovely."

"Check it out." I tilt my head toward the view.

For the first time since we sat down, her eyes aren't focused on me or her plate. Instead, she gazes across the dining room table, where the sun kisses the horizon in a vibrant display of gold, orange, and purple.

She inhales. "My God, Troy. I feel like I need to say a prayer." Her eyes are wide and filled with tears as she takes in the sun beginning to dip below the horizon. She wipes under her eyelid with her finger. *Damn*. I didn't mean to make her cry.

"Are you okay?"

"Yeah. It's just...it's so beautiful. How do you ever leave this place?"

"Would you like to go to the edge?"

"Of the mountain?"

"No. There's a spot just beyond the pool where you can sit. If you want to watch the sunset, I can reheat the food after."

"Let's watch the sunset."

I stand, hold my hand to her, and help her up. "Chris, patio one," I call out, and the glass wall slides to one side, providing us access to the outdoor space.

"Who is Chris?" she asks, holding my arm as we walk.

"My home computer system." We stroll across the patio, past the pool, to a descending staircase. "May I?" She nods. I lift her gently and carry her down five steps, then set her back on her feet and guide her to a pair of chairs. "You can sit here."

I stand beside her with my back against the wall. We watch silently for the next ten minutes as the sun dips below the horizon. It's a sight I've witnessed many times before. Yet, seeing it with her makes my soul sing. I shouldn't feel this way, but I can't control it. She leans forward, still staring into the distance. She senses my gaze, looks over her shoulder, and smiles at me. "You ready to go in?" I ask.

"Yeah."

When I help her this time, I carry her up the stairs, past the pool, across the patio, and into the kitchen. "Have a seat here. I'll get our plates and reheat them."

"Does Chris respond to my voice commands?"

I grab the plates, put one in the microwave, turn, and lean against the counter, saying, "Of course."

"Chris, play some jazz."

Just as *Bridge over the Stars* by Keiko Matsui begins to play from the speakers, the microwave dings. I take out the plate and set it on the countertop in front of Kennedy, along with fresh silverware. I repeat the process for my dinner.

"I never asked if you wanted wine."

"I prefer cocktails. That's why I brought a list of things along, plus items from our grocery run."

"Did you want one?"

"No, I usually do that on the weekends. My friend Sasha and I have a tradition of trying out new recipes. Do you drink?"

"No."

She stares at me for a moment, as if deciding what to do with that information, sighs, and then eats her salmon. She eats a few more bites and then asks, "Troy, should I be worried about these people coming after me?"

"We don't know who they are yet, but as long as you're with me, you have nothing to fear. You're here to focus on healing and your project."

I tell her what she needs to hear, not to appease her, but because it's true. Seeing her and sensing our connection, it's clear to me...I would die for her.

Chapter 15

An Agreement

"The key is not to prioritize what's on your schedule, but to schedule your priorities."
– Stephen Covey

Kennedy

Waking up yesterday, I certainly didn't expect to be the headline news topic or the target of someone seeking access to my work. I also didn't foresee being flown by helicopter to the remote residence of my smoking-hot bodyguard. Life said, "Hold my beer."

Last night after dinner I retreated to my room early under the pretense I was exhausted from the day's events. While partially true, I mainly needed a break from Troy. To be free from the scent of leather and musk drawing me in, the strong arms I want wrapping around me. To silence the sound of Barry White stroking my soul with every word. To focus. To get back to reality. To stop wanting something that isn't mine.

This morning, I woke up at my usual time. The difference is that the city noises weren't there to greet my day. No sirens. No horns. No neighbors. There's only silence and a spectacular view of the sprawling property, and beyond that...more mountains. Before yesterday, I had never been anywhere where you didn't need to close the curtains to avoid being seen. This place takes privacy to a whole new level. I'm curious if anyone else has been here and make a mental note to ask.

Getting ready doesn't take me long. Troy considered everything, including teak stools in and out of the bath, allowing me to take care of business without reinjuring myself. I can't wait to get rid of this boot. Conveniently, I can remove it when necessary...it's the part about needing to do anything regarding it that I dislike. I check the time. Six-thirty. Perfect. No commute means extra hours to work on my project. I put on a white logo T-shirt dress and knee-high white socks with black stripes at the top. I strap the boot on one foot and slip my other foot into a black platform slide before heading down the hall to the kitchen.

I'm not sure how he knows I've entered the kitchen, but Troy turns, cup in hand, to face me before I reach the counter. It's the first time I've seen him without a suit, and he...well, let's just say I'd love to press my fingers against the ripples in his black T-shirt or slide my hands into his jean pockets as I sneak in for a hug. *He's not yours*, I sing-song the words in my head. He leans against the counter, one leg crossed over the other, and sips his drink.

"Morning. Coffee?" Troy raises his cup, the faint steam curling between us like an unspoken invitation.

I shuffle over as gracefully as my boot-slide combo allows, biting back a wince. "I'm disappointed," I tease, resting my hand on the cool counter for balance. "I expected you to be waiting outside my door when I got up. You know, protecting me."

And there it is. His smile. Damn, it's unfair, the way it transforms his whole face, softening the sharp angles into something...warm.

Troy steps closer, his large hand gently cupping my elbow as if he can sense the wobble in my balance. His touch is steady, grounding. "Have a seat. Are you okay?"

I plop myself onto a bar stool, brushing off his concern with a tentative laugh. "Yeah, just fine. I told you that smile of yours is dangerous."

He presses his lips together, but it doesn't quite hide the amusement in his eyes. "Breakfast is ready if you're hungry. I made a spinach and cheese omelet with a selection of fruit, or there's yogurt if you'd prefer."

I blink, caught off guard. A man whose muscles suggest he could bench-press a mountain made me breakfast. "You don't have to cook for me every day. Despite my appetite for unhealthy eating, I'm pretty good in the kitchen. Besides, a pastry and coffee work just fine for breakfast."

Troy doesn't argue. Instead, he turns to the stove, moving with a strangely mesmerizing efficiency. Within moments, he places a plate in front of me, the omelet's cheesy aroma mingling with the fresh scent of coffee as he pours a cup for me.

"We should discuss a meal plan to help with your healing process," he says, his tone matter-of-fact but kind. "Have you started your exercises?"

I take a sip of coffee, stalling. "No. And why can't I eat what I want?"

"You can," he replies, setting his own plate down and sitting across from me. "But disregarding the doctor's orders and not eating right will prolong your recovery. Your next visit is in—"

"Three weeks," I finish his statement.

"Right. What's your expectation for that visit?"

"I expect the doctor to tell me I can ditch this boot and walk well enough to go home."

Troy's brow slightly furrows. A quiet intensity in his gaze makes me feel as if he sees right through me. "It'll be a while before you're back to normal. As for the boot, you're running behind schedule based on what I noticed while examining your ankle yesterday."

A flicker of frustration stirs in my chest. "My main priorities are regaining my mobility and advancing my project. Part of the reason I'm here—and not tucked away in some hotel—is my difficulty moving fast if something happens."

"And that's exactly why I suggest establishing a routine to achieve your mobility goals. This means setting aside part of your day for therapeutic exercises and eating the right foods."

"I don't have time for this."

"You have twenty-four hours," he counters evenly. "I'm asking for two and a half each day. Your choice."

"Why so many?" I ask, narrowing my eyes.

"Thirty minutes each for breakfast and lunch. An hour for dinner. An extra thirty for exercise."

"And you're going to make all those meals?"

He doesn't answer right away, his steady gaze betraying nothing. His contemplation is enough confirmation for me.

"Why would you do that?" I press, my voice softer now.

"To help you. And I like cooking. I don't get to do it often."

"Because of your job?"

"That's right."

I push my fork around the plate he has so carefully prepared for me, the vibrant reds and yellows a stark contrast to the grab-and-go meals I'm used to. A strange knot forms in my chest, a mix of gratitude and resistance. "I need to think about it," I say, the words tasting bitter. Committing to another man's care—even in something as simple as a meal plan—feels like stepping onto thin ice. The last time I let someone into my routine and my life, it didn't end well.

I dedicated three years to Ford. Reflecting on it, I was going along with his plan. His idea was to keep separate residences, even though we saw each other daily. He persuaded me that it wasn't advisable to travel together for business. So, when he had business trips, I didn't go, and vice versa. It was always his way, his plan—all the way up until he decided we couldn't be together.

It didn't register until he returned a few months ago. *"Have lunch with me," he stated, not asking.* I accepted. *"Have dinner with me," he insisted.*

I held out until I couldn't—until he showed up at the hospital as my emergency contact. That was his idea, too. *"Your parents are retired and travel a lot. You should list me as your emergency contact," he argued.* At the time, it made sense. Now, it feels like he was slowly lulling me into a false sense of security with him. But why? I thought his pressure signaled that we were moving toward marriage, or at least that he was becoming my person. He's not. I wonder if he ever felt anything for me. I can't go through that again.

But Troy isn't pressing. He isn't insisting. He's just...present. And perhaps, for now, that's enough.

A bird passing by the kitchen window pulls my attention across the room. Like all the other spaces in this house, it boasts a spectacular view. With no visible roads leading here, building this place would have taken a lot of money and a strategically executed plan. What does that say about Troy?

"Troy, I need to get some work done. I plan to deliver the first iteration of my project before Rose goes on maternity leave. Thanks for breakfast," I say, then stand.

"You good for lunch at noon?"

"Sure."

I turn and walk down the hall to the library on the other side of the house. I open my laptop and power it on. I have a few hours to catch my breath before I decide whether to trust another man again...even if he vowed to protect me.

***

Albert Einstein said, *"It's not that I'm so smart, it's just that I stay with problems longer."* I've adopted this quote as my motto and use it as the reason I put in so many hours on the job. The lack of distraction has been beneficial to being productive. I rerun my program for the next few hours, testing different variables with protocells to determine which will yield sustained results that mimic normal cells. Three hours into my work, I introduce another variable and watch with bated breath as the algorithm runs, learning as it goes. If I can create an algorithm that produces the desired results, I can advance the testing to the lab phase. The difficulty in developing protocells lies in achieving self-awareness, allowing the cells to act as if they're naturally performing—in essence, demonstrating the same eight key properties of animated life that an autonomous cell would. Biting my lip, I watch the simulation on the screen. The cell implodes. *Damn.*

I press my fingers to my eyes and rub them. I'm overthinking this. I put my boot back on, swivel the tufted leather chair, and visually explore the room. The library is the one space that deviates from the modern aesthetic found throughout the house. With its floor-to-ceiling, dark-stained book-shelves and ornate fireplace, it has an atmosphere reminiscent of a private gentleman's club I've seen in movies.

As I glance at my watch, I reflect on my last conversation with Troy. He seemed genuinely interested in my recovery. I can't remember a time in my relationship with Ford when he showed concern for me. When I was sick, he would say things like, *"It's just a cold. It'll run its course."* He would head off to work and leave me to fend for myself. Sure, sometimes it was merely a cold, but that's beside the point. Surprisingly, he appeared attentive after picking me up from the hospital. It's so unlike him. I'm wary that he's only acting this way because I turned down his dinner invitation and he's searching for ways to reenter my life. My injury has likely created an opportunity. However, with Troy, I don't feel any ulterior motive. He seems genuinely invested in me. The real question is whether he's doing this out of duty or something more personal.

It's almost noon. I haven't seen Troy since this morning. I half-expected to run into him a few hours ago when I went to the kitchen for bottled water. Frustrated and hungry, I make my way to the kitchen. On the counter is a serving tray with a wooden salad bowl filled with spinach, shaved almonds, and blueberries. Beside it are matching salad tongs, two bottles of sparkling water, stacked plates, silverware, and several accompaniments for lunch. Beyond the patio door, Troy is standing at the outdoor grill with his back to me. I pick up the tray and head toward him.

Setting the tray on the outdoor table, I say, "Please tell me those are burgers."

He turns with metal tongs in hand. There's a familiarity in his eyes that makes me think he's trying to mask his happiness at seeing me. I smile, hoping it will relax him a bit.

"Grilled chicken. Have a seat. I'll bring it over."

I comply, sitting where I have a clear view of his assets. He flips the chicken, checking it for doneness, then places it on a platter. He slices the chicken with quick, precise strokes and then brings the platter to the table.

"Is this part of my meal plan? Because I could really go for a burger right now. Not that this doesn't look good," I say, placing a plate and utensils in front of him. I take the other plate to put my salad on, along with a few grilled chicken strips, which I drizzle with dressing. I take a bite. "This is good. Did you make this dressing?"

"It's premade strawberry vinaigrette. If you were to follow a plan, this would be on it." Troy fills his plate with salad and follows the same steps I do.

"Who taught you how to cook?"

"My mom, but I learned grilling from my dad. I think he was secretly competing with his buddies to see who could cook the best. My mom does a good job grilling, too, but she let him do his thing," he says, surprising me by sharing something personal.

"Would you believe me if I told you I never used a grill before?"

"Obtaining several degrees simultaneously and living in a downtown high-rise—I don't find that unusual. While you're here, I can teach you if you're interested."

"I'll take you up on that."

"How was work? Did you make headway?"

"Ugh, one of my tests failed. It's a setback, but I have an idea of possible modifications."

"You're accomplished in biophysics and data science. I don't imagine many people possess your capabilities."

"True. Scientists usually have a strong grasp of one but not both. However, there are a few of us around."

"Sounds complicated. I'll stick to what I do."

"The concept is not as complicated as you think; it's replicating how nature works that's tricky." I grab a blueberry from the salad bowl, slice it in half, and set it on the table, skin-side down. "Okay, imagine this blueberry is a cell." I point to the shiny, purple skin. "The skin's like the outer layer of the cell, protecting everything inside. But it's not just a shield—it's busy. Think of it like a gatekeeper, deciding what comes in and what goes out. Nutrients, waste, signals—it manages all of that."

Troy nods, chewing thoughtfully.

"Now, inside the blueberry? That's where the real magic happens." I tap the juicy part. "It's sending messages, like little electrical signals, telling the cell how to behave. But here's the thing—cells aren't just following orders. They *know* when something is off. If there's too much of one thing or not enough of another, they adjust, trying to balance themselves out."

I glance up to make sure he's still with me. He is—his eyes are locked on mine with the same steady intensity that always gets under my skin.

"Instincts."

"Precisely. But in the lab," I continue, "we can't recreate that natural *knowing*. Instinct. We can build structure, but it just sits there unless something tells it what to do. That's where AI comes in. Kinda like the bracelet you gave me." I lean in a little, my voice dropping like I'm letting him in on a secret. "I write algorithms—basically, instructions—that help these artificial cells learn and adapt just like real ones do. The more they process, the smarter they get. It's like teaching them to think."

I pick up the other half of the blueberry and hold it out to him. "Nature figured out how to turn this into a blueberry instead of a grape. My work is trying to teach artificial cells to know what they're supposed to become. Go ahead." I hold it closer to his lips. "Taste it."

Troy leans in and I place half of the berry in his mouth. A shiver runs down my spine when his tongue touches my fingers. When I pull my hand away, he licks his lips. I eat the other half, but I'm still in my Troy haze. I inhale and say, "There are eight gates or algorithms I need to develop."

"How long do you think it'll take to reach the stage where you're ready to present to the board?"

"A few months. If I can get them right, it will speed up the process, and then I can get in the lab. That's the most important part."

"Have you ever missed a deadline?"

I smirk. "Somehow, I have a feeling you already know the answer to that question."

"You have this thing about time. You should consider my suggestion."

"Follow your plan and get out of here sooner?"

"This is not about rushing you. It's about getting you back to doing the things you love. The things you do when not working."

"Which is not a lot."

"I'm surprised—bright woman like you. I imagine you out exploring."

"I wish. Research consumes most of my time. This project could be the pinnacle of my career. If successful, maybe I can finally do some of the things I've been missing out on."

"Like?"

I pick up my fork and separate the meat from the salad. Troy stills, waiting for my response.

I take a deep breath, exhale, and say, "You don't want to hear it. You might think I'm simple."

He tilts his head slightly. "You think I'd judge you for having a life outside the lab?"

"I wish I had time to spend at the beach walking barefoot in the sand or having a picnic in the park. Maybe hang out at museums on the weekends—nothing complicated. Then, if I had more time...travel."

"Sounds doable. You'll do that and more. Step one starts with healing your foot."

I huff. "Your plan." He nods. "What do I get out of this besides a speedy recovery?"

A smirk tugs at his lips. "That's not enough for you?"

A set of rules governs conduct in every situation, including sports, civilizations, genetics, and everything else. If Troy wants me to do what he says, I want something from him in return. Something more than I can give myself.

"I'll recover no matter what. I want to leave with a fresh perspective." I cut a piece of chicken and eat it. "You say you want to help me be ready for my next appointment, but I assume you want me out of your hair quickly. Whatever the right answer is—I'll bite."

"So, you agree?"

"On one condition."

"I thought we covered this."

"How about you fly back to town to get me junk food before I go on a hunger strike."

"You wouldn't dare."

"No, I wouldn't, but I want something in return."

"Name it."

"Can I trust you'll follow through?"

He purses his lips, unimpressed. "You've already entrusted your life to me. Anything you ask for is yours as long as you stick to the plan I lay out."

"Okay. So, at the end of this, if I want to learn to fly your helicopter or how to grill, whatever I ask, I get?"

"Anything."

I tap my index finger against my chin. This man has no idea what he's getting into. I push back my chair and stand.

Troy stands, too. "What are you doing?"

"Getting a piece of paper to write down what I want. Then I'll seal it in an envelope. If the doctor clears me in three weeks, you can open it and read the request. If I don't pass the physical, I'll burn the envelope. Fair is fair."

"Have a seat. I'll get it." He walks inside to the credenza beneath the picture that covers his TV, retrieves some supplies, returns to the table, and hands them to me. "Here you go."

"Are the bedroom and bathrooms the only spaces without cameras in your house?"

"Yes."

"Then I'll be back. You might cheat and check your surveillance footage to see what I wrote."

"That's not necessary." He takes out his phone, taps it a few times, and then shows me the screen where he deactivated the cameras. "You have twenty seconds." He leaves the phone on the table near me, then turns his back to me.

I smile to myself as I write my request in the tiniest script. I fold the paper in on itself four times, place it into the envelope, and seal it. "Okay, done. Let's lock this away somewhere."

I take a deep breath to calm the butterflies. *What did I just do?*

CHAPTER 16

Just the Two of Us

"One of the hardest things in life is having words in your heart that you can't utter."
– James Earl Jones

Troy

SHE'S NOT MINE. SHE'S my client, I remind myself, holding her calf as I carefully remove her orthopedic boot. Honey and lavender linger in the air, embracing me, making it hard to focus when I only want to slide my hand up her thigh. Taking a deep breath, I recite my mantra.

Yesterday, Kennedy agreed to follow my plan, which includes a relatively strict diet of protein, low-fat dairy, and leafy green foods. Having experienced similar injuries in my youth and with the advice of a brother who's also a surgeon, I understand the importance of diet and exercise in relation to healing broken bones. Kennedy did good last night—not a single complaint about the stuffed turkey breast. She even surprised me by eating two helpings. However, she was hesitant about letting me guide her through the foot exercises, so after dinner, she chose to try them on her own before going to bed.

"I'm positive I did it wrong," she says as I put the boot on the floor beside us. I slip off her sock and lay it on the floor, too.

"I'm going to bend your knee. All I want you to do is stretch your leg until the bottom of your foot is flat to my hand," I say, holding my hand like I'm taking an oath.

During breakfast, Kennedy confessed that she preferred me to guide her through the exercises because it hurt too much when she tried on her own. We agreed to work out twice a day, once after lunch and again after dinner, for thirty minutes each time. So here we are on the exercise mat in my gym. I brought a red sand hourglass from my office to time our session since she's a stickler for time, and we decided this would be a tech-free zone.

She extends her leg until her skin makes contact with mine. Her foot is cold compared to my warm body, likely due to immobilization. "That's good. Now, push my hand back toward me and tell me what you feel. Don't worry, I won't resist."

She presses her foot gently against me like the touch of a child placing their hand in yours. "It feels ok."

"Good. You might feel something with this next move. Tell me the moment you do."

"Okay."

I place a pillow on the mat beneath her calf and ankle. "I'll demonstrate the move on your good foot, and then I'd like you to replicate it on this one." I touch her big toe on the injured foot. Then I take her good foot and arch her toes until they point toward me. "Now try the same move on your other foot. Pretend you are pumping the brakes, but not too aggressively."

"I'll try." She angles her foot slightly, pointing her toes toward me. Her eyes narrow.

"Do you feel anything?"

"Yeah. It hurts."

"Grade the pain like you're grading my biochem exam. A fail is equivalent to the pain you felt on campus the day you hurt it."

"Fifty percent."

"I thought I'd do better than that."

"Are we still talking about my pain?" She smirks.

"Let's try again." She repeats the gesture, then straightens her foot. "Again." She repeats the gesture twice more. "What grade?"

"Fifty-nine."

"That's good. Let's try a few more times."

Kennedy flexes her ankle. It's so small that it fits easily between my thumb and forefinger. I feel her gaze, heat pressing into my skin. My attention follows the line of her body, drawn to the pull of her stare, unrelenting when our eyes meet. We share an unspoken connection, a signal passing between us that neither of us can act on. Our time on the mountain is limited. I need to remain clear-headed to protect her.

"You're an enigma, Troy, and I'm determined to unlock your secrets."

I blink. "What do you want to know?"

"Where do I start? What kind of man builds something like this yet is willing to take a bullet for someone?"

"My purpose is to protect my clients, not take a bullet."

"But you took one for Rose."

"I did my job."

"Have you ever killed someone?"

"Yes."

"I don't suppose the man who shot you is still alive?"

"No."

"Rose and June call you their man of steel. In the short time I've known you, I understand why. But I don't get why you need this...," she gestures as if presenting something, "if.... Sorry, I'm being too personal. It must feel powerful to have no fears."

I'm unsure how to respond to that, so I address the first part of her statement by asking a question: "How did you feel when we were on the mountainside watching the sunset?"

"Like we were the only two people on earth. For a moment the world fell away. The only thing on my mind was the spectacular view and...you."

Her words wrap around my soul, squeezing while my heart races as it does around her. My mind drifts back to the moment we were taking in the view. I don't share with her that while she was watching the miracle of nature, I was gazing at something more beautiful than a thousand sunsets...*her*. Kennedy must sense my thoughts because she presses her toe against my hand. "It was lovely, Troy. You built this to escape it all. No one can find you here. This is a place without worries."

"That's right." I cup her foot in my hand and gently massage it, careful not to hurt her.

"Are your parents still alive?"

"Yes."

"Have they been here?"

"Many times." I glance at the hourglass; it's almost half full. After I finish massaging Kennedy's foot, I put her sock and boot back on. I stand and extend my hand to help her to her feet. "I'll let you get back to work. I'll see you at dinner."

When Kennedy stands, she rests her hands on my forearms to steady herself. She's close. Too close. I want to wrap my arms around her and pull her in. I want to make her mine. I want to tell her she'll never have to worry about anything. I shouldn't feel this way, but I do.

With a tilt of her head, she holds my attention. "What does the Man of Steel do when I'm working?"

Memorizing her features, the curve of her lips, the sparkle in her eyes, I tell her. "One man showed up at your workplace several times looking for you. Seventy-two people downloaded your latest research paper. One hundred and fifty people attended your last lecture in New York. Two hundred thirty-eight people entered your apartment building the day you wondered whether you left a glass out." I open my mouth to mention another figure, but she presses her fingers against my lips. I hold my breath—her eyes are filled with tears. I want to wipe them away, but I can't hide the harsh truth.

"Okay. I understand. Thanks. I'll let *you* get back to work," she says. She turns and I watch the woman I want more than anything...leave.

CHAPTER 17

Overture

"There is a charm about the forbidden that makes it unspeakably desirable."
– Mark Twain

Kennedy

THE MOUNTAIN AIR MUST be getting to my head. I close my laptop with a decisive snap, exhaling a breath that feels like it has been trapped all day. The equations and notes can wait; my ankle can't. And if I'm honest, neither can I.

The idea of seeking out Troy sends a wave of warmth through me, even though I attempt to rationalize it away. I need assistance with the exercises—his skills are practical, not personal. At least, that's what I tell myself.

I find him leaning against the porch railing, the wind tugging at his shirt as he watches the horizon. He turns when he hears me, his eyes scanning me with that ever-watchful gaze that makes me feel both safe and seen.

"Done for the day?" he asks, slightly lifting his brow.

"For now," I reply, trying not to focus too much on the way his voice wraps around me like a protective cocoon. "I could use some help with my ankle exercises before dinner. If you're not too busy."

He nods, straightening. "Let's do it inside. Less wind."

I follow him into the living room and pass the credenza containing my note, where he quickly and efficiently sets up the space. The couch becomes my perch, a folded towel his impromptu tool, and his strong, steady hands provide the reassurance I didn't realize I needed. On the table sits an hourglass—a symbol marking the time, reminding me that for thirty minutes, he's mine.

"Alright," he says, kneeling in front of me, his face mere inches from my elevated leg. "Let's start with some gentle flexes. Tell me if it hurts."

As he guides my foot through the first stretch, his fingers light and firm against my skin, I can't help but study his face. The sharp lines of his jaw, the skillfully cut beard, the slight crease between his brows as he concentrates—it all fascinates me.

I shouldn't be looking, shouldn't be wondering what it would feel like to trace my fingers along his cheek or what might be hiding behind the stoic exterior he wears like armor. But I can't stop myself.

His thumb shifts slightly, pressing into a tight spot on my ankle, and I inhale sharply. It isn't pain I feel—it's something else entirely. His gaze flicks up to mine, his eyes darkening for a moment before he shifts his attention to my ankle.

"Too much?" he asks, his voice carefully neutral.

"No," I respond quickly, my voice a little breathless. "It's fine."

Fine isn't the right word. The warmth spreading from his touch isn't fine—it was electric, heady, and terrifying all at once. It's something I've never felt before...not even with Ford.

He continues, his movements steady and measured, though I can't help but notice the slight tension in his jaw. Is he feeling it, too? The charged energy that seems to fill the room whenever we're this close?

When we finish the last stretch, he doesn't pull away. Instead, like before, he begins massaging my foot, his strong hands moving with a tenderness I've come to expect.

"This will help with circulation," he murmurs, his voice softer now, almost intimate.

I bite my lip, fighting the urge to close my eyes and just melt into the sensation. His touch is deliberate, professional even, but I can't ignore the undercurrent of something deeper. He glances up briefly, and for a heartbeat, our eyes meet. There is something in his gaze—a flicker of emotion he quickly masks, but not before I catch it.

I want to say something, anything, to break the tension, but the words catch in my throat. So, instead, I let the moment stretch between us, heavy with everything we aren't saying.

When he finally pulls his hands away, I feel their absence like a cold breeze. He stands, his expression unreadable once more.

He glances at the hourglass, then me. "That should do it for now," he says, his voice back to its usual steady tone.

I nod, my heart still racing. "Thank you, Troy."

"We stick to the plan, we help you heal," he says, his eyes lingering on mine for a fraction of a second before he turns and leaves the room.

As he heads down the hall, I exhale a shaky breath, my foot still tingling where his hands have been. I'm unsure of whether either of us is ready to name whatever is happening between us.

***

Following my exercises, I answer a few emails before I freshen up and go to the kitchen. The aroma of garlic and rosemary fills the air, mingling with the faint hum of soft jazz playing from the sound system. He stands at the counter, his broad back to me, slicing cherry tomatoes with precision. Despite his intimidating presence, there is something calming about watching him work in the kitchen—his movements deliberate and unhurried, as though cooking is the most natural thing in the world.

"Does your week wind down like the rest of us?" I ask, leaning against the doorframe.

"Define wind down," he replies, his focus still fixed on the cutting board.

"You know, hang out with the guys. Go for a drink. Pick up women. Things like that." I smirk. "Wait, do you even have friends?"

He sets the knife down and turns to me, one eyebrow slightly raised. "Which question do you want me to answer first?"

I chuckle. "The wind down."

"I work seven days a week unless my client doesn't require my services. Rose and Niall are usually on the go, so my shift ends around midnight."

"And when you do have free time, do you have friends to share it with?"

"A few of us get together now and then," he says, shrugging. "But they're part of my crew."

"Is that code for dangerous men like you?"

A small smile tugs at his lips as he returns to slicing tomatoes. "What do you do on Fridays?"

"Wind down," I say, stepping closer. "I mentioned before, if I were home and Sasha were in town, we'd be in one of our apartments making drinks and catching up on the latest gossip. That was the plan for last weekend, but life had other ideas."

"A temporary setback," he assures me, his voice gentle. "You did a good job with your foot flexes today."

I smile at the praise. "I have a great instructor." My gaze drifts to the ingredients he's laid out: fresh herbs, a bottle of olive oil, and a beautiful cut of swordfish. "I'm going to make a cocktail. Would you like one?"

"You know I don't drink."

"Just testing."

He glances at me, his eyes warm. "But don't let that stop you."

"If I make you a nonalcoholic version, will you drink it?"

"If it's good."

"Challenge accepted," I say, moving to the counter. "I'm going to make a blueberry blitzer. Do you have ginger ale?"

"I do."

Troy leans against the counter, watching me as I gather the ingredients: blueberries, champagne, and ice. For his version, I swap the champagne for ginger ale. His gaze follows my hands as I crush the blueberries in the shaker, his intensity making my skin prickle.

"You're very serious about this," he says, his tone teasing.

"I take cocktails seriously," I reply, sugaring the rim of two glasses. "Besides, you don't seem like the type to settle for mediocre."

"Fair point." His voice is laced with quiet amusement.

I pour the first glass for myself, garnishing it with fresh-cut rosemary, then repeat the process for Troy's drink. I slide his glass across the counter and watch as he takes a sip. He licks his lips, a faint smile playing on his face. I quietly celebrate inside, having put it there.

"Not bad," he says, setting the glass down. "I might even ask for a second."

I laugh. "High praise from the man who doesn't drink."

"You forgot something," he says, holding his glass up. "To groundbreaking experiments." He clicks his glass to mine.

"To mountain hideaways."

"Cheers," we say in unison.

He tilts his head, his gaze locking with mine. "I could get used to this. Quiet nights, good company." His words are soft, but they land heavy in my chest.

I swallow, feeling an unfamiliar warmth spread through me. "Me too," I admit, barely above a whisper.

For a moment, the kitchen falls silent except for the low hum of music and the crackle of the skillet. It isn't an uncomfortable silence—it feels full, charged with something unspoken but undeniable.

After dinner, Troy takes me up on that second drink. He grabs our drinks, and slowly, I follow him down the hall, past his office to the rear of the house. The glass door leading to the back patio opens.

"What in the world is all this?"

Troy sets our drinks on the outdoor table where, at some point, he prearranged snacks: fruit, nuts, and cheese. Large pillar candles provide extra light alongside three easels—two are blank and one displays a Richard Mayhew abstract painting featuring a vibrant swirl of blood-orange clouds against the golden sky. Neatly arranged in front of the blank easels are paintbrushes, paint, and water—all the essentials needed to recreate one of our brilliant Black artist's masterpieces.

I sit, holding my hand to my mouth in shock.

"There's no museum on this mountain, but there is art," Troy says, sitting beside me at his easel. "Paint and sip?"

There's a glimmer of something in his eyes. I study the painting for a moment. Reaching out, I grab his arm as I realize what's happening. "My God, Troy, tell me this isn't the original."

"I built this place with this painting in mind. The colors—"

"They mirror the sunset we watched."

"Perfectly."

I take a deep breath and collect my thoughts. This man continues to astonish me with his care and kindness. *I'm not going to cry this time.* I exhale deeply, pick up a paintbrush, open my paint colors, and paint. As I focus on my activity, mixing colors on my palette: red and yellow to create blood orange, and brushing them onto my canvas, I smile at him.

"What's the name of this painting?"

"Overture II."

"It's beautiful."

As I sit back, taking in the swirls of color on my canvas and the way they mirror the masterpiece before me, I realize Troy isn't just giving me an activity—he's giving me a moment, a glimpse of something bigger than both of us. An overture. The beginning of something not yet fully formed but full of promise. And for the first time in a long time, I'm not afraid to see where it will lead.

CHAPTER 18

Smile

"Laughter is the sun that drives winter from the human face."
– Victor Hugo

Troy

I STAND BY THE kitchen window, my palm pressing against the warm glass. The sun hugs the landscape as bees busy themselves, floating between flowers, keeping our fragile ecosystem intact. Everything's in its place, serene and unbothered—a sharp contrast to the chaos swirling in my head. My phone vibrates on the counter and I snatch it up when I see Anita's name flash across the screen.

"Anita," I answer, my voice clipped. "Tell me you have something."

Her voice comes through calm, methodical. "We tracked down the guy. He's not talking, but we ran his prints through every database we could access. Turns out, he's a ghost—no record, no ID, nothing concrete except the fact he's been using aliases linked to shady jobs overseas."

Just as I figured.

"Damn it," I mutter, pinching the bridge of my nose. "Who hires someone like that for a job like this?"

"That's where it gets interesting," Anita continues. "I dug deeper into Kennedy's file, specifically the disappearance of her old professor, Dr. Rutledge. There's a pattern, Troy. Rutledge went missing weeks after someone tried stealing a prototype from his lab. No one ever figured out what happened, but the chatter at the time suggested corporate espionage. Guess what? The guy we just caught? He was spotted on campus during that period."

I go still, the weight of her words settling over me like a storm cloud. "You're saying this isn't random. Whoever's targeting Kennedy now—they've done this before."

"Exactly. Whoever it is, they're methodical, patient. They're playing the long game. And they want whatever breakthrough Kennedy's working on."

Her words confirm my worst-case scenario.

"Any leads on who hired this guy?"

Anita sighs. "Not yet, but I'm digging. I'll call as soon as I know more."

"Do it fast," I say. "We're running out of time."

I end the call, my chest tight with frustration. The threads are connecting, and the picture they're forming is murky at best.

I glance at the clock. It's late, and Kennedy's been holed up in the library for hours. She hasn't said much since she limped through the door earlier, her ankle still a mess. She needs to eat, and I need to clear my head.

I head to the kitchen, pulling out ingredients for pasta. Simple, comforting—something we both can use right now. As I chop garlic, my thoughts churn. Someone out there is orchestrating this, and it's my job to stop them.

The faint sound of Kennedy's footfalls on the floor pulls me from my thoughts. I glance over my shoulder and see her leaning against the doorframe, her gaze soft but questioning. *God, she's beautiful.*

"You're cooking?" she asks, a small smile tugging at her lips despite the exhaustion lining her face.

"Yeah," I say, forcing a grin. "Even superheroes have to eat."

Her laugh is quiet but warm, and for a moment, the weight on my shoulders feels a little lighter.

"And their heroines." I nod. "I never asked what security handle you've created for me."

"You won't need one until we return to the city for your appointment. Have a seat."

With slow, steady movements, she eases over and onto a barstool. "You're being cagey, which means it's likely something bizarre like 'cupca ke.'" Caught off guard by her humor, I bark out a laugh. Kennedy smiles, then spontaneously bursts into singing a song.

"I smile even though it hurts me….," she croons, closing her eyes and singing several lyrics of the Kirk Franklin song. Her voice is lovely, like that of an angel. Mesmerized, I listen. Then, as if she realizes what she's doing, she covers her mouth. Her eyes fly open and my heart clenches because, instead of happiness, they're filled with tears. It's the second time she's surprised me with her vulnerability.

Instinctively, I go to her and wrap my arms around her. With her head pressed to my chest, tears soak my shirt.

When her breathing comes under control, she says, "I'm sorry. It's…there's so much meaning in that, and…"

"It's okay."

"No. You need to know." She tilts her head. "I may appear like none of this is getting to me, but it is. I just want to do my work without constantly looking over my shoulder, wondering who's after me. The pressure of my research is already overwhelming—so much to prove, so much at stake. And now this… I just—" She swallows, her voice unsteady. "I don't want to end up like my former professor."

"I won't let anyone get near you."

She touches my lip. "When you smile…when you let go like you did a moment ago…when you're just Troy, the fear falls away. And I'm lost in how beautiful it is. That song reminded me of your smile but also pointed out what I've been hiding. I didn't mean to lose it like that."

Fuck. How do I resist her? I blow out a breath at her revelation while fighting the urge to dip my head and kiss her fears away. "You have to trust me. Everything will be fine. Anyone trying to get to you has to get past me. That. Will. Never. Happen." I emphasize my words to breathe life into them on her behalf.

"I understand what you're saying, but for a short time, at least while we're here where no one can get to me, can you just be *Troy*?"

Staring down into pleading brown eyes, what do I tell her? Do I confess that she can have all my smiles? That I live for those moments when her eyes light up when she sees me. That I am her protector. That I am human. That for the rest of my life, I'll be both...*for her.*

I brush her hair over her shoulder and then cup her cheek. "Let's get you fed."

CHAPTER 19

Friends and Firsts

"Wishing to be friends is quick work, but friendship is a slow ripening fruit."
– Aristotle

Kennedy

THE SOUND OF BIRDS chirping outside wakes me, providing a pleasant contrast to the cacophony of alarms and sirens I'm accustomed to in the city. Since arriving at Troy's mountain house, I've allowed my internal clock to dictate my days, an unfamiliar yet welcome luxury. I stretch lazily under the warm blanket, my mind already cataloging the long list of things I want to accomplish today. My algorithm is coming together, and I'm almost excited to sit down and tweak it some more—almost.

But the truth is, I miss my life.

The edges of my mind are filled with longing. For everything I left behind. For familiarity. For my friends. For Sasha.

I slide out of bed, pull myself together, tug on a hoodie dress, and head toward the kitchen, where I know Troy will already be. The rich aroma of coffee greets me before I even see him. Sure enough, he's at the counter, sipping coffee and scrolling through something on his phone. When I walk in, his eyes wander the length of my body, his lips curving into a small smile that does ridiculous things to my chest. Taking in everything that's him makes me so glad I confessed my concerns.

117

I've spent days trying to figure him out, peeling back the layers he guards so fiercely. Some parts he reveals in quiet moments, yet others remain locked away, impenetrable.

"Morning," he says, his deep voice smooth but carrying that ever-present edge of control.

"Morning." I grab a mug and pour myself some coffee, letting the warmth seep into my palms as I steal a moment to gather my thoughts. "Hey, Troy, can we talk?"

His brow lifts and he leans slightly against the counter, phone forgotten.

"My friend Sasha's back in town," I begin, settling onto one of the stools across from him. "We usually hang out on Fridays. You know, have cocktails, catch up, and...I miss her. I was wondering if you could fly her out to visit this weekend." I pause, meeting his gaze. "Before you say it, she's not a security risk."

Troy places his coffee on the counter, his expression sharpening as his hand moves to rub the back of his neck. It's a rare sign, one that says he's weighing something serious. "How important is this to you?"

I want this. My chest tightens, but I hold his gaze. "If she can't come here, you may as well take me home," the words come out firm, layered in conviction. Sasha has been my anchor in so many storms, just as I've been hers.

Troy's jaw ticks, his eyes darkening as he weighs my request. His need to protect me wars with something else, something more human.

"Does she know you're here?" he asks, his voice calm but tinged with a warning.

"She knows I'm away until I can stabilize my ankle and that I have security. I followed every protocol. No location. No details."

He exhales slowly, the tension in his frame shifting into resolve. "I'll have a member of my tactical team fly her in. Take out your phone."

"Why?" I blink at him, thrown by the abruptness.

"Text Sasha the following message, nothing more. Drinks at my place. Pack for the weekend. Usual time. Doc will drive."

I hesitate, my thumb hovering over the screen. "Doc? Does this Doc person know how to fly?" This feels oddly familiar, like when I was with Ford, allowing him to take the lead. That's not happening again.

"He dropped me on campus," he says, his expression hardening.

My mind spins as I piece things together. There's so much I still don't know about Troy—the dangerous edges he keeps hidden, the world he operates in.

"Mr. Armstrong," I say his name the way I did the day we met. Reminding him who we are to each other...what we've become. "Is it your intent to intimidate me?"

"No. I'm trying to protect you."

I gesture to the stool near me. "You told me once that as long as I'm with you, I have nothing to fear. I'm here."

Cup in hand, he joins me at the counter. A quiet understanding passes between us. Refocusing on my phone, I type the message exactly as Troy dictates, each word bearing the weight of the unknown.

"Done," I say softly, glancing up to meet his steady gaze.

Troy nods, the faintest trace of something unspoken flickering in his eyes. "She'll be safe. You have my word."

And somehow, despite everything, I believe him.

***

René Descartes said, "I think, therefore I am." But is that really the case? Or are we simply the sum of intentional molecular interactions: a cascade of chemical decisions that mimic what we call self-perception? This is the heart of my project—proving "self-perception via chemical cognition"—the missing piece that prevents AI from replacing humans.

I retest my algorithm, simulating the first three of eight key properties of animated life. The results are promising, enough to coax a flutter of hope in my chest. If I can sustain this trajectory, I'll prove my thesis and move beyond simulation into lab testing. However, time is of the essence, and I need to successfully complete eight programs before I can move to lab testing and then go before the board.

Hours pass as I refine variables, adjust inputs, and recalibrate outputs. My focus is razor-sharp until the final test. I set the system to learn on its own and lean back, my breath caught somewhere between my lungs and throat.

The screen pulses with activity, a continuous stream of data. And then, it happens.

The cell collapses.

"Damn." The word tears out of me, sharp and bitter. My fingers hover over the keys, itching to dive back in, but I force myself to stop. I know this spiral all too well. I check my watch. Time to walk away.

I shut everything down and head outside to the patio, where Troy is prepping one side of his dual grill. The late afternoon sun bathes the area in a golden glow and the scent of charcoal mingles with the crisp mountain air. His broad shoulders are stern against the view, his movements deliberate, efficient. Watching him is oddly soothing.

I step closer. "I guess there's no better time than now for a lesson."

Troy turns, a smile tugging at the corner of his mouth. His expression softens when he sees me; something in that look makes my frustration ease just a fraction. "Hey. How did the experiment go?"

I move to his side, watching him arrange paper beneath a pile of coals. The frustration I'd been holding bubbles over and I blow out a sharp breath. "It crashed and burned. I'll start again on Monday." I nod toward the grill. "Can I?"

He hands me a stack of crinkled newspapers. "Sure. First, we build the layers to get the fire going."

I stand beside him, following his lead as we tuck balled-up paper beneath the coals. His quiet confidence is grounding.

"You'll figure it out," he says, his tone resolute. "You always do."

The conviction in his voice comes as no surprise to me. I glance up, meeting his eyes. There's no doubt, no patronizing reassurance—just a solid belief in me. Unlike Ford, who felt it was his job to fix me. "Thanks," I murmur, carefully lining the coals as he instructed. "What time will Doc be here with Sasha?" I ask, shifting the conversation.

"They should be here by the time we get the meat on."

"What do I need to know about Doc?"

Troy leans back on his heels, a faint smirk playing on his lips. "For starters, his real name is Daxton. Dax for short. He's an ex-military surgeon."

"Thus, the nickname," I say, nodding as I place another coal.

"Exactly."

"Is he part of the team watching out for me?"

"Yes." His response is pithy as usual.

"You don't like to talk about all this...security stuff, do you?"

His movements still for a beat before he answers. "I'd rather you focus on the things that matter to you—your work."

"Friendships," I add, a note of challenge in my voice.

His lips quirk in response. "Your friend will be here soon."

I shift my focus to him fully. "Will we ever be friends, or is that not part of how you operate?"

The question hangs in the air, and for a moment, I think he won't answer. But then he looks at me, his eyes searching mine, a flicker of something vulnerable breaking through his usual composure. "We should go in and prep the meat," he says, his voice softer than usual.

The words are practical, but the way he looks at me lingers—like there's something unsaid. And just like that, my frustrations over the experiment feel smaller. At this moment, learning how to grill with Troy is enough.

Abandoning the discussion, I follow Troy inside. We prep food trays at the counter, shoulder to shoulder: I make chicken skewers and Troy seasons the ribeye. Surprisingly, we move in sync like we've done this before, and he seems at ease with it all despite his lack of response earlier.

"The coals should be at the right temperature now. I'll grab the trays. You open the grill," he says, picking up the trays. I follow him outside. He sets the trays down and I read the temperature gauge.

"A little over four fifty. Is that good?"

"We can put these on now. Are you ready?"

"Ready," I confirm, picking up a skewer with one hand and preparing to lift the lid with the other.

"Don't stand too close. There'll be a lot of smoke."

He raises an eyebrow at me until I step back a little, then nods. I open the grill, and he isn't lying; a cloud of smoke hits me, making me cough. I lean in, but he extends his arm, keeping a safe distance between the grill and me. I place the skewers one by one on the grates. They sizzle upon contact. The aroma of chicken cooking brings back memories of family barbecues in the park, sitting on wooden benches in front of a table full of covered dishes: beans, potato salad, buns, and all the fixings.

"Congratulations."

After placing the last skewer on, I smile smugly at him. "Thank you. You know, I was thinking about when I went to barbecues as a child. There was always something red to drink."

"Ah, man, I had plenty of red punch back in the day." He nods, lost in the moment. "I'm sure you can concoct something for us." Earlier, he mentioned that like him, Dax doesn't drink.

"Yeah, but nothing stains your tongue like the red punch. How about I make a strawberry spritzer? It's close but without the dye."

"Sounds like a winner."

Seconds later, the thunderous roar of a helicopter reverberates in the distance. *She's here.* I want to run to meet my friend, but circumstances prevent me.

Troy senses my nervous anticipation, touches my shoulder, and says, "Give it a minute. Doc's got her."

Chapter 20

Something in the Way She Moves

"The heart is like a candle, longing to be lit!"
– Rumi

Troy

There's something utterly captivating about the way Kennedy moves—an effortless grace that draws me in with a magnetic pull I can't seem to shake. God knows I've tried. When she leans her elbow on the counter, resting her delicate chin in her hand, a picture of casual elegance steals my focus. And when she glances over her shoulder at me—those eyes catching the light just right—it's more than a look. It's a challenge, a siren's call laced with an invitation, daring me to cross the line between duty and desire.

Kennedy surprised me when she asked if I was her friend. *No*, I want to say. You're more than that. You're the woman I want beside me, beneath me, because...I want to be your everything. You are more to me than you'll ever know. But I can't say any of that or even allow myself to consider it. My job is clearly defined. Protect her at all costs, even if it means breaking my heart in the process.

"Man, when you send me on a mission, you could at least warn me who I'm transporting," Dax says over the squealing of Sasha and Kennedy, who are rocking back and forth, locked in an embrace.

We clasp hands and then lean in for a man-shoulder bump hug.

"What did you do?" I ask accusingly. My eyes shift to Kennedy, who's deep into a whisper discussion with her friend. She catches my gaze and I lift my chin in acknowledgment.

"Sasha, this is Troy, the man who whisked me away to this lovely hideaway." She waves her hand toward the house.

"Sasha, nice to meet you," I greet her.

Her eyes size me up. "So, this is Troy. Definitely, doctor approved," she says with an instigative smirk. Like Kennedy, she doesn't mask her inner monologue.

Kennedy tilts her head, giving Sasha a *What are you doing* stare. "Uh, okay, thank you for that, Sasha Geneviève Duval."

"Ooh, Geneviève. I like that," Dax says.

"You did not just out my government name."

"I did."

Watching the dynamic between Kennedy and Sasha is cute. They have a bond similar to what I have with my brother. I clear my throat. "Kennedy, this is Daxton."

"Nice to meet you, Kennedy. You can call me Dax."

"Or Doc," Sasha adds, smiling.

Dax's eyes shift to Sasha and he says in a low, smooth tone, "You can call me whatever you want, Geneviève."

I shake my head in disbelief at what I'm witnessing from Dax. "Man, now I need to know what you did on the way here."

"That makes two of us," Kennedy says. Then something grabs her attention. Her nose wrinkles and her eyes widen with concern as she tries to signal me. "The chicken," she mouths to me before quickly turning toward the grill and losing her balance in the process. I reach out and place my hand on her lower back, steadying her. The warmth of her hip in my palm sends blood rushing to places it shouldn't. *God, this woman.*

"I got you," I tell her. She lifts the grill lid, pressing her body closer to mine like we belong this way. "It's just the juice dripping onto the coals. You're doing good. We can take them off now."

"Well, what have we here?" Sasha's voice cuts through the moment. Still, I don't let go of Kennedy. "Girl, you never grilled a day in your life."

"Well, I am now. Thanks to the Man of Steel."

Dax joins in. "You're asking what I've been doing—what have you been doing?" he redirects.

"Girl, I got this." Sasha picks up the meat tray, takes the tongs from Kennedy, and shoos her away. "Shouldn't you be resting your foot or making us a drink?"

I release Kennedy. Carefully, she walks over to Dax. "Don't think you're off the hook. Just what did you two talk about on your way here?"

"Drinks?" Sasha calls over her shoulder.

"In a minute." She eyes Dax.

"My boy here didn't tell me that I was escorting the famous author of 'What's Wrong with Dorian Gray?'"

"And you know about a book on genetics and the study of perceived aging because...," she says, her eyebrows raised as she draws out the words, expecting him to fill in the blank.

"Because he's almost forty, but people think he's much younger," I chime in.

"He looks good to me," Sasha murmurs, still minding the grill.

"Thank you, Doc," Dax smirks.

"Thank *you*, Doc," Sasha replies.

"Okay, I've heard all I need. Troy...can you help me with the drinks?"

I lead Kennedy inside. We immediately start preparing the drinks at the kitchen counter. She muddles the strawberries while I gather everything else. The sound of a buzzing phone catches my attention. I don't check mine since I would have felt it in my pocket. Kennedy slips her hand into her dress pocket, takes out her phone, frowns, returns it, and resumes mashing the strawberries—with added force this time.

I step closer. "Everything okay?"

"Yeah. It's nothing."

"Nothing or something you don't want to talk about."

"I'm fine. Nothing affecting my security if that's what you mean. How about you? Our friends seem to have formed a bond in the short time they've known each other."

I run my hand through my beard. "Yeah, you noticed that."

"I notice a lot, like how you watch me like a hawk. I appreciate you catching me out there."

"I told you I got you."

Kennedy takes the cocktail shaker I prepared, dumps the strawberries in, and then places the lid on.

"I'll do that." I pick up the cocktail shaker and give it a shake. The ice pounds against the sides, creating a frost that chills my hand, signaling that it's ready. I set it down on the counter. Kennedy slides four glasses toward me. I open the shaker and pour an equal measure of the mixture into each glass. She tops two glasses with champagne and two with ginger ale, then garnishes each with a sprig of rosemary. Our fingers touch as she hands me a glass, sending a spark between us.

"Sorry about that."

"Troy, you don't have to apologize for touching me. You realize you've been massaging my ankle since I arrived."

"I'm not trying to make a move on you."

"I wish you would." She says the words aloud that I've felt the past few days—words I want to act on.

"I can't."

"You mean you won't. When you held me at the grill, it was the first time you seemed..." She hesitates for a moment, contemplating her words, as if anything she says could offend me. "Human." I'm touched by her revelation, confirming what I've known all along—we're connected.

I surprise myself by saying, "I am human. I just can't be who you want me to be—not right now. My job is to protect you, Kennedy. I don't know if I could think straight if it were any other way." I let those words linger in the air, capturing everything that remains unspoken.

Something changes in her eyes. She steps closer, placing her hand on my chest, her warmth radiating between us. I'm sure she can feel my heart pounding.

"I get it. But I will need you to try at some point, Man of Steel," she whispers. Kennedy holds my gaze, tracing an invisible line down my jaw with her fingers, willing me to feel her words.

The glimmer in her gaze signals me, a silent taunt that stirs a hunger I've buried far too long—her touch tugs at my soul. Every second in her presence becomes a battle between logic and longing, each moment unraveling my carefully constructed walls.

My resolve is firm, but with her...it's fraying fast.

CHAPTER 21

'Round Midnight

"Each friend represents a world in us, a world possibly not born until they arrive, and it is only by this meeting that a new world is born."
– Anaïs Nin

Kennedy

THE SUN IS A few hours from setting. We moved everything indoors as the wind picked up over the mountaintop. That doesn't matter. Every space is an experience in this place. Wherever we are feels magical.

Sitting around the table, passing plates as we help ourselves to seconds, reminds me of the holidays. Classic jazz plays softly in the background as we share stories, hinting at who we are outside this mountain hideaway. Here, there are no exes or enemies searching for me, no genetic codes to crack. It's just the four of us enjoying the good vibes, trash-talking, high-fiving, and...laughing together. It's been so long—too long—since I felt this free.

"Let me get that for ya," Dax offers, sliding Sasha's plate toward him as he carefully cuts strips of meat from the skewer so she doesn't have to.

"Man, you just can't help but show off your cutting skills," Troy teases.

"Listen, Geneviève shouldn't have to deal with something I can handle."

"You did good, Ken," Sasha says, holding up a piece of chicken on her fork, entirely in her element, unfazed by the attention.

"Not like I didn't have help from everyone in this room."

Surprising me, Troy touches my hand beneath the table. "Take the compliment."

"Thanks," I add. My reward: a slight smile.

I curl my fingers around his hand, indulging in the rare glimpse of Troy that he shares only with me. The current song comes to an end, and *'Round Midnight* by Miles Davis plays through the speakers. For a moment, I shut my eyes, absorbing the music and feeling each note. I open them to find Troy watching me. I glance around the table.

"So, Dax, is jazz your thing like Troy, or are you into something else?"

"Oh, I feel this. I love jazz, but I also like neo-soul. However, this...*'Round Midnight* is the tune. Miles Davis can do no wrong. He once said, 'It's not the note you play that's the wrong note–'"

"'It's the note you play afterward that makes it right or wrong,'" I say, finishing the quote.

Troy winks at me. "Yeah, talk about a great jazz artist. Herbie Hancock learned that lesson firsthand from Miles while playing sets with him."

"Ah, say no more. Herbie is the man. Can we get some 'Rockit' over here?" Sasha adds, moving her fingers back and forth like a DJ scratching a record and humming the tune.

"I'm sticking with Miles as the greatest because, as the Man of Steel points out," I say, using my index finger to emphasize my point. "Herbie had lessons to learn from Miles. He even mentioned how he messed up a chord once, and Miles improvised, playing a few notes that made it seem like it was the right chord all along. There's a lesson to take from that." I nod, processing my own words. Yeah, there's a lesson: the right person can help you turn something that seems bad into something beautiful. I hold Troy's gaze. He gives me a tight-lipped smile, signaling that we're on the same wavelength.

"Yeah, he learned: don't fuck with Miles. However, I think Geneviève is on to something. I'll see your 'Rockit' and raise you 'Cantaloupe Island,'" Dax announces, bringing me out of my Troy haze.

"Thank you, Doc," Sasha tells him.

"You went somewhere when this song first came on. Where did you go?" The deep richness of Troy's voice captures our attention. The room goes quiet, and all eyes fall on me.

I take a sip of my drink, purse my lips, and absorb the vibe of the people who somehow make me feel safe. Sasha, Doc, Troy. They are my world, if only for this brief moment. I blow out a breath and say, "I went to where I believe the song begins. It feels like the moment you leave the club after midnight, after the last dance, when all the conversations have taken place and the drinks have stopped flowing. As you walk down the slightly damp sidewalks toward the car, you feel your man's arm securely around you." I smile at Troy. "You know, that feeling when you're leaning against him, inhaling his essence, knowing that when you arrive home, he's all yours."

"I can see that," Sasha says, nodding.

I continue. "That goes on for a while—until the drive ends. Then the music picks up. You're home, you're in love; he takes off your coat, his slightly parted lips hover just above yours, and the best part begins."

Dax claps, and Sasha joins in, as does Troy. "That's beautiful."

"Girl, you got us all in our emotions and other things over here," Sasha says.

"Blame it on the Man of Steel."

"I just asked a question. But thanks, Kennedy, you paint a very vivid picture."

"Okay, y'all, let's put this stuff away. Who's up for a game?" I ask.

"Pictionary," Sasha calls out.

"I'm in, but only if Sasha's on my team," Dax announces, raising his eyebrow at her.

"Okay, Doc, you have a deal."

Dax lifts a chin to Troy. "You in, man?"

"I'm in. We can use the touch screen TV."

***

Cleaning up doesn't take long. Sasha and I manage the indoors while Troy and Dax are outside on the patio discussing whatever superheroes talk about. Meanwhile, I update Sasha on the past week—a life I don't recognize as my own but more like something out of a suspense movie. However, it's not something crafted for a general audience, nor is it the latest release waiting for a positive Rotten Tomatoes review. This is real.

"Enough talk about my failed experiments and people searching for me. You seem to be into Dax."

"Girl, Doc is fine," she elongates the word "fine." "And he has a helicopter. What man do we know, besides Troy, who has a helicopter? I think I'm in love." She pauses for a second as if thinking. "Do you think he kills people?"

"I think they both do if necessary."

"But he would have taken an oath like me."

"Not necessarily—you know that. Besides, he's saving lives in a different way now. Does that bother you?"

"I don't know. If anything comes out of this—which I hope it does, I'll figure it out."

"Don't overthink it. You're right; he is cute. Anyway, he wouldn't be working for Troy if he was a bad person. So, he's not a danger to you, at least."

"Speaking of Troy...." She leans in, nudges my shoulder, and whispers, "What's going on between you two? I see how he looks at you. Please tell me you've sampled that."

I shake my head. "These guys have rules. They don't date their clients."

"Bullshit. That man is salivating like he's starving and you're his favorite dessert. Did you at least talk to him about it?"

"You know me. I don't hold back, but he won't give."

"What's going on with Ford?"

"That's a different story. He won't stop calling and texting. He says he wants to talk."

"Please tell me you're not falling for his b.s."

"No. But there's something there...something unresolved. I can't put my finger on it."

"See, this is how I know he's bad for you. You've got this beautiful man at your beck and call, ready to die for you, and Ford's got your head stuck in the past. Forget about him."

"I'm trying. There's something I can't figure out about our situation. If it was all really about him and his job, why is he dragging me back into his life?"

"'Cause he's a fucking idiot. You should have let me kick his ass."

I let out a laugh at the image her statement brings to mind. "Yeah, I should have, huh? Oh, well." I tilt my head toward the patio. "The guys are coming back in. Let's see if the brains match the brawn. Oh, and just so you know, Dax is doctor-approved." I smirk, lock arms with Sasha, and head into the living room to join the guys.

Dax rubs his hands together and says, "All right, let's get this game going. Who's keeping time?"

"I've got it." Troy opens a drawer in the console beneath the TV and retrieves an hourglass that matches the one he gave me, except smaller. "This gives us sixty seconds per play."

"Whose got the cards?" Sasha asks.

Dax walks over to the coffee table and pulls out his phone. "We can use my phone. I'll pull up the word generator."

Troy touches my elbow and says, "You can choose where you want to sit. When you're not drawing, I want you to elevate your foot—you've been on it most of the day." Concern laces his voice, making me want him even more. No, Ford was never like this.

"The chaise lounge will do." I walk over and sit. He positions an ottoman near the chair and lifts my leg to set it on the ottoman. "Thanks."

"Since my bestie is getting comfortable, we should be first up. Do you want to draw or select the word?" Sasha asks Dax.

Dax flips through the phone screen. "I'll choose. You draw, and then we can switch if they don't get it."

"Are you two conspiring against us already?" I ask. Troy pulls up a chair beside me.

"We'll let them believe they're going to win." He closes his hand and positions his knuckles for a fist bump. "Team?"

I press my knuckles to his. "Team." And somehow, saying those words feels like more.

"Are you all ready?" he picks up the hourglass.

"Ready," we all say in unison. Troy flips the glass.

Dax stands next to Sasha, holding the phone and shielding it from Troy and me. They exchange a knowing glance, sealed with a nod. Sasha turns toward the TV screen and begins to draw. She creates two horizontal lines at the top, indicating that the word has two syllables. Below that, she quickly sketches several stacked ovals, with a small square on top of one and a makeshift vessel resembling a glass or cup pouring something onto the stack.

"Pancakes," Troy calls out. She and Dax shake their heads, wearing smug smiles.

The sand keeps pouring into the bottom half of the hourglass. Beside the stack, she draws a square with three rows of tiny squares inside. I turn to Troy.

"I got this," I tell him and mouth the answer to him. He nods in agreement. "Waffles," I call out before the time runs out.

"Damn, she's good," Dax says.

Troy high-fives me. We're up next. "Do you want to draw?" he asks.

"Heck yeah."

"Okay," he says, helping me up. He retrieves the phone from Dax, scrolls, and shows me the word.

"No way. Did you do that on purpose?" I ask in astonishment, reading the screen that says Superman.

"Luck of the draw."

I lean in and whisper, "Seems you're destined to be my superhero."

"I'm not complaining. You ready?"

"I can't draw this; pick another word."

"What are you doing over there? This is game night, not date night," Sasha chides.

"Yeah, yeah. Don't be so anxious to lose." I laugh. Troy swipes the screen and shows me another word. "I can work with that."

The timer is set, and I turn toward the TV. Instead of sitting, Troy stays by my side. Like Sasha, I draw two lines to indicate the number of syllables in the word. Then, I draw a narrow vertical cylinder with one arrow pointing to the top of the cylinder and another pointing upward at the bottom.

Sasha bursts out, saying, "Straw."

Troy stares down at them. Sasha rolls her eyes, which is comical. I concentrate on my drawing. I X out the drawing, and next to it, I draw a circle with an arrow pointing down at the circle.

"Ball," Dax calls out. I frown. My gaze shifts to Troy, who watches me with an unreadable expression that makes me want to abandon the game and cuddle in his lap. He winks and raises his chin, prompting me to focus on the game.

Next, I draw a line at the right, left, and bottom.

"North," Dax blurts out.

I point to the second line on the screen. Then, I draw the narrow cylinder again.

"North pole," Sasha screams, correctly guessing the word.

The game goes on until Troy and I make it to ten points, winning.

I lean back into the chaise as Sasha plops onto the sofa with a dramatic groan.

"You did good," she says, pointing at Dax. "But sadly, my girl here overtook us."

Dax grumbles something about needing a rematch, but my focus has shifted. My eyes wander to Troy, sitting across from me, arms crossed, a hint of a smirk still lingering from our victory. He's so composed, so in control. The steady calm he brings into every room is magnetic. It makes me want to lean into him, to burrow into that strength and let it envelop me.

But he's keeping a distance.

I notice it in the way he doesn't sit too close. The way he shifts his gaze just before our eyes lock for too long. The way he hasn't once touched me beyond the brief brush of fingers passing the phone or the accidental bump of knees. Each time, I caught him pulling back as if reminding himself that he shouldn't linger.

And I get it.

I do.

I'm not blind to what this situation means for him—a job. A mission. I'm not just a woman to him; I'm a client, someone he's sworn to protect. There are lines he's convinced himself he can't cross, rules he's living by because they've kept him steady for years.

But I hope he can see how much I want him to forget all of that.

Because I'm not afraid of crossing lines. Not with him. Not when he looks at me like he wants to strip away every layer I've built around myself these past years and see me.

The ache that's been building between us isn't just in my head. It's there in the way he watches me when he thinks I won't notice. It's in the way his voice softens when he says my name. It's in the way his presence steadies me in ways I don't think he even realizes.

And right now, I don't want him to be my bodyguard.

I want him to be mine.

As Sasha and Dax take their conversation to another part of the house and head down the hall, I'm left with him. The room quiets and the only sound is the wind whooshing through the trees beyond the glass walls.

Troy stands, stretching his arms over his head, his shirt pulling tight across his chest. I bite the inside of my cheek to keep from staring too long.

"Good game," he says, giving me that rare smile—the one that's real. Warm.

I nod, my heart tripping over itself. I should let him walk away to wherever he goes when he retreats to his own head. I should keep the boundaries as neat and tidy as he seems to want them to be.

But I don't want to.

"Troy." His name comes out softer than I intended, more vulnerable. He stops and turns to face me fully.

For a moment, we just look at each other. His jaw tenses and there is that flicker of hesitation in his eyes again. I can see the war he's waging inside—the push and pull of what he wants versus what he's telling himself he can't have.

I stand, taking a step closer. The air feels heavier, charged with everything we've been avoiding.

"I'm not afraid," I say quietly. My voice doesn't waver. "Of you. Of this."

He swallows, his gaze dropping to the floor for a beat before meeting mine again. His eyes are stormy, conflicted.

"You should be," he whispers.

But I shake my head. "No, I shouldn't." I take another step closer, my heart pounding. "Because I trust you. And I know you'd never hurt me."

His breath comes out in a slow exhale, and for the first time, I see the cracks in his armor—the man behind the Man of Steel. Vulnerable. Human.

And mine, if he'd just let himself be.

The silence stretches, thick with unspoken things, until finally, he lifts his hand, brushing a strand of hair behind my ear. His touch is gentle, reverent.

But it's not enough. Not for me.

"Troy," I whisper, leaning into his touch. "Don't make me keep waiting."

For a heartbeat, he doesn't move. Then, slowly, he steps back, his hand falling away. "You're not a job to me, Kennedy." His voice is low, rough around the edges. "That's why I have to be careful."

I watch him walk away, my chest aching with want and frustration. But there's something different in his retreat this time. He didn't say he doesn't want me. He said he has to be careful.

And I'll wait—for now.

Because I've seen the way he looks at me.

Careful won't last forever.

CHAPTER 22

Duty Verses Desire

"Accept the things to which fate binds you, and love the people with whom fate brings you together, but do so with all your heart."
– Marcus Aurelius

Troy

I LEAVE THE LIVING room and step out into the biting wind on the patio, hoping the cold will shake me from this trance I've been in all night. Being with Kennedy—so close, so natural, as if we were more than we are—messes with my head. I've never been one to lose focus. Not on a mission. Not in life.

But everything about her pulls me in.

I want to be the man who stands beside her, not just the one who stands guard. But that can't happen. Not yet. Maybe not ever. There are people out there who want to hurt her, and I need to stay sharp to keep her safe. That's my priority. It has to be.

I hear the door open behind me, and Dax steps out. Sasha stays inside with Kennedy, their voices low, comfortable. Dax walks up beside me, and I nod toward the far end of the patio, where we can talk without the wind cutting through. I flick on the electric fireplace, watching the soft glow chase away the darkness.

"You and Sasha seem to be hitting it off," I say, breaking the silence.

Dax grins. "Yeah, we're planning to grab dinner after leaving here tomorrow. See where things go."

"That's good." I give a slight nod. "She's a great woman. Kennedy needs friends like her. People she can trust."

"She's got you too," Dax points out, his gaze steady.

I don't respond to that. I don't know if I'm the right kind of protector for Kennedy—not when my feelings are tangled with my duty.

"Any updates from our source?" I ask, steering the conversation back to business.

"Nothing new," Dax replies. "We're keeping eyes on everyone connected to the break-in and her former professor's disappearance. When you take her into the city for that doctor's appointment, we'll have a team in place."

I nod, already running through the plan in my head.

"You need me to cover her when you and Marcus head to your parents' next week?" Dax asks.

"No."

His eyes widen in surprise. "You're not going?"

"I'm taking her with me," I say before fully processing it. But the decision feels right. She's safer with me. And maybe...maybe I need her there, too.

Dax raises a brow. "Are you two...an item now?"

"No."

"How's that going to work? And why not? There's chemistry brewing between you two, and you know it."

I grit my teeth. "You know the rules. I don't date clients."

Dax gives me an "I've heard this before" look and replies, "Rules only matter if you let them. You've been breaking your own rule since the day you met her."

He's not wrong. I can't deny what's there between us. But the weight of what I can't do presses heavier.

"We've talked," I admit quietly. "We both want the same things."

"Then what's stopping you?"

I stare into the fire. "I can't give her half of me. I want to be the man who holds her, who worships her the way she deserves. But I also need to keep her safe. And those two things—wanting her and protecting her—don't mix. Not when there's still danger out there."

"Sounds like you've already made your choice."

"I'm doing my job."

Dax claps me on the shoulder. "Is that what you're telling yourself?"

I glance back toward the house, toward the woman waiting inside. She said she'd wait for me to figure it out—to figure us out. But how long can someone wait for a man too afraid to reach out and take what he wants?

"I can't be reckless," I tell him. "I've seen what happens when a protector gets too close. He loses sight of the danger."

"And if you don't get close?" Dax asks, his voice quieter now. "What happens when the real danger is losing her?"

His words hang in the air. I don't answer.

Because I don't know what terrifies me more—failing to protect Kennedy...or losing her because I was too damn scared to try.

Sands of Time

"Love recognizes no barriers. It jumps hurdles, leaps fences, penetrates walls to arrive at its destination full of hope."
– Maya Angelou

Kennedy

T H E H O U R G L A S S I S S E T. The crimson sands of time pour through its narrow waist, each grain marking stolen moments with him—moments I crave more with each passing day. These have become my favorite hours—the quiet interludes spent in physical therapy under Troy's watchful eye. His touch, gentle yet grounding, anchors me. His every glance, more than mere observation, speaks volumes he keeps locked behind an iron will.

In these fleeting moments, he feels human. Touchable. Almost mine.

I've progressed to standing foot flex exercises—a milestone I hadn't thought possible weeks ago.

I bend my knee, point my toe downward, and then flex upward. The movement, though simple, is a triumph. Troy stands beside me, ever cautious, his steady hand resting on my elbow to ensure I don't falter. His light touch radiates strength, and the warmth seeps into my skin.

Carefully, I press my foot flat against the ground, mindful not to put my full weight on it—not yet, not until the doctor gives me the all-clear.

"Great job," he praises, his voice low and soothing.

"You think the doctor will be pleased with my progress?"

Troy's lips turn into that rare faint smile that feels like a private reward. "I'm sure he will be." He gestures to the exercise bench, signaling me to sit.

As I settle in, he kneels beside me, one knee bent, the other planted firmly on the ground. Carefully, he stretches my leg across his knee. His strong hands glide across my ankle, massaging the tender joints with a softness that makes my pulse race.

The hands I've dreamed of roaming my body, now soothing my ache.

"When we go to the city," I start, watching him closely, "can we stop by my apartment before heading back here?"

He lifts a brow. "Did you forget something?"

"Eventually, I will need more than a pair of slides and sneakers."

His gaze sharpens. "No heels."

I can't help but laugh. "I may be delusional about some things, but not that."

His brow furrows slightly, amused curiosity replacing his usual stoicism. "What are you delusional about?"

I hesitate a moment before taking a leap. "You. Thinking there's a chance you'll set aside these strict rules you have."

Boldly, I reach out and brush my fingers through the neat, tiny black waves of his hair. The strands are soft, smoother than I imagined, and he doesn't pull away. My heart skips a beat as I trace the shell of his ear, my fingertips gliding down to cup his jaw. His stubble is rough against my palm, but it grounds me.

There it is—the faintest upturn of his lips. A smile. I brush my thumb across his lip's corner, confirming the smile.

He's letting me in.

Troy continues working my ankle, his focus split between the task and the tension thickening between us.

"I have a job to do," he says softly. "I promise you—we'll find the people after your research."

I knew he'd say that. His duty always comes first.

But I'm not done pressing. "And what about me?" I whisper. "Will you ever put down the armor long enough to see what's standing right in front of you?"

His hands are still. For a fleeting second, he says nothing. Then, slowly, he lowers my leg, replaces my boot with meticulous care, and rises to his full height.

"Our trip to the city," he says, breaking the silence, "will be brief."

Something in his tone shifts, more personal, more intimate.

"My parents' anniversary is coming up. I plan to spend the weekend with them in Palm Springs."

I blink, confused. He can't be serious. He's leaving me here? On this isolated mountain, with only Dax or one of his other team members for company?

Before my mind can spiral, he adds, "I'm taking you with me."

The words hit me like a lightning strike. My heart soars. He doesn't want to leave me behind. He could have sent a dozen men to protect me, but he *wants* me with him.

"Can you lean down for a second?" I ask, my voice soft.

His brows knit in confusion, but he obliges, leaning closer.

Without hesitation, I wrap my arms around his neck and pull him in for a hug.

"Thank you," I whisper into his ear, holding him tight, savoring the feel of him.

For a moment, he lets himself melt into the embrace, his arms hovering before they rest lightly on my back. His body warms me, and I hear him whisper, "Kennedy."

There's something in his tone—a softness, a longing.

Slowly, he untangles himself from my grip but doesn't let my hands go.

"I get to meet the people who made the Man of Steel," I tease, trying to lighten the mood.

He smirks, his response classic Troy. "Back to work."

I laugh, but my heart feels lighter. He's letting me in, bit by bit. And as I return to my algorithms, the smile on my face refuses to fade.

Because now I know.

He doesn't want to be away from me.

And maybe, just maybe, I'm starting to break through his armor.

Chapter 24

This Is Personal

"We don't see things as they are, we see them as we are."
– Anaïs Nin

Troy

Taking a deep breath, I uncurl my fingers, which have been in a tight ball since I answered my phone. My knuckles are stiff, and the imprint of my nails lingers on my palm. "We're leaving in five minutes. I want a report with names by the time we land," I tell Anita, forcing my voice to stay even. The anger simmering inside me isn't meant for her.

Another damn attempt. This time, a direct hit on Ross Enterprises' systems. They're getting bolder. Sloppier, too. They don't realize the trap I've laid—my anti-hacking measures are far superior. And even if they managed to break through, they'd find nothing. Kennedy's research has been locked down on my private server, air-gapped from any network. The only way anyone is getting to it is over my dead body.

But now we know for sure. A mercenary hacking group is involved. Which means this isn't some random opportunistic attack. Someone powerful—and ruthless—is pulling the strings.

"On it," Anita assures me before I end the call.

I roll my shoulders, release some tension, and head toward the kitchen, where she's waiting.

The moment I step into the room, I feel it—the pull of her presence. Kennedy sits at the counter, the soft glow of the pendant light catching in her hair, making her curls shimmer like black diamonds. When sees me, her smile cuts through the weight pressing on my chest.

God, that smile. It lights up the room—and my soul. How the hell am I supposed to keep my distance from her?

I walk toward her, my footsteps slow and deliberate. She slides her glass of sparkling water across the counter toward me with a playful raise of her brows. "Thirsty?"

The corners of my mouth twitch despite myself. Beautiful, intelligent, witty...irresistible. Everything about her draws me in, even when I know I should hold back.

I pick up the glass, letting my fingers brush where hers just were, and take a sip. The cool fizz of the water does nothing to ease the heat simmering under my skin.

"What am I going to do with you?" I say, shaking my head.

Her smile softens as she tilts her head, studying me. Her hand lifts toward my face, and I instinctively grab her wrist before she can touch me. The warmth of her skin seeps into my palm.

"I was just going to ask what that scowl is for," she says softly.

"Business."

Her gaze sharpens. "My business or yours?"

"Our business." I hold her gaze, making sure she hears the weight behind those words. "Your business is mine."

She doesn't flinch. Of course, she doesn't. Kennedy is too damn brave for that. "Then I want to know."

I hesitate for a beat, then decide there's no point in sugarcoating it. "Hackers. They're after something you have."

Her brows knit together and I see her mind racing through possibilities. "Why?"

"That's what I need you to tell me." I set the glass down and step closer, my grip on her wrist softening until I cradle her hand in mine. "What makes your work worth this kind of risk?"

Kennedy exhales slowly, her lips pressing into a thoughtful line. "It depends. When complete, my research will allow us to create new life from scratch and do so at an accelerated rate. We intend to cure diseases—genetic disorders, autoimmune conditions, even organ failure. We're talking about regenerating life, not just preserving it."

Her voice is steady, but there's an underlying tension in her tone. She knows exactly where my mind is going.

"And in the wrong hands?" I press, already dreading the answer.

She swallows. "It's a key."

"To what?"

She meets my gaze, unwavering. "Depending on which of my algorithms they're after, it could be used to dominate the synthetic life and AI hybrid market. In military applications, it could be weaponized to create bio-enhanced military assets. Autonomous drones, self-repairing machines...even synthetic soldiers."

I let out a slow breath, the implications settling heavy in my chest.

"And you didn't think to tell me this sooner?" I ask, my voice rougher than I intend.

Her eyes flash with defiance. "Because I never intended it to be used that way. And it won't be—not on my watch."

There's no way around the next question. I hate myself for asking it, but I need to know.

"Is this similar to the work of Dr. Rutledge?"

I don't realize I'm still holding her hand until she squeezes mine, grounding me.

A flicker of pride flashes in her eyes, but it's tempered by something heavier. Resignation. "Some of it," she admits quietly. "But I've surpassed what he was attempting to do."

Fuck.

They're not just after her research.

They want Kennedy.

And that makes this personal.

I take a step closer, my grip tightening. "They're not getting you," I vow.

Her lips part, and I see the faint tremble there. Whether it's fear or something else, I don't know. But I do know one thing.

I'm not letting her out of my sight. Not now. Not ever.

CHAPTER 25

Their Sights Are Set

"You are the bows from which your children as living arrows are sent forth."
– Khalil Gibran

Troy

I DIDN'T KNOW HOW Kennedy would respond to spending the weekend with my parents, but I knew whatever the response would be, it would be genuine. Since then, another veil has fallen between us. One by one, she's wearing down my defenses—each loving smile, every light touch and lingering glance slowly chips away at self-induced barriers. Ones I didn't know could be broken...until I met her.

Her eyes dance with mischief as I return from loading the helicopter with our things. "Piggyback ride?" she teases.

"No," I tell her flatly. "I need to have eyes on you." She rolls her eyes, but I carry her in my arms across the patio to the helipad anyway. One arm is wrapped around my neck, and her hand presses against my chest. Even after I put her in her seat, I can still feel the imprint of her touch, the warmth of her fingers. Her scent—lavender and honey—clings to my clothes, refusing to let go.

The helicopter ride to my parents' house is quiet. Kennedy stares out the window, soaking in the view of Southern California. Her face lights up whenever we pass something interesting—the mountains, the coastline, the clusters of desert homes. I'm hoping in these moments, her mind is far from computer codes, criminals, or anything that can dim the smile I've come to cherish.

It's a short flight to my parents' sprawling property in Palm Springs. Noise from our transport alerts them to our arrival. We exit the craft and round the corner. My mom is already at the door waiting to greet us, looking lovely as always, wearing a blue linen wrap dress.

"Baby boy," she calls out as I help Kennedy up the walkway. I shake my head, resigned that asking her not to call me that is useless.

When I reach her, she pulls me into a hug, squeezing me tight. "Mom, this is Dr. Kennedy Green," I introduce her, pausing ever so slightly before adding, "My client." The word seems off, too formal for what we're becoming. "She's been at the mountain house for the past few weeks. Kennedy, this is my mom, Tanya Armstrong."

Kennedy extends her hand, but Mom pulls her into a hug. "None of that hand-shaking nonsense," Mom says warmly. "Dr. Green. Welcome to our home. You must be in quite the situation to be held up on that mountain."

Kennedy laughs softly. "Mrs. Armstrong, it's lovely to meet you. You can call me Kennedy."

"And you can call me Tanya." Mom hooks her arm through Kennedy's, leading her inside, already fussing over her. I follow, carrying the bags.

"I saw Marcus' car out front," I say as we head into the house. The smell of baked goods and hot coffee wafts through the air, making me hungry. "What are he and Dad up to?"

Mom sighs. "You know your brother. He's checking the medicine cabinet, making sure our doctors are not overprescribing things."

"Why does Dad need medicine? Last I knew, he got a clean bill of health."

"I pulled a muscle last week," Dad announces, his deep voice echoing down the hall.

"Dad," I greet. "This is Dr. Kennedy Green; I mentioned her on the phone. Kennedy, this is my father, Maurice Armstrong."

"Dr. Green, it's a pleasure to meet you. My son mentioned how brilliant you are, but he left out how beautiful you are. By the way, you can call me Maurice."

"Maurice, behave," Mom chastises.

"It's true," Dad says with a shrug.

"Thank you, Maurice. You can call me Kennedy."

My brother walks into the room with his usual swagger. Instead of the crisp white shirt and slacks he wears at the hospital, he is dressed down in jeans and a black t-shirt. "Ah, the voice of an angel," he says, extending a hand. "You must be the famous Dr. Green. I've heard a lot about you. I'm Marcus."

"Marcus? You're chief surgeon Dr. Armstrong—I didn't make the connection until now." Kennedy tilts her head, her eyes bouncing between us. "Are you two fraternal twins?"

Marcus lets out a bark of laughter. "I'm the older, better-looking one."

"Hardly. He meant to confirm he is the chief of surgery."

"Boys, enough of that. Kennedy, brunch is almost ready. I hope you're hungry."

"Absolutely."

We all follow Mom into the kitchen. I help Kennedy to the table. "Would you like something to drink?" Mom asks Kennedy.

"I'll have coffee. I can help if you need it," she offers.

"I got it," Mom says, eying my brother and me. "Baby boy, Marcus, you two can set the food on the table."

"I'll get the hot stuff, you get cold stuff," I tell Marcus.

"Your girl is stunning," Marcus whispers, nudging my shoulder.

"She's not my girl," I mutter, even though I don't believe it.

"Right. And I'm Superfly. Tell it to someone who doesn't know you like I do."

Ignoring him, I grab the quiche, asparagus, and fresh-baked biscuits and set them in the center of the table.

"How's your ankle, Kennedy? Hopefully, you don't have much walking to do at the house," my dad asks.

"Getting better," she replies, glancing my way with a soft smile that strokes my soul. "Troy has me on a strict recovery plan."

"Compliments of my advice," Marcus adds. He's right. I texted him when I knew Kennedy was coming home with me, wanting only the best care for her. "You should let me take a look at that."

Kennedy laughs. "The chief of surgery as my doctor? I'd be honored."

I clear my throat. "It's more of a security thing."

Mom sets cups on the table along with the coffee pot and creamer. Kennedy examines her mug, brows furrowed.

"Is this a picture of you as a baby, Troy?"

"That's Marcus. I believe he was about two in the picture," Mom answers. "Isn't he cute?"

"And the others, are they him and Troy at various ages?"

I roll my eyes. "Those are him, too," I hate to admit. Kennedy pours coffee into her mug and smiles.

"Just how many of these are there?" she asks.

"Eight," Marcus punctuates proudly. "She needed a new set of cups. These fit the bill perfectly."

"It's the cutest thing," Mom says, cutting a slice of quiche and plating it.

Kennedy covers her mouth, stifling a laugh, and I can't help but smile at my brother's absurd antics.

Mom sets the plate of quiche in front of Kennedy. "We hope one day we'll have a set of our own grandkids," she says.

Marcus and I cough in unison, caught off guard by the not-so-subtle hint. Although I expected my mom to bring up the topic, I thought we'd have a reprieve in the presence of company. In the past, when she brought up the topic of starting a family, it seemed like some idealized version of life beyond my grasp. Admittedly, Kennedy has me rethinking everything.

What would it be like to have her permanently by my side? Does she want kids? Do *I* want kids? Can I stay true to myself and my commitment to protecting others?

Kennedy raises an eyebrow, amused, as her eyes shift between me and Marcus.

"What do you think, Kennedy?" My dad asks.

She blinks, as if surprised by how quickly the conversation changed, as she gets drawn into my parent's agenda. "Um, yeah, I suppose that would be ideal in your situation."

Marcus smirks at me, leaning in. "This is all you, man."

Ignoring him, I turn the conversation to work. "Marcus, are you still expanding your department?"

"I hired a few more staff. I was thinking about bringing your guy, Dax, to the team. He's got talent. Is he still thinking about retiring from medicine?"

"If you're interested, you can talk to him. He has his reasons for stepping away."

"Do you have any siblings, Kennedy?" Marcus asks.

"I'm an only child." Kennedy turns toward Mom. "Tanya, what was it like to raise these two?"

"Oh, it was an adventure. Marcus was always wandering off, studying or watching medical shows. Troy, on the other hand, never wandered far. He was always watching people, pointing out things the rest of us didn't notice. And in school...well, Troy had a bit of a reputation."

"For what?" Kennedy asks.

Dad pipes in, "Beating up bullies. We couldn't blame him, though. He was preventing them from terrorizing other students."

"Some people need to be taught a lesson. Pick a fight with someone your size and never put your hands on a woman."

Kennedy's eyes shift to me. "So, protecting people has always been in your nature."

"I suppose."

"Kennedy, Troy, and Marcus host a big birthday bash every year since their birthdays are days apart. Will you be there this year?" my mom asks.

Kennedy eats a biscuit, giving herself a few moments before she answers.

"Mom," I warn. "She's a client."

Marcus sits back in his chair, wearing a smug smile. Of course, he's enjoying this.

"We...haven't discussed that. I wouldn't be opposed to attending."

"You hear that, Baby boy?"

"I did, Mom."

Eventually, we make it through brunch without my parents marrying me off. However, it's obvious my parents have their sights set on Kennedy. Later in the day, when we have a brief reprieve from my parents, I give her a tour of the property.

Afterward, to celebrate their anniversary, Marcus and I take them out to dinner.

"Let's toast," I announce.

"I'll lead it," Marcus says. He holds up his glass. "To Mom and Dad, the two people who demonstrate that true love is possible. Thank you for continuing to be great role models. Cheers."

"Cheers," we all say in unison.

I clink my glass to Kennedy's. She fits right in; she belongs with us. Her movements and interactions are so carefree. Watching her, my heart races. When she tosses her head back and laughs at something, my dad says she seems at home. This feels so right, and I never want the night to end.

At one point in the evening, Marcus pulls me aside and says, "She's the one man. Don't let her go."

I'm trying to hold on.

***

The sun has long since set, replaced by the moon casting a silvery glow over the pool. The desert air is warm, wrapping around us like a blanket. It's after ten, and my parents have settled in for the night. Marcus is inside, taking an emergency call from the hospital. Kennedy and I sit in companionable silence that says more than words ever could.

"Your parents are lovely," she says. "Marcus is a hoot."

Sitting back, one leg crossed over my knee, I stare at her. The glint of light from the moon catches the sparkle in her eye just right. "That's one word for him."

"Your mom said you've always been protective. That kind of instinct comes from something deeper. What made you this way, Troy?"

I stare at her for a long moment, deciding how much to share. The thing that's eaten away at me all these years. Not even my parents know.

"I was eight years old," I begin, my voice barely above a whisper. "We were out as a family, eating at a restaurant with a view of the bay. When we finished, we waited in the lobby while Mom used the restroom. Marcus and I stood by the window, looking down at the courtyard below."

Kennedy watches me, her gaze steady.

"There was a young woman sitting on a stone bench. She had two kids—a boy and a girl, maybe three or four years old. At first, I thought they were playing. The sister had something in her hand. He slapped it out. When she went to pick it up, the boy started hitting her. But he didn't stop. Even when she fell, he kept hitting her."

Kennedy's hand flies to her mouth. "Oh my god."

"The mother didn't move. She just...sat there." I take a deep breath, pushing back the familiar ache in my chest. "The girl was crying, her hands in a defensive posture, trying to protect herself and get him to stop, but he didn't. When he stomped on her, I couldn't take it anymore. I ran for the elevator. I had to help her."

Kennedy reaches out, her fingers brushing against mine. We don't voice the reasons why a mother wouldn't react in this situation. We don't talk about the children's learned behavior.

"When I got down there, they were gone. I was too late."

I close my eyes for a moment, swallowing the knot of guilt in my throat. "I never forgot that. I couldn't protect her. But I swore I'd never let that happen again. I'd protect the people who couldn't protect themselves."

She squeezes my hand. "Troy...."

Her voice is soft, full of compassion. I don't pull away. I hold on. Because I never want to let her go.

CHAPTER 26

Doctor, Doctor

"Be careful what you wish for, lest it come true!"
– Aesop's Fables

Kennedy

SOME DAYS ARE A struggle. Then there are rare days when I'm firing on all cylinders—today is one of those. I finally figured out how to replicate the seventh key property of animated life. It's a huge step forward—one I've dreamed about since I was a student under Dr. Rutledge. If I can decode the eighth one, I will have accomplished something the world never thought possible. I credit my focused effort to the atmosphere Troy creates. Something about the seclusion and safety I feel when I'm around him fuels my creativity and critical thinking.

After spending the weekend with Troy and his family, we turned a crucial page in our relationship. He's still my protector, staying true to his self-imposed boundaries. But last weekend offered me a glimpse behind the steel façade he diligently defends. Occasionally, he gives me tiny hints, tender touches, a wink, a whisper...his smile. God, I crave that smile. All the things that signify...he's mine.

I'm anxious about today. Soon, I'll learn whether the sacrifices I've made—quiet seclusion, daily exercise, and adjusting my diet—have paid off. On the downside, in anticipation of going into the city, Troy has

158

transformed into protective mode. The extent of his emotion today is a tight-lipped smile over coffee.

Our flight to the city is short. At the airport our car is waiting when the helicopter lands. When Troy opens the car door, I want to touch his hand, but I don't dare—not now. Not while his mind is on preventing anyone from getting near to me. As the driver navigates the streets of San Francisco, I glance at Troy in the rearview mirror. Instinctively, his eyes lock on mine. Something about the "I've got you covered" look he's giving me settles my nerves, and I wonder if he knows the effect he has on me. Perhaps he's doing it because he does.

"When we arrive at the hospital, wait for me to open the car door," he says authoritatively. I nod in response. "I'll escort you to the exam room and wait for you. You don't need to check-in. Everything is prearranged."

"Got it."

The car comes to a rolling stop in front of the hospital, and I follow his instructions to the letter, letting him take the lead. I'm not surprised to see Dax standing guard, his face stoic, at the building entrance. Gone is the playful giant who threw flirty smiles at my best friend. I give him a small smile as we pass, neither expecting nor receiving anything in return.

Once inside, Troy and I head straight to the elevator. The doors open, and I stand with my back against the wall, holding the handrails for extra support. He stands opposite me, and I hold his gaze in a futile attempt to read the mind behind the beautiful mask he portrays. But I can't. He won't let me in. The elevator dings, breaking the trance and alerting us that we have arrived at our floor. I wait for the door to open, take a deep breath, and curse the divine or whoever brought me a man I can't have. *Damn you.*

Just as Troy mentioned, everything is in order. Upon arriving on the floor, we're welcomed by a hospital staff member who guides us to a room. Troy assists me onto the exam table, takes off my boot, gives me a reassuring smile, and then steps out. Shortly after, a nurse comes in, asks me a few questions, and checks my vitals.

"Dr. Armstrong will be in shortly. Afterward, I'll escort you for X-rays."
I nod and wait.

The next time the door opens, Marcus welcomes me with a smile.

"Dr. Green, it's good to see you again. How are you feeling?"

"I'm good, Dr. Armstrong." I take a deep breath. "I'm hoping you have good news for me."

"We'll see." He washes his hands in the sink, dries them, and then puts on gloves. "I'm going to examine your foot. Tell me if you feel any pain."

"Okay."

He rolls a chair over and sits. He slides off my sock and examines my ankle. His touch is gentle yet deliberate, reminiscent of Troy's, as he presses on certain spots and flexes my foot. I study the similarity in his hands and features; everything about him reminds me of Troy, yet he seems so different. Even without the playful banter I experienced in Palm Springs, his doctor's manners still feel human. I think about Troy and wonder whether he could let the Man of Steel veil down to be with me...truly be with me. *Would he want that?*

"Your ankle is looking good. We'll take an X-ray and verify how you're healing."

"And if it looks okay...what's next?"

"You discontinue wearing the boot and initiate physical therapy over the next two weeks."

"Will therapy consist of exercises similar to those Troy had me performing?"

"That depends. What were the last few exercises you did together?"

"I...I laid on my back with my boot on as a weight and was able to lift my leg. Yesterday, I put pressure on my foot and walked a few steps without the boot."

He smirks at me. "My brother is committed to getting you back on your feet."

"It's not his fault. I'm a bit anal when it comes to time constraints and commitments. I'm anxious to regain my independence. Besides, I have a big project to complete."

"I understand. Well, let's get your X-ray," he says, returning my sock in place. The room's down the hall. I'll have the nurse help you into the wheelchair."

"I don't need that."

He locks eyes with me, and it's filled with the same questioning "did I stutter" look that Troy gives me. "Dr. Green, I prefer it."

He stands. When he opens the door, Troy is standing there waiting.

He tips his head to Troy and says, "Wheelchair." I roll my eyes, not caring who sees.

Marcus disappears into the hallway, and Troy enters the room, closing the door behind him. He rolls the wheelchair in the corner over to the exam table and locks the wheels. He leans over me. The door clicks and opens.

"I can help with that," the nurse says, entering the room.

Troy holds up a hand, halting her. Then he slides an arm under my legs and one around my waist, lifts me, and sits me in the chair.

"I think he's got this," I say in jest. "You lead, we'll follow," I tell her.

Chin over my shoulder, I give Troy a tight-lipped smirk. He doesn't respond—just continues pushing me down the hall. Once in the X-ray room, he assists me again and waits. When the process is over, we rinse and repeat. This time, when we return to the exam room, I don't get out of the wheelchair. Troy turns to leave.

"Don't go."

"I'm giving you your privacy."

"I haven't had any for weeks." His eyebrows raise. "You know what I mean. My business is your business. Have a seat. You don't plan to intimidate me and your brother, do you?" I say the words I know will tame the giant and bring Troy back to me. Reluctantly, he sits. "Thank you. This is my least favorite side of you. I understand you have to act this way, but...."

I don't finish my statement, not because I'm afraid or think I'll hurt him. I don't finish because there's no reason—he knows. He can read me, and I'm learning to read him, too.

We sit in silence for I don't know how long before I say, "You know if I get the all-clear, you have to open the envelope."

For the first time since we got into the room, he's not focused on me but on something beyond my shoulder, only briefly, and I wonder what he's thinking. Then it dawns on me: I'm playing with fire.

Let's hope I don't get burned.

CHAPTER 27

High Stakes and Hot Coffee

"Some of us think holding on makes us strong but sometimes it is letting go."
– Hermann Hesse

Troy

TWO STOPS. I ESTIMATE no more than fifteen minutes per stop—store, apartment, and then back to the airport. We still haven't tracked the criminals to their source, but we're getting close. I don't want to take any chances, but more importantly, I won't stifle Kennedy's creativity by making her feel captive. My reward for compromising is a smile from Kennedy that lights up my soul. But I can't lose focus.

Kennedy picks up a few comfort foods at the store, while I grab items to restock my supplies. Back in the car on our way to the apartment, I check the rearview mirror. Something on her phone has her attention split between me and whatever's outside the window. Something is bothering her.

"Everything good?" I ask.

"Yeah, it's been a while since I've been home. I guess I'm just in my feelings."

"Understandable. I'll be with you every step of the way." She holds my gaze in the mirror and nods.

We round the corner to her block, and her apartment building comes into view.

"Same protocol. Follow my lead, okay?"

"Of course."

Everything appears normal at first glance. Kennedy confirms that there is no mail waiting for her in the lobby. All her necessities are paperless, and after joining Ross Enterprises, she had all her mail redirected to a PO Box following our security protocol. As we exit the elevator on her floor, I notice her glance toward the apartment of her neighbor, who has a coir doormat in front of their apartment.

"Have you seen that before?" I tip my head.

"That rug? No. Sometimes someone puts out a small plant when they have a guest coming, to help them easily find their place, but never a rug."

I take note of the apartment number so my team can look into the occupants. Once I open her door, she stands just inside the entryway while I check each room.

"All clear," I tell her when I'm done.

Her face relaxes. She says, "I'll just be a few minutes," before disappearing down the hall.

My earpiece beeps—it can only be Dax.

"Speak."

"You still good on your ETA?"

If Kennedy sticks to the plan, we'll be out of here and back to the airport as scheduled. "We'll be down in ten."

"Copy that," he says, ending the call.

Kennedy appears with an overnight bag. "You sure we have enough space?"

"I'm sure. Is this everything?"

"It is. But..." She hesitates, and I feel another compromise coming. I can't help but give in to this woman, yet I refuse to risk her safety. "Can we make one more stop?" I open my mouth to speak, but she interjects, "I just want to grab coffee. It's my favorite." She checks her watch. "We have time. I promise it won't take long."

"Where is this place?"

"The shop is at the end of the block." Her eyes plead.

"Grab it to-go."

"That'll work."

I tap my earpiece again. "Doc, detour to corner coffeeshop." He acknowledges, and I grab Kennedy's bag as we head out the door.

At the street level, I place her belongings in the trunk and instruct the driver to take us to the corner. The lead car with Dax should already be there waiting. It's a short drive. We could have walked, but Kennedy has accomplished more today than she has in the past few weeks. I'm worried she may have overextended herself. However, her actions demonstrate her eagerness to return to normal life. Unexpectedly, being with her feels normal, even though I won't allow myself to think we could converge our worlds. I tried that before and failed.

I think about my conversation in the hospital with Marcus before he went to examine Kennedy.

"Man, tell me she's my future sister-in-law." His expression showed he was serious.

"Naw, man. I can't go there. My job is to protect her. When this threat is over, we both have to move on with our lives. It can't work."

"Troy, this is not Justine. Put that shit behind you. Everything about Kennedy tells me she's committed to you for the long run. You may be doing your job, but the way you two move in sync, like you're connected, is special. You can't tell me you don't feel it."

Justine. Ten years ago, we were on the path to becoming something more. I did what I believed was necessary to make us work. What I didn't realize was that she had her own hesitations—or rather, her father had more sway over her than she had over her own heart. She was looking for security. Husband. House. Home. Not the kind at the end of the barrel of a gun. I still don't know if she truly loved me. Maybe she did in her own way. That doesn't matter now. The important lesson I learned from that relationship is that I couldn't stop being myself while I was with her. It takes two to make it work. That's why I can't give in to the feelings I've developed for Kennedy. I won't risk giving my all again only to have it rejected because someone can't handle the kind of work I do.

"This isn't about Justine," I told him. "Kennedy has her own life to lead. Once we uncover who's behind the threat, she'll return to her routine, and I'll get back to protecting the Ross family."

"That's not a life. You're the CEO of a multi-million-dollar company. Run your business, man. Give your team a chance to lead in the field. You and I both know you need to step away from fieldwork at some point. But that doesn't mean you have to stop protecting others."

"I'll think about it," I told him, using those words to satisfy him, knowing in my heart he was right.

I help Kennedy out of the car when it stops in front of the modern steel-and-concrete building that houses the coffee shop on the street level. Dax stands to the side of the glass entrance. I nod to him as I guide Kennedy inside and toward the counter.

"Double tall latte," she tells the barista. I reach over and tap my phone to the payment scanner. "Thanks."

She slips her hands in her pockets and wrinkles her nose at me as we step aside to wait for her drink. She's so freaking cute.

Someone approaching quickly puts me on high alert. Instinctively, I extend my hand to stop them from getting any closer. A fair-skinned brunette tries to push past me. When we arrived, I noticed her sitting in the back, scrolling through her phone.

I say, "Stand back," and it grabs Kennedy's attention. She is unaware that someone is trying to get near her. She turns and ends up face-to-face with me.

"Dr. Green?" the woman calls.

"Lisa?"

"Hi, I'm surprised to see you here."

Kennedy touches my arm. "She's a former student of mine." I lower my arm to give her space to address the woman while still keeping my position between them. Lisa is not on Kennedy's security list, suggesting that their relationship is superficial.

"I was sitting in the back. I'm expecting someone."

Kennedy nods. "You moved back to San Francisco?"

"No, I'm still in Seattle—just here on business. How are you?" Her attention is drawn to Kennedy's boot. "I guess I should ask whether you're okay."

"I'm good. It's just a temporary setback. So, you have a business meeting here?"

"Oh no. Not today. I'm meeting my friend."

My earpiece signals. I tap it. It must be Dax. "Incoming. Familiar," he says, indicating someone else Kennedy knows has arrived—this time, someone on my list.

"Latte for Kennedy," the barista calls out. She steps forward to get her drink. I move in sync with her.

"Kennedy?" someone else calls out. I recognize his voice—Ford, her emergency contact from the hospital.

Kennedy turns, and her voice rises an octave as she says, "Ford?"

Lisa walks towards Ford and leans in for a hug. He hesitates before awkwardly returning it as if caught doing something he shouldn't. She kisses him on the cheek. Once he untangles himself from Lisa, he moves toward Kennedy, but I don't let him get close enough to touch her. We exchange warring glances. Heat crawls up my neck as I stare him down. The door opens again, and I mentally note everyone entering: two women and a man.

"Why didn't you tell me you were back? I've been texting." Ford's voice is a blend of surprise and irritation. "How are you doing?"

"Do you know Dr. Green?" Lisa asks as though she's probing for information she already has. He remains silent, his gaze fixed on Kennedy.

"I'm okay, Ford." Kennedy tilts her head slightly. "How do you know Lisa?"

"We met in Seattle."

"Seattle," Kennedy repeats. The atmosphere in the shop becomes heavy. It's a situation I've faced many times in my career when no one dares say what they're thinking. It doesn't help that I have an overwhelming desire to crush Ford.

Kennedy shifts her weight onto her boot. Even when exhausted, she's stunning. However, the feelings she's masking at the sight of these two aren't helping. I'm getting her out of here.

"We need to get moving, Dr. Green," I announce, tracking everyone's movements.

"Wait," Ford holds up a hand. I take a step closer. "What are you doing? Why are you here?" he asks me, his tone unnecessarily aggressive.

He doesn't know who he's dealing with.

Stepping closer, I glare at him and say, "I'm here to stop you from getting closer. Dr. Green, do you have any further business with these people?"

Her voice is soft yet firm as she replies, "No. I'm all done here."

"Kennedy, talk to me. Will you be back later this evening? Let's talk."

"It doesn't seem like either of you has ordered a drink yet. Don't let me stop you. I have to go," she says, linking her arm with mine.

"Kennedy."

This time, she doesn't respond. I guide her through the door, past Dax, and to the car. Once she gets in, I notice that a gentleman who came into the shop after Ford is leaving without a drink. I tap my earpiece.

"Detain him. He didn't make a purchase." Dax nods.

I get Kennedy into the car and away from the shop as quickly as possible. Something about her exchange with Ford and Lisa is unsettling. I sense that Kennedy feels the same. She's quiet the entire drive to the airport. Aside from thanking the staff when we arrive and expressing gratitude to me for carrying her to and from the aircraft, she doesn't say much else. She doesn't need to—not until she's ready.

When she is, I'll be there.

CHAPTER 28

SOS

*"You may not control all the events that happen to you,
but you can decide not to be reduced by them."*
– Maya Angelou

Kennedy

What the hell was that back at the coffee shop? I keep repeating the words in my head in the car on the way to the airport and during our flight back to Troy's house. The way Lisa hugged and kissed him felt more than casual. Everything about their interaction signals they're a couple. But what the hell? Why is he constantly trying to get together with me? I don't know this man anymore. After all these years, I continue to discover new things about him. Or maybe I overlooked things, like confusing his control for concern. This is something new. He travels a lot. Does he have a girl in every city? What the hell were we then? Was *I?*—one of many? *Shit.*

I'm silent on the trip back and as Troy carries me into the house. While he retrieves our belongings from the helicopter, I head to my room to take a bath. Purposely, I put my phone on DND and set it within reach of the tub, ignoring the numerous texts from Ford. The entire ordeal has left me spent, stunned, and starving. The good news is that I'll finally be rid of the boot. Tomorrow, I'll be walking on my own.

I maneuver to stand and get out of the tub, using my hands and one good foot to steady myself as I sit on the edge. Only when I swing my legs over do I realize I didn't put down a rug. Water drips from my legs onto the floor. *Shoot.* There's no way I'm jeopardizing my progress by slipping on wet marble. I reach for my towel and wrap it around myself. It'll be fine if I put my boot on—it has good grip. But it's not fine because I was so mad at Ford that I threw the boot across the bathroom after I took it off. Why does this bathroom have to be the size of an apartment? I have no idea. I'm in a no-win situation.

I do the only thing I can to escape this mess and avoid injuring myself again. I text Troy.

Me: SOS

I watch the screen. There is no text response. Instead, two seconds later, he bursts through the bathroom door. Not bursts through like he is breaking it down, but if I were locked in, God help that door.

He rushes to my side. "Kennedy. What happened? Are you hurt?" His voice is steady, yet filled with concern.

I tilt my head toward my boot. "I forgot to put down a rug, and my boot is—"

I don't get to finish. He grabs a rug and my boot, then returns to me, laying the plush white bath mat over the water. I place my feet on the mat.

"How's your ankle?" he asks.

"I think I overdid it today. It's sore when I put pressure on it."

"You've been on your feet most of the day. No more walking tonight. I'll be your feet."

"You're insane. After we eat, I won't be doing much other than reviewing code."

"Like I said, I'll be carrying you. Hold on."

Before I can protest, he lifts me and carries me to my room, where he sets me down on the bed. I'm stunned when he asks, "What are you wearing?"

I think, "Nothing right now," but for once, I hold back my inner thoughts. Instead, I fumble with my words, distracted by everything that belongs to Troy: his strength, his thoughtfulness, his care. All the things that make me want him even more. "Uh..." I point. "Top drawer. Olive green T-shirt dress. Oh, and lotion."

In only a few strides, his long muscular legs carry him to the drawer, where he retrieves my dress. After that, he heads to the bathroom to get my lotion. Returning, he hands everything to me and says, "I'll be outside the door. Let me know when you're ready. You won't need the boot. I've got you." After he leaves, closing the door behind him, I blink, confused by his actions.

I take my time getting ready, processing everything that happened at the coffee shop. I keep questioning whether I should talk to Ford and give him a chance to explain himself. But why? He means nothing to me now. If that's true, why does he live rent-free in my head? Why won't he let me go? Why didn't he introduce Lisa as his girlfriend? I don't care if they're a couple. *Do I?*

The clock on the nightstand ticks. It's time for dinner. Sticking to the schedule means I get in a few hours of work despite the busy day.

"Troy."

He opens the door, his eyes examining me as he approaches. He kneels and then lifts my sore ankle, checking it as he does before we exercise. "Where are your socks?"

"It's a warm night; since you insist on carrying me, I don't need them." He nods.

Standing to his full height, he announces, "Dinner is ready. You get a cheat night." He lifts me from the bed.

"Pizza?"

He gives me a small, press-lipped smile. "Yes."

"Let's eat in the great room overlooking the view."

"Movie or jazz?" he asks.

A soft trumpet melody by Chris Botti drifts through the speakers. The music is a lovely constant here—part of what makes this place feel so calming. The other reason is beside me, watching me with quiet intensity.

When Troy is like this—holding me in his arms, gazing at me like I matter—I can see a future with him.

Does he see it too?

"I prefer music."

Troy sets me gently onto the couch, positioning me so I face the massive windows overlooking the valley. I settle in, finally able to take a breather from today. Moments later, he returns with two trays, setting one on my lap and the other on the coffee table.

"Did you want anything besides sparkling water?"

"Not tonight. Maybe this weekend I'll create a new cocktail." I take a bite of my pizza. The cheese stretches before snapping back, the blend of tomato and spices warm and familiar.

"I'm looking forward to it." His half-smile flickers, but there's something guarded about it.

I swallow, watching him. "What's with the...." I point, moving my finger in a circular motion.

"There are a few things we need to discuss."

"Now?"

"Now."

I straighten slightly. "Is this about my security?"

"Partially." He leans forward, resting his elbows on his knees. "The neighbor you mentioned—the one with the rug? He didn't put it there. He's been in India for the past two weeks on family business."

A chill spreads through me. "Then who—?"

"The man who entered the coffee shop after Ford has been living in his apartment."

My stomach knots. "House-sitting?"

"No."

I grip the tray tighter. "Oh my god."

Troy exhales slowly, his voice controlled. "We suspected something like this would happen. The evidence suggests he was watching you."

My pulse kicks up. "Is he in custody?"

"Yes."

I let out a breath, but it doesn't help the unease curling inside me. "Did he have a weapon? Was he there to hurt me?"

"Kennedy." His voice drops, firm but reassuring. "I didn't tell you this to scare you. Your instincts were right about the rug. If anything feels off—emails, calls, texts, people—you tell me. No exceptions."

I nod, throat tight. "I will." I pause, then push forward. "You said that was only part of it. What else?"

Troy leans back slightly, assessing me. "What happened at the coffee shop? You seemed unsettled when Lisa showed up. And then Ford..."

I roll my shoulders, trying to loosen the tension there. "Lisa was one of my students. We didn't interact much outside of class."

"But you interact with Nate."

"He was my top student. Lisa..." I hesitate. "I caught her cheating."

Troy doesn't react immediately, just watches me with those unreadable eyes. Then, quietly, "You don't trust her."

It's not a question. He already knows the answer.

"No. Liars and cheaters rarely change. They just find new ways to hide it."

He nods once. "My team is looking into her background."

My grip tightens around the water bottle in my lap. "You think she has something to do with this?"

"I think everyone is a suspect—including Ford."

He says it casually, but there's something more behind it. Something that makes me uneasy.

Then he looks at me, piercing and direct. "Kennedy, why didn't you tell me about Ford when I asked for the names of people closest to you?"

I blink. "Because...there was no reason. He's been in Seattle for the past year and a half."

"He's still your emergency contact."

"That was a mistake. My parents should be listed."

Troy's jaw tightens, and I feel the weight of his scrutiny. "You two dated."

It's not a question.

"For three years. It ended two years ago."

His gaze darkens slightly. "Kennedy, these are things I need to know to protect you. Whether he's involved or not, I can't afford to leave any stone unturned."

I take another bite of my pizza, chewing slowly, measuring my words.

"I understand." I glance up, meeting his gaze. "I didn't think he was important enough to tell you about."

"If you ever hesitate about something like that, err on the side of telling me."

"You're right."

A beat passes. His voice is softer when he says, "Did he hurt you?"

I frown. "Physically?"

He nods.

"No. If someone ever tried that with me, I'd be the one in jail."

Troy surprises me by laughing. "You are fiery."

I arch a brow. "I'll take that as a compliment coming from you."

He sobers slightly. "Something shifted when he arrived. Do you want him back?"

The question throws me. I expected Troy to push about Ford's connection to Lisa, not about my personal feelings. If we were a couple, it would make sense. But we're not—at least, not officially. But this isn't just business. This isn't just about protection. This is about us. And if he's considering me, he deserves to know.

"No," I say, my voice firm. "Ford has been pursuing me since he returned from Seattle, but I don't want him." I hesitate, then add, "The interaction between him and Lisa confused me. It seemed..." I can't bring myself to say it.

Troy does. "Close. Like they're a couple."

I nod. "That's right."

"What caused your breakup?"

I swallow. The only other person who knows the whole story is Sasha.

Still, I tell him everything. Troy listens without interrupting, his pizza forgotten on his tray. His eyes never leave mine. And somehow, telling him is effortless. Somehow, with him, it feels safe.

When I'm done, he asks, "What did you feel at the restaurant when you saw him again after all those months apart?"

I contemplate my answer before responding. "Confused at first. I didn't understand why he wanted to meet with me. I was disappointed when I learned his true intentions. But I also experienced a wave of relief because he *was* trying to reconnect. I'm not sure what that says about me...."

"You want closure. He returned, opening the door for you to get it."

He's right. The issue is that I haven't been receptive to getting the closure I need. I keep shutting the door when Ford wants to talk about what happened in the past. Maybe I'm afraid of the truth.

"I've been trying to forget who he was to me, but seeing him with Lisa today brought it all back. Our time together wasn't bad, yet it wasn't great either. I should have felt devastated when he left."

"You weren't in love with him."

I shake my head. "I was never in love with him. Maybe that's why his leaving didn't affect me as much as it should have. I was angry. My feelings were hurt. But my heart and soul were spared."

"Only love can cut that deep."

"So, I hear," I whisper.

He has a slight upturn at the corner of his lip when he asks, "Did you do what Angela did in that movie and burn all his shit?"

I laugh, picturing the scene. "He left a few things at my place. I didn't burn them, but I did toss them in the trash chute."

"No, you didn't."

"I did. Leather shoes, silk ties, dress slacks, all of it. It felt freeing."

"Everything?"

"Except for a sweater I bought him. I gave that to a homeless man."

"Damn, woman."

"I know...petty, huh? So unlike my poised, professional persona."

"You did what you thought was right given the circumstances."

"Thank you. I did." I exhale sharply, attempting to brush aside a strand of hair that has fallen against my cheek. Troy holds my gaze, leans over, and carefully tucks the hair behind my ear. Before he pulls away, he gently glides the pad of his thumb across my cheek, sending a shiver throughout my body.

I want this man.

He stands. "Did you want any more pizza?" I shake my head. He collects my dishes. "I'll put these away."

He turns toward the kitchen, but I stop him. "Hey."

"Did you change your mind?" he asks.

"No. But your brother gave me the all-clear today, which means following your regimen was the right move. Thanks for suggesting it."

"You did good."

"I'm glad you agree." I hesitate for a moment and add, "You know what this means. We can open the envelope."

CHAPTER 29

Until...

"To truly love we must learn to mix various ingredients - care, affection, recognition, respect, commitment, and trust, as well as honest and open communication."
– bell hooks

Troy

PRESSING MY PALMS AGAINST the kitchen counter, I gaze at the evening sky. The sun still hangs above the horizon. I love the long summer days. Some of the happiest moments in my life were summer vacations spent with my family during childhood. Each year, our parents took us to a different country. *"You need to understand there's life beyond our own country. Learn about other cultures and open your mind to all that our planet has to offer,"* my father would say. I could never have imagined that protecting others would be the catalyst for seeing the world. Looking over the horizon, I recall those days and wonder if I'll have a family to share the same experience with.

I take a deep breath.

Kennedy.

When I picked her up from the edge of the tub, consumed by lavender and honey, heat from her body permeating my skin, it took all my willpower not to remove her towel, pull her into me, and claim her as mine. In my mind, I already have. I close my eyes and see hers taunting me—willing me to give in to the feeling.

I can't.

I need to protect her, not give in to my desire to taste every beautiful inch of her. I open my eyes, go to the fridge, and retrieve my treat for her. When I return to the main room, she's vibing to Keiko Matsui's *Bridges Over the Stars*, her eyes closed. She's stunning.

"I got you something," I say, sitting on the coffee table in front of her. "Your favorite."

When she opens her eyes, they land on me but are quickly diverted to the brilliant colors of the red velvet cupcake in my hand.

"Wow, this really is a cheat day." She takes the cupcake, peels back the liner, and takes a bite. "Mmm. Oh my God." She mutters with her mouth full.

"Glad you like it."

"You're not having any?"

"You know I don't eat that stuff. Besides, you held up your end of the bargain. It's the least I can do." I stand.

"Where are you going?"

I walk over to the credenza, lift the vase, and retrieve the envelope from beneath it. "I'm finding out what your request is."

Her eyes dance before she says, "Can you take me to watch the sunset?"

I don't hesitate. I grab her cupcake and the envelope, then place them on the table before picking her up. "I was just thinking about all the sunsets in all the countries I've visited."

The glass door slides open as I approach and step out onto the patio. Kennedy's arms are wrapped tight around my neck. Her face is so close that I can feel her breath when she says, "I want to travel the world."

Looking out over the horizon I say, "You will."

"It's so beautiful here. It'll be hard to leave."

A chill passes through me at the thought of her no longer in my life. "I'm happy to bring you back whenever you want respite."

"No. This is your spot to bring your family, friends, and...that special...." She talks as if she's changed her mind, given up on me, or both—either, unbearable. Perhaps she's offering me an out I don't want.

"You're the only woman besides my mom and your friend Sasha who has been here. I'm not the kind of man with many women on my arm. My life is dangerous...complex."

"I understand complex." Kennedy lays her head on my shoulder and trails her nose along my neck toward my ear. My desire for her presses against my jeans. "Let me in, Troy. We're smart enough to figure this out...together," she whispers.

"I won't risk your life."

"I'm not asking you to. Tell me, would we be having this conversation if the circumstances were different and people weren't after me?" She runs a finger along my jawline, and I'm tempted to press my cheek against her palm.

She holds my gaze, waiting for a response. Daring me to speak, like she already knows what I'm thinking. Like she wants me as much as I want her. Every glance, every touch, makes it harder to hold the line. She's not just under my protection—she's under my skin.

I take a deep breath. I can't lie to her. "In another lifetime, had we met, you'd be in my bed, beneath me."

"Troy."

"Let's go in so you can finish your cupcake."

I carry her inside. When I bend to lower her to the couch, she clings tighter.

"You're stuck with me for the moment."

Craving the warmth her closeness provides, I concede, sitting with her on my lap. When I hand her the half-eaten cupcake, she offers me a bite—once more, I decline. She tips her head toward the envelope. I pick it up.

"So, we finished our barbecue lessons. You enjoyed most of your favorite meals tonight. What's next? Don't tell me. You want flying lessons so you can come here more often."

"Oooh, I didn't think of that. Is it too late to add?"

I laugh. "No. If you're serious about learning, I'll teach you."

Flipping the envelope, I slide my finger beneath the small opening at the corner and across the seam, freeing the contents. The paper feels impossibly light in my hands, but the weight of it presses against my chest. *Three weeks.* Three damn weeks this thing has been sitting here, unread. I told her she could ask for anything. And now, I'm about to find out exactly what that means.

Slowly, I undo the micro-folds—Kennedy's cute attempt to conceal her wish. In the background, Brian Culbertson's *Journey* plays over the speakers, the smooth jazz a stark contrast to the tension curling in my gut.

Kennedy scoops icing with her finger and licks it, completely unaware that my entire world just tilted sideways. I should be focused on the implications of this note, on how to handle it. Instead, I'm watching her mouth, thinking about how soft her lips would feel if I kissed her.

I raise an eyebrow, wondering what was on the mind of the woman I brought here three weeks ago. A time she realized her life could be in danger. A time when we were virtually strangers. Even then, I felt a connection to her. Now we dance a delicate dance—more boundaries crossed than I care to admit.

I open the paper and read her handwritten note.

"For one night only. I want all of you. Completely. Mine."

The words hit me like a blow to the ribs. My grip on the paper tightens before I force myself to let go, dropping it onto the table like it burned me. My pulse slams against my throat, and for a second, I forget how to breathe.

I should have expected this. Kennedy doesn't do anything halfway. But this? This isn't a casual request—it's a line drawn in permanent ink. I promised her anything. I promised to protect her. But what if those two things aren't the same anymore?

Three weeks ago, she was a woman in trouble, a client, a responsibility. But now? Now she's the reason I lose sleep. The reason I catch myself looking too long, wanting too much. The reason my carefully built walls have cracks running straight through them.

Kennedy searches my eyes for answers, and I don't have any.

"Kennedy." My voice carries a blend of surprise and caution.

"You said anything I want. I want you."

That was my promise. But this...this isn't just a request. It's an invitation. A challenge. A line I can't uncross. And yet, I already know the answer. Hell, I knew the second I met her.

She eats the last bite of her cake. I smile tentatively, my mind weighing everything. White and red icing covers her lips. Cupping her chin, I turn her face to mine.

It's now or never.

"You have icing on your face. I'm going to lick it off. When I'm done, I'm going to take you to my bedroom and have you for dessert. After that, I'm going to make love to you. Can you handle that?"

She gives me a throaty, "Yes."

Slowly, I trace her lips with my tongue. Her mouth falls open, and I cover it with mine, indulging in something I've wanted for months—our first kiss. I take my time at first, savoring the first feel of her soft, plump lips on mine—lips I want all over my body. I want more. I lick into her, mingling my tongue with her. She tastes sweet, like cream cheese frosting with a hint of her. I deepen the kiss as she sucks my tongue, desperate for more of me. Freely, I give it to her—kissing her like she's my life-saving oxygen. Because at this moment, she is—she makes me feel more alive than I ever felt. My body thickens beneath her.

Lips still pressed to mine, Kennedy maneuvers her body so she's sitting astride me. I break the kiss while grabbing the shin of her injured leg, lifting it so there's no pressure on her ankle.

"We have to be careful. You have to follow my lead. I won't let you reinjure yourself. Understood?"

She gives me a breathy "Okay," before crashing her lips to mine. She grinds against my hardened shaft, and I want to be in her so badly. But this is her night, her gift. I have to take it slow. We kiss like that, my hands roaming her body over her t-shirt until she comes up for air.

I reach beneath her t-shirt and palm her breast. It fits perfectly in my hands. She dips her head and nibbles at my ear. "I want you, Troy," she whispers.

"Enough to put it in writing, apparently. Sit up, beautiful," I tell her. She obliges, and I lift her shirt over her head and toss it aside.

I palm one breast while sucking the other. Her nipple hardens in my mouth as I make circles around it with my tongue, alternating between them. Then I reach between her legs—*my god.* I close my eyes briefly, taking it all in. Feeling her heat makes my dick twitch, and I coat my fingers in the hot, slick evidence of her yearning for me.

Her breath hitches as I stroke her body. "Oh, God," she moans when I insert my fingers. Her back arches and I smile against her breast, anticipating soon she'll be coming on my hand. Her walls grip my finger. I lift my head and watch her as she rides my hand, eyes closed, mouth hung open.

"Come for me, beautiful," I encourage.

"Oh, god, not yet." She places a hand on mine. Her eyes snap open. I stop moving my fingers and lock eyes with her.

"What do you need? Whatever it is, take it."

"I meant it when I said I wanted you to be mine. When I come, when I call your name for the first time in pleasure, I want you to capture my moans. I want you to know I'm yours, Troy. I mean it. I don't want anything or anyone else."

This night is much more than I anticipated. This is our point of no return. Once I take her—she's mine.

Carefully, I lay Kennedy on her back. I cradle her head in my hand, cover her lips with mine, and kiss her hard. I reach between her legs, and her body responds immediately, pulsing at the slightest touch, drenched with desire. As I work her body, I capture every moan, every whimper in my mouth. The vibration sends a signal through my body to my soul—*she's mine.* Her body moves in time with the rhythm of my hand. She's coming. Her wall close in around my fingers and pulse erratically: she sucks my tongue in time with the rhythm, and I hold her, kiss her, give her everything she needs.

Until her walls stop pulsing.

Until her breath settles.

Until she's mine.

"Troy."

CHAPTER 30

Kenni

"It is an absolute human certainty that no one can know his own beauty or perceive a sense of his own worth until it has been reflected back to him in the mirror of another loving, caring human being."
– John Joseph Powell

Kennedy

WHAT WAS I THINKING?

When Troy swallows my cries, he inhales my soul. After my first orgasm, he carries me to his room, lays me on the edge of the bed, and lifts my legs over his shoulders. Like he so calmly articulated, he eats me for dessert, feasting until I see stars.

He's not done.

He hovers over me, trailing kisses down my body.

"Now I understand why God rested on the seventh day; what else could He do after creating someone as beautiful as you? Your skin is like the finest silk, and every brush against it me leaves me craving more." He licks one breast and then the other. His tongue trails a line down my stomach. My back arches, anticipating each caress, each stroke of his tongue. I desperately want him in me as he licks between my thighs. "And you taste like ambrosia of the Gods. How is that even possible?" He continues licking my sweet spot while his arm is stretched across me—his hand pinching my breast.

"Oh, God, Troy." I palm his head between my legs, clawing at the tiny waves of hair, desperate to have him in me. "I need you." He responds, picking up the pace of his tongue, devouring me until I can't hold out any longer and come on his face. When my pulsing subsides, he crawls up my body and trails his nose up my cheek.

"That's my girl." He kisses me, giving me a taste of myself. When he stands, evidence of his need for me presses against his jeans, and all I can think is...my man. Bending, he gathers me in his arms and places me in the center of the bed. "I think you're ready now." He smirks, satisfied with hand and mouth work. He is so fucking fine. I'm here for all of it.

"Seems I'm not the only one ready." There's still a slight hesitation warring within, but he's mine. There's no turning back from what we're about to do. "Don't make me wait."

He takes off his t-shirt, then undoes his belt and zipper. When he slides down his slacks along with his briefs, I gasp. "Holy...." I cover my mouth. He's huge. "Troy." I swallow. "That's not going to fit," I say, my voice a blend of excitement and panic.

He smiles and shakes his head. "You're cute."

He gets in bed and crawls up my body, bringing all his heat. When he kisses me, I cup his cheek and whisper, "I'm serious, Troy."

He smiles against my face. "I promise I'll fit." He kisses me behind my ear. I reach between us and stroke his length, familiarizing myself with what I'm about to get myself into. Troy reaches for the nightstand. I grab his hand.

"No. I'm yours, Troy. I meant that. What do you want?"

"I want what's mine."

"Then claim me."

Troy gently lifts my injured leg over his shoulder. I position his length to my entrance, holding my breath as he slowly sinks into me. With each inch, he pushes in and then pulls out, gradually getting me used to his size—acclimating me to what's mine. It's a beautiful pain that has my walls clenching him at first push.

"Kennedy, you feel amazing." His breath is heavy as he works my body at a slow, steady pace. I lift my hips to meet each thrust, feeling my body expand, welcoming him. "That's it. Feel me glide into you." His mouth latches onto my breast, and I almost come from the pressure and pleasure of it all.

"Troy." My voice comes out in a whimper.

"I'm here, beautiful. Take me." He continues a constant rhythm until it feels like he completely bottoms out within me. "You got this." Troy lifts his head and locks eyes with me. "I want to watch you coat me with your love." He pushes harder and deeper, our rhythms in sync. My eyes fall shut as the pressure builds. It's too much and everything at the same time. Yet it feels so good I can't breathe.

"Open your eyes, beautiful, and come for me." He pushes again, sending me over an explosive edge. My walls grip him as they pulse against his thick length. I don't even recognize the guttural scream that comes out of me as I come around him. "That's it."

I reach for his hips and hold them in place in search of respite, but there is none. I'm full of him. Just the feel of him against my walls makes them pulse. "Give me a second. It's too much." I pant.

He smiles against my cheek, then kisses me. Slowly, he eases his length out, but not all the way, just enough to gradually fill me again. He maintains the pace while kissing me until my body begs for more. More of him. More of the feeling. More of...his love.

Instinctively, Troy already knows what I need. He increases the pace, faster, harder, until his sweat covers my face. Until the only sound is our heavy breathing and our bodies slamming into one another. Until he says, "Come with me."

I do.

It's everything, and I can't imagine living another second without Troy.

When he comes, he calls my name like he's scoured the universe to find me. "Kenni."

***

One night. That was his promise expertly delivered. I tried not to think about it when Troy took me the second time. He said he'd fit—I don't know how, but he did. It was bliss. I savored the moment of having him in me again. We made a mess of the bed, so we changed the sheets. Now I'm sitting in the tub while Troy is in the shower because he insists I can't do weight-bearing walking or stand without my boot until tomorrow. I smile, staring at the silhouette of his body, his arms outstretched, touching the wall as water streams over his head. *I had all of that man in me. Holy fuck.* I'm sore thinking about it, but I want more. I want him in me the entire night.

"Troy," I call above the noise of the shower. He opens the glass door.

"You okay?" he asks.

"Yeah."

"Ready to get out?"

"Hum. Not quite. I want to rinse off in the shower."

"I'm not letting you stand in here."

I extend my hand out of the tub, and he leaves the shower to come to me. "What are you doing?"

"About to have a shower with you." I toggle the lever to let the water out of the tub. Troy lifts me out and takes me into the shower, holding me astride him, allowing the water to flow over my back. I take the handheld shower head and wash my front before replacing it.

"You're something. You know that?" He dips his head and kisses me. His body rises, and I reach down and take hold of him.

"Take me," I tell him.

Troy cradles my hips, allowing me to position him in me. He doesn't place my back against the shower wall when he enters. Instead, he holds me—one arm wrapped around my hips, his other hand pressed against the wall, balancing us both as I ride him hard. The cacophony of his grunts, my cries, our bodies clashing while water pours over us is a symphony of love. When we come together, his juices mix with mine, running down our bodies, circling the drain, and I cry. I cry because I never want us to end.

For the first time, I lose track of time. When Troy sits me on top of a towel on the bathroom counter and dries me, I stroke his arms and stare at him. *He's mine.* "You're a beautiful man. You know that?"

"If you say so, then I am."

"Do people tell you things like that? Like...when you're standing guard, do they walk up to you and go, 'You're so fine.'"

He laughs; it's beautiful. It bounces off the walls, making my heart soar because I get to experience what no one else does—his happiness.

He presses his nose to mine. "No. I suppose I'm too intimidating for that."

"Rose never told you?"

"Niall would try to kill me if he knew she said something like that. Not that he could."

I wrap my arms around his neck. I dust my lips across his and whisper against them. "You're so fine." He kisses me again. When he breaks the kiss, I say, "I'm tired. Take me to bed."

He lifts me and carries me to bed, my towel falling to the floor. I lay on my side facing him, wrapped in his protective arms, enjoying the feel of our skin touching until I fall asleep to his heartbeat. I remain that way until my eyes open hours later.

When I wake, he's watching me. I cup his cheek and pull his face to mine. He kisses me, waking every cell in my body. And when he rolls me onto my back and pushes into me—I'm home.

CHAPTER 31

Home

"The minute I heard my first love story, I started looking for you, not knowing how blind that was. Lovers don't finally meet somewhere. They're in each other all along."
– Rumi

Troy

EVERYTHING ABOUT KENNEDY GREEN feels right. Like mine. Like home.

Reading the slip of paper that revealed her desires left me feeling conflicted. We talked about possibly waiting until our situation changed. Until my feelings for her wouldn't cloud my judgment. Until I could love her openly without endangering her life. Because I do love her. I would have forfeited my promise if I didn't wholeheartedly believe that we were meant for each other.

Having her. Tasting her. Coming inside her. Everything about her...*about us* is perfect. When she smiles at me, it strokes my soul. When she touches me, I see flashes of our future. I shouldn't feel this way, not about her. Not now. Not when someone is trying to get to her. I need to protect her, not give in to my desire to pull her close.

I tried.

I wake up and move to get out of bed to shower, determined to be satisfied with my brief taste of her. But before I can leave, she grabs my hand.

"I know I said one night, but I can't get enough of you," she says, her eyes pleading.

"Kenni."

She doesn't say anything—just holds her arms open...waiting for me. Giving in, I lift her leg, lowering myself to her. When she comes, her moans, like music, bounce off the walls, reverberating through me. When we shower, all our love spills between us as I take her again. Afterward, finally satiated, we get dressed.

"Put. Me. Down," she says, punctuating each word as I carry her to the kitchen. I set her down on the counter. "You know I can't hop down."

Standing between her legs, I smooth a curl from her face and gaze into eyes that, less than an hour ago, reflected the depth of her desire for me. I memorized each expression: when I kissed every inch of her body, when I entered and claimed her, when she came calling my name and I swallowed her cries. I wonder if she knows that she has completely consumed me. I cup her cheek, smoothing my thumb across it.

"Smart, sexy, and spirited—the best of everything." My words hold her attention. She tilts her head in my palm and smiles. "I'm making breakfast, then we can acclimate you to walking without a boot. You good?"

"I'm great."

I turn on the coffee pot and set a tall glass of water on the counter next to Kennedy. "You should hydrate. You didn't drink much last night."

"There wasn't much downtime."

"You'll have plenty today." My words have a double meaning. It's Friday—Kennedy has experiments to conduct, and our time of lovemaking is over.

I can't let what's developing between us affect me more than it already has. Although my experience with Justine left me unsure about whether a woman would accept my career, I trust Kennedy when she says she'll wait.

"Don't make anything heavy. I'm not that hungry."

"Hot or cold?"

"Cold. I like that granola you make."

I gather ingredients for a quick, healthy, high-protein breakfast: Greek yogurt, homemade granola, and fruit. After washing and slicing the fruit, I place the bowl on the counter next to Kennedy. I take a berry and feed it to her. When her tongue brushes against my finger, I resist the urge to pull her into a kiss. I set her on the barstool before getting the yogurt and granola. After preparing our yogurt bowls, I hand her a spoon and coffee and then sit beside her.

"You have two weeks of intense therapy to get through," I tell her.

Kennedy eats several spoonfuls before saying, "Then I go home?"

"You'll be strong enough to handle more challenging situations on your own, but you still have a few more weeks before you can wear heels and feel a bit more normal. But yes, you can go home."

"And if I need to return before then. Like for a meeting or something?"

"I'll escort you. My team will be nearby as well. We will find those responsible for this, Kenni."

She grabs my hand and squeezes. "I know you will. I'm not afraid of them, but I don't understand why I can't go home now. Not that I want to be away from you...it's just that I—"

"You want to get on with your life."

"Yeah, this project is important to me. *You're* important to me."

"Don't base your decisions on me."

"What?" She moves to slide off the stool.

"Don't." Reflexively, I stand and grab her waist before her bare feet hit the floor. "What are you doing?" When I try to sit her back on the stool, she clings to me the way she did last night. "You're going to hurt yourself."

"Standing up to you."

Resignedly, I sit back down, bringing her with me. "You're too short for that. Don't do that again. You'll end up back in that boot."

"I didn't realize the drop was that far."

"Talk to me, Kenni. What's bothering you?" I prod, trying to ignore the effect her closeness has on me. How her scent envelops like a warm hug. How her breath caressing my face makes my dick twitch.

"We need to discuss how we do this moving forward. Telling me not to consider you in my decision-making won't work. It's too late for that. I made up my mind days ago. After last night—"

"You asked for one night."

"I don't know what I was thinking when I wrote the note. At the time, I just wanted to see your human side."

"And that was the only way you thought I could show it?"

She laughs tentatively. "Honestly, I just wanted to hook up. I didn't even know whether you were dating."

"I'm not seeing anyone." She raises an eyebrow as if I could forget the woman on my lap who I spent the night buried in. "You know what I mean."

"Anyway, my point is that after spending all this time with you, I changed my mind. I want more. When you indicated there was a chance for us, when you told me in another lifetime you would have taken me already—I knew one day, we would be together. What we shared last night and this morning was the start."

"Kenni—"

She rubs her hands along my arms. "I love it when you call me that." She smiles. Her face softens when she says, "I don't want this to end."

"My job is to protect you. There can't be an *us* right now. I told you before."

"Too late."

"I need you to focus on healing and meeting your deadline. Give me time to solve who is after you. I need my head in the game, not thinking about how soon I can be buried in you again." I tell her the truth, but how do I make her understand without telling her I've fallen in love?

"Do you really want me to wait?"

My voice is stern when I say. "This is not a game. I would die for you, and I will kill anyone who tries to hurt you."

"I get it."

"Do you really?"

"You said we have two weeks before I'm strong enough. Can anyone find me here?"

"No."

"And you won't leave my side until this is over?"

"If this isn't resolved before you leave here, I remain your chief of security. Like with other clients, my team and I will work in shifts."

"You won't stay with me in the city?"

"No, Kenni. I'll be nearby. I told you, you need to live your life. You have important work to do."

She sighs heavily. Her eyes shift to someplace beyond my shoulder, then back to me. She bites her lip and I wonder what's going through that brilliant mind of hers. "I need something else."

"I don't read minds, Kenni. Talk to me or at least eat." My voice is straightforward. Having our first disagreement with her in my lap should feel odd, but it doesn't.

"Kiss me, Troy."

"We had our night."

She reaches her hands behind her, placing them on top of mine as I hold her hips. "I'll wait."

"Kenni, beautiful, you need to eat." Leaning back, Kennedy stubbornly stares me down. She's feisty and utterly unafraid of me. I laugh internally because I wouldn't want her any other way. "You want me to feed you?" Still no response.

We stare at each other for a few minutes, and then I touch my forehead to hers. I don't know how to do this—but I don't want to lose her. "I broke every rule in the book last night. Touching you. Tasting you. Breathing you. Being inside you. Everything about our connection is something I've never experienced before. Kennedy Green, when you came into my life, you made it better by simply being there. I love you. I can't imagine living another day without you." I take a moment, letting my confession linger between us. "But Kenni, it's hard to focus when you're around. I need to focus because I can't lose you. Ever. Do you understand that?" I finally receive a response when she nods, tears streaming down her cheek. I exhale deeply and continue. "With all my love I'm telling you we need to find a compromise. Let me do what I need to keep you safe. I promise, if you feel as strongly as I do, we'll figure this out. We'll get through this...together."

She wraps her arms around my neck and brushes her lips against mine. I pull her close and kiss her passionately, surrendering to her desires and mine. She breaks the kiss and says, "I love you. I'm scared of what loving you means, but I promise I won't let that interfere with figuring it out."

"We will. I'm not going anywhere." She nods. "Will you eat something now?"

"One more thing."

"Kenni," I warn.

She slides her hands under my shirt and smooths her fingers over my muscles. Her touch is so gentle as she explores my skin. I hold her in place, letting her do whatever she wants. She brushes her lips against my ear. "My man of steel," she whispers. She straightens, seeming calmer after our admissions of love. I reach into the bowl for a strawberry and feed it to her, then pop one into my mouth.

I manage to get her to eat a few more pieces of fruit before she presses her lips to mine. I deepen the kiss, sucking the last of the berry juice from her tongue. Even without the fruit, she tastes sweet. I cup her chin and pull back from the kiss. My girl is strong, smart, sassy, yet there's a vulnerability about her.

"Kenni, honey, talk to me. Tell me what's going on. Tell me what you want."

"Since I met you, I've been trying to get you to show me your human side." She smiles. "Last night, you gave me that and so much more. We can't go backward."

"We won't, but moving forward won't always be like last night."

"And in the meantime, until we return to the city?"

"I told you. You need to heal. You have your work."

She squeezes the muscles on my arms like she's testing them for ripeness. They don't give under her fingers' pressure. She slides her fingers under my shirt and does the same thing with my pecs, sending sparks of electricity through me. "You know me by now. I'll accomplish both." She hugs and kisses me again, taking what she needs from me. "Make love to me, Troy." She whispers against my lips. "I don't want to be here and not be able to have you the way I did last night."

There she is—the woman who tells me her inner thoughts.

"That's what this is about?"

She nods and tugs at the bottom of my shirt. I allow her to pull it over my head. She drops it to the floor, takes off her T-shirt, and tosses it. I palm one of her breasts because I know she loves that—so do I. My body hardens in response. I dip my head and suck her breast briefly—her breath hitches.

"I want to spend the day with you. I can't focus on anything else right now." She grabs my hard length between us, and I groan. "Your body says you want the same."

"I do. But beautiful, you need to eat. You need to hydrate." She undoes my slacks and grabs my length, stroking it between us, and I'm about to explode, undone by the sensation.

"Lift me," she commands. I stand, and she pushes my slacks down; I sit back down and lift her, allowing her to position herself to receive me. As she slides down my shaft, I close my eyes, engulfed in the feeling of her surrounding me.

"My God, woman."

She feels it, too. "Oh, Troy."

She leans back, and I hold her hips as I rock her to a steady, fast rhythm because I won't last long with her on me like this. I lean into her and wrap my mouth around her breast and suck hard.

"Troy," she screams, signaling that she's coming, but I already know. Last night, I memorized every detail of the perfectly constructed path to her pleasure.

"Come with me, beautiful." I pump up into her, and she screams my name as we come together, me pouring my love into her in waves while she rides me. When we're done, I hold her in place—still thick inside her. Juices, evidence of our love, spill between us. Connected in a way that feels right. Perfect. Like home.

CHAPTER 32

Business, Bad Decisions, and Bare Feet

"If you want to fly in the sky, you need to leave the earth. If you want to move forward, you need to let go of the past that drags you down."
– Amit Ray

Kennedy

I'M MISSING SOMETHING. *DAMN it.* I push back from my desk, rubbing my temples. This program has undergone millions of iterations, yet it still won't execute the final task. The answer is here—I know it is—but I can't see it. I need to step back, reassess. *What am I overlooking?*

This is the final cell property. If I can solve this, I can take it to the lab weeks ahead of schedule. Fresh eyes might help. But not just anyone—someone with deep experience in this niche overlap of biophysics and data science. Someone like...

Nate.

I grab my phone and swipe through a string of missed messages. *Damn. Twenty?* Ford must be losing his mind. I can't keep dodging him. But right now, the algorithm comes first. I exhale sharply and tap the screen to call Nate.

He picks up immediately. "Nate here."

"Nate, it's Dr. Green. I hope you're well."

"Dr. Green, it's great to hear from you. What can I do for you?"

"I'm in the final stages of programming but hit a roadblock. The algorithm stalls at a critical point."

"I'm happy to take a look."

"Still interested in joining my team?"

"Absolutely."

"Good. I'll contact headquarters and have them get you onboarded. Expect a formal offer soon—I'm sure you'll be impressed by the package. As a reminder, all offers are contingent upon successfully completing background checks. Once that's set, I have my EA schedule a debrief."

"You just made my day."

"There's more," I add, glancing out the library window, curious about which part of the house Troy is in. "If we crack this and secure product approval, you'll be credited alongside me. Expect to have something in hand by Monday."

"I've studied all your work to date. If you need me to review anything beforehand, let me know."

"Let's get you officially onboarded first. And, Nate—be prepared for some strict security protocol."

Silence stretches across the call before Nate says, "Meaning?"

"Meaning, people who would do just about anything to get their hands on this work, including taking a life."

His voice is steady, but I catch the slight hesitation. "That's why you've been off the lecture circuit."

"Yes, that and my injury. Be cautious."

"I understand. Thanks for the heads-up."

"Have a good weekend, Nate." I hang up, exhaling slowly.

Now, I need to deal with Ford.

I read through the string of messages conveying the same sentiment: "We need to talk as soon as you can." *What is there to talk about?* If he's seeing Lisa, he should just come clean and tell me. If he went to Seattle to be with her, then I want to know. Maybe that's the closure I've been seeking.

Nothing about his abrupt decision to leave me and go to Seattle for a job without discussing it with me first makes any sense—unless he went to be with Lisa. I'm a grown woman; he could have told me.

I flex my ankle, stretching it before I stand, just as Troy taught me. This past week with him has been one of my best yet. Waking up in his strong arms each morning is everything I've ever wanted and more. Loving Troy makes every flaw of Ford's stand out even more.

Taking a deep breath, I swipe my finger across my phone. Ford answers right away. "Kennedy, finally. Where are you?"

"Ford, I'm away working." He doesn't need to know where I am. I couldn't tell him if I wanted to. I don't trust him. "You left me a few messages."

"Are you in the city? Can you meet me so we can talk?"

"This is your chance to talk. What was that between you and Lisa at the coffee shop?"

"It's not what you think."

"Oh, please. You expect me to believe you two are just friends?"

"We aren't dating," he says.

I let out a dry laugh. "Just friends. Friend with benefits, maybe? Whatever you want to call it, Ford, it doesn't matter anymore."

"I wanted to discuss us."

"There is no us, Ford. That ended two years ago, remember? When you decided to break up with me to go to Seattle? It seems Sasha was right. You went there for another woman. You should have just told me."

"Kennedy."

"Don't Kennedy me. Why can't you just admit you were cheating on me? That's what they call it when you're dating one woman and sleeping with another. God, I can't believe I fell for all the travel talk—you saying it was a bad idea to travel together. How many other women are there like Lisa?"

"Come on, Kennedy. Meet me for dinner. Wherever you want to go—you name it."

My fingers tighten around the phone—my pulse hammers in my ears. Ford's voice is too smooth, too familiar, and for a split second, I remember what it was like to believe him. Then I remember the look on Lisa's face at the coffee shop—the way she leaned into him, like they had years of history.

"Are you serious? I'm not interested. As far as I'm concerned, I dodged a bullet when you left. Answer this: were you already with Lisa when I mentioned she was a former student? Or did you seek her out after you left? Never mind. Forget I asked; it's not important."

"Kennedy, we had something real. We can have it again. Just meet me for dinner."

His voice drips with practiced charm, the same voice that once convinced me to ignore my instincts, to wait for him while he "figured things out."

"Been there, done that. I don't want you, Ford. Please stop calling me."

"Why are you with that guy? Troy? That's his name, right?"

I shake my head. "You really don't get it, do you? The difference between you and him? He doesn't lie to me. How about for once in your life Ford just tell the truth."

Silence stretches across the line. "I met her at a conference," Ford says. His voice carries that guilty hesitation I know too well—like he's trying to soften the truth, as if that'll make it any easier to swallow.

"And what? You didn't think to tell her you were dating someone?" My tone is sharp, controlled, but my pulse betrays me, thrumming with the force of unspoken anger.

"It's not like—"

"What's it like, Ford?" I cut him off, my patience evaporating. "Explain it to me. Why did you even come back?"

He exhales, the sound strained. "She's not like you. I made a mistake."

A bitter laugh escapes me. "A mistake?" I repeat, the word foreign on my tongue.

"The other day, I didn't even know she followed me back to San Francisco," he rushes on. "Believe it or not, all she talks about is you. How great—"

"Save it." My stomach turns, fury and exhaustion tangling in my chest. "I don't need affirmation from your side chick. I don't need anything from you."

"I'm just—"

"You're just selfish, Ford. Selfish and controlling," I say, my voice colder now. "You don't get to rewrite history to ease your conscience. You left. You made your choice. And I'm finally making mine."

"Kennedy."

"Goodbye, Ford." And good riddance, I don't say. Instead, I hang up. I can't believe him. What is he thinking, that I would fall back into his arms? This isn't how I envisioned the conversation going, but it's for the best.

I lean back in my chair. A weight I didn't even realize I was still carrying lifts off my chest. The years I spent wondering, second-guessing, blaming myself—it was never about me. It was always about Ford, about his narcissism, his inability to be honest. And now that I see it, I don't just feel relief. I feel free.

My suspicion that he never loved me was correct. I was just one of many—the one he didn't want to let go of.

I turn off my phone and shut my laptop. I don't need to think about Ford ever again. What I need is Troy. I need the steady presence of the man who has never made me question my worth. The man I love.

Heading down the hall, I debate whether to update him on my conversation with Ford. Passing through the living room, I spot him outside, sitting on the outdoor sofa. He's the highlight of my day.

"I don't care what it takes—I want full surveillance. No gaps, no mistakes. If they so much as breathe near her, I want to know before they do." His voice is deep and commanding as he talks to his caller. "I expect the report on their activities over the past five years in my email within the hour," he says before ending the call. He removes his earphones as I approach him.

I block the sun with my body as I stand in front of him. "Hey, handsome," I say, sitting on his lap and draping my legs across the sofa. Leaning in, I touch my cheek to his, inhaling the hint of leathery musk he wears so well.

He snakes an arm around my waist. "Hey, beautiful."

"Was that about me?"

"There's nothing for you to worry about." He brushes my hair away from my face. "How's work going?"

"Just one more code to crack, but I might need help getting across the finish line."

"You have staff at your disposal."

"My thoughts exactly. You did say everything came back all clear with Nate, right?"

"He's only partially cleared. There's still one report pending. Why?"

"I just made him an offer."

He gently cups my cheek, his thumb tracing a smooth path along my skin. "I love that you trust your instincts, but check in with me first next time, okay? At least until we're sure."

"I will," I say, my voice more contemplative than confident.

"In the interim, I'll expedite his investigation." I nod, biting my lip. "Something happened." He senses my mood. "Talk to me."

I run my hand along his arm, reflecting on the strength they provide. Troy is constantly helping me when I can't help myself, caring for me, and ensuring I'm on the right course when I don't even notice I'm off track, like the care regime he implemented. If it weren't for him, I'd still be fumbling around in that boot. Everything about him is so unlike Ford.

"I talked to Ford."

His jaw ticks when I say his name. "Do I need to pay him a visit?"

I bark out a laugh. "No. I set him straight. He won't be calling anymore. I just wanted you to know it's done."

"I don't trust that guy."

When I respond, "For good reason," Troy's eyebrow lifts as if he knows something more. It passes quickly.

"Scoot back, beautiful. Let me check your ankle."

I move from Troy's lap to the cushion until my calves are on his legs. Carefully, he removes my tennis shoe and sock. He smooths his hand over my feet, sliding it up my leg beneath my pants to my knee. I start to say something sassy like, "That's not my ankle," but I don't do anything to distract him from making me feel seen—wanted. Every night since our first night together, I have fallen asleep tucked in his arms, sore, satiated, and spent. When I wake, it's to the sound of his heartbeat, his length between us, and the love in his eyes when he calls my name as his seed runs down my thighs.

He bends my knee and examines my ankle. Applying slight pressure to it, he asks, "Any pain?" I shake my head. "Good. You're walking much better."

"I feel better because of you." I hold his gaze, giving deeper meaning to my words.

"Don't give me that look, Kenni," he warns.

"What?" I ask, pretending to be innocent. He doesn't respond. Instead of putting on my sock and shoe, he takes off the others, then grabs me by the waist and pulls me onto him, knees on either side of him. "Why'd you take my shoes off?"

"You won't need them the rest of this weekend. You'll be too sore to walk."

I lean in and kiss my man. He palms my hips and pulls me closer, and I can feel every inch of his promise growing beneath me.

He breaks the kiss and says, "You good?"

Panting, I reply, "Barefoot. Check."

Chapter 33

A Familiar Voice

"I can do all things through Christ who strengthens me."
– The Bible, Philippians 4:13

Kennedy

"THERE IS NOTHING YOU cannot do." That's the motto my parents instilled in me. That's what I repeat in my head as I take a deep breath. My face is pressed to Troy's chest as his strong arms lock me in place.

"You good?" Troy pulls back, seeking confirmation in my eyes. And I give it because I love him.

Troy is my force, my flame, my friend. Even now, as the bearer of bad news, he's my rock. Nate failed his security clearance. But unlike when others deliver bad news, Troy came with a solution: my best friend.

I sigh. "Yeah. I need to call Sasha."

He grabs my hips and presses me into him. "Everything will be fine. I'll make it up to you."

I laugh tentatively. "You better."

Untangling myself from my man, I head into the library to call Sasha. She picks up right away.

"Hey, girl. When are you heading back here?" Her voice is cheery and just what I need.

"Hey, Sash. Hopefully soon. That's what I'm calling about. I need help with the final leg of this project and you're my last hope."

I give her the low down on what I've done so far. The milestones, the setbacks. Everything.

I pace the length of my office, my phone held out as Sasha's familiar voice fills the space.

"Let me get this straight," she says, her tone sharp with curiosity. "You're asking me to partner with you on decoding the eight sequence?"

I smile despite the tension coiling in my gut. "I need someone I trust, and you're the best geneticist I know."

"Flattery will get you everywhere, Dr. Green," she teases, but I hear excitement creeping into her voice. "Of course, I'm in. I'd be crazy to say no. This could change everything."

Relief washes over me, the first real breath I've taken in what feels like days. "Thank you, Sash. I don't want to go into details over the phone, but let's just say the security stuff is...getting to me."

She makes a noise of understanding. A low hum in the background. "Troy?"

"Yeah. He ran a background check on Nate." I walk across the room and sink into my chair, staring at the model of my digital research on the monitor. "He failed. The company he contracts for? Doesn't exist. And there are gaps in his employment history that make no sense."

Sasha swears under her breath. "So, what's the next move?"

"Troy's handling it," I say trying to push down the unease again. "I'm just focusing on the work. And I need you on this, Sash. I can't afford distractions."

"I'm in." Her voice softens. "You know, Ken, you're never in this alone. Not with me around."

I swallow hard. "I know. Thanks, girl."

There's a pause before I let out a sharp exhale. "Speaking of cutting out distractions, I had it out with Ford."

Sasha huffs. "Finally. What happened?"

"He admitted to cheating."

A sharp inhale. "That bastard."

"Yeah, well, I blocked him. For good this time." I close my eyes, pressing the heel of my hand against my forehead. "It felt...final. And freeing."

"As it should." There's satisfaction in her voice. This has been a long time coming. "He was a weight you didn't need."

"Exactly." I shake my head, needing to move on from the topic. "Anyway, enough about him. Tell me something good."

Sasha chuckles. "Well, I'm seeing more of Doc."

That pulls me upright. "Oh? More how?"

"More as in...the doctor's in the house." She sings the last part, dragging out the house.

My jaw drops. "Sasha Geneviève Duval, are you telling me you actually like this man? Like for real, for real?"

She groans. "Ugh, don't make a thing out of it."

I laugh, a real, honest laugh that lightens my chest and bounces off the walls. "Oh, I'm definitely making a thing out of it. Spill."

We fall into an easy conversation, shifting away from security threats and past mistakes into something lighter—something hopeful. And for the first time in days, I feel like I can breathe again.

CHAPTER 34

The Good and Bad of it All

"In every conceivable manner, the family is a link to our past, bridge to our future."
– Alex Haley

Kennedy

"WE DID IT." I raise my hand to high-five Sasha. Her palm meets mine with a satisfying clap.

"Congratulations, Ken," she says, beaming. Her energy is infectious.

Bringing her on board was the right decision. Within twenty-four hours of starting, she identified the variable that had kept me stuck for weeks. We had been on a video call together, watching in disbelief as the algorithm cleared all eight stages without a hitch. She was so elated. And as for me...I was astonished.

I had achieved the impossible.

Everything is happening faster than I expected. I was still at Troy's house when we finished the algorithm. Turns out the lens of a medical geneticist was precisely what I needed all along. Being in her element, I let Sasha lead the lab testing while I took the time I needed to heal. With her brilliant mind she easily took over while maintaining a scaled back version of her lecture schedule.

Now, after presenting to the board, I'm back in my office waiting. Troy stands guard outside, a silent but constant presence.

"You're sure we'll hear back today?" Sasha asks.

"Yes. Their meetings usually go ninety minutes." I glance at my watch. "Why don't you go grab lunch with Doc. His eyes haven't left you." I tip my head to the glass window looking into the main office area beyond my door. "I'll text you when I get word."

She looks at Dax then back at me. "Alright, girl. But text me the second you know."

As soon as she steps out, Troy enters, closing the door behind him. He doesn't speak. Just stand there, legs slightly parted, hands in his pockets, watching me.

"Before you ask," I say, "I haven't heard back yet."

"You will, soon."

His voice is steady, certain. Like he's been here before. And I suppose he has, with Rose and June. But this is different.

Troy isn't just my protector. He's my everything.

We arrived Wednesday, a day earlier than planned. June pulled strings to get us on the board's calendar today instead of next month. Troy insisted on handling security as he does with any other client. Keeping a professional distance. Following protocol.

But last night, when we arrived at my apartment, I put my foot down.

Troy had just signaled Doc that he was heading out when I walked over and wrapped my arms around him. "You're not leaving me at midnight to sit in some random place to rest."

He cupped my face, his gaze steady. "We talked about this."

"Tell me this...how much sleep will you get knowing I'm here alone, even with your most trusted team member nearby? Be honest."

A muscle ticked in his jaw. "None."

"Neither will I."

That's all it took.

Doc took over his shift, and Troy took me to bed.

This morning, when we woke up, we started embracing what has become our new normal.

If we were at home, I would walk over to him now, wrap my arm around him, then press my lips against his jaw. But here, I promised not to distract him from his job.

Instead, I ask, "Have there been any more attempts to access my work?"

His expression tightens. "None. There are several individuals we're monitoring."

I exhale slowly. "They're being low key."

He huffs a quiet laugh. "You sound like me."

"What are they waiting for?"

He hesitates. "You don't want to hear this."

"Troy," I press, stepping closer. "What are they waiting for?"

His gaze sharpens. "Something indicating you were successful."

My stomach drops.

Flipping my wrist, I check my watch. The board has already made their decision. My hands feel cold, despite the warmth in the room. I clasp my bracelet—a reminder of the good and bad of it all. If they approve my work, word will eventually reach the wrong people.

Troy reads the concern in my eyes.

He steps closer, voice firm. "Kenni, no one will get you. Not through me."

I nod, swallowing past the lump in my throat. Allowing his words to seep through the fear and comfort me. Then my phone buzzes.

June.

June: Congratulations.

My fingers tremble as I type a response.

Me: Thank you.

I lift my eyes to Troy, my heart pounding. "I did it. Troy, I did it."

He doesn't hesitate. He opens his arms.

I rush into them.

"You did it, beautiful." His voice is low, reverent. Leaning back, I see it—pride in his eyes, raw and real. He brushes his thumb across my cheek. "Let your team know. I'll be outside until you're ready to leave."

A soft ache blooms in my chest as he pulls away. He cups my cheek, just for a second, then he's gone.

The news should be exhilarating. This is what I've spent my career working toward. But it's bittersweet. Because I know that somewhere out there, someone is still trying to steal what I've created.

But I have Troy.

And no one is getting past him.

***

Standing by the wall windows overlooking the city sprawling beneath me in Troy's penthouse, I reflect on the announcement. *I did it.* Despite injuries, exes, and people trying to steal my work, I did it. With the board's stamp of approval, I can move on to developing life-saving solutions.

I sip my cocktail. The champagne bubbles frolic on my tongue with undertones of Ube—yet another one of my creations. *Europa* drifts through the sound system, its notes curling around me like smoke. I can't help but think back to Professor Rutledge's class. I used to sit in those stiff lecture hall chairs, staring out the window, dreaming of this day. Dreaming of what it would feel like to unlock the mysteries—not just of life, but of consciousness. To solve the unsolvable.

But I didn't do it alone. Troy's quiet strength, his unwavering belief in me, pushed back the shadows of self-doubt I never wanted to admit existed. His presence gave me room to breathe, to let my mind stretch and my ideas take shape. Without him, I might've still been chasing answers in circles, never daring to trust myself.

If it weren't for the weight of my own skin, the pull of gravity anchoring me here, I swear—I'd be floating. Staring out the window, I catch Troy's reflection coming into view—his strong arms snake around my waist. The warmth of his body presses to my back, anchoring me.

He rests his chin on my shoulder and whispers, "A kiss for your thoughts."

I turn in his arms. "Just thinking about us—how much I love you."

"I love you, too. You've had a long day. You should rest."

"Have a drink with me." His eyebrows raise. "I'll make a special one for you," I add.

"Finish that." He tips his head to my glass. I drink the last sip. As quick as the glass leaves my lips, he cups my chin in his hand and kisses me, sucking my tongue and the last of champagne from my mouth. It's striking and sensual and makes my sex clench.

Somewhere between the moon and the stars, I find myself in a Troy haze. My hips in his palms, my legs wrapped around his waist. My lips never leave his as he walks past the credenza heading down the hall. The buzz of my phone cuts through the fog. *Shit.*

I break the kiss. My parents' ringtone. "I need to get that."

Troy takes me back into the living room and sets me on my feet. "I'll be in my office." He kisses my forehead before giving me privacy.

"Mom," I answer. I can hear my father in the background asking whether I'm there. "You made it back."

"Kenni, we've missed you."

"I missed you too, Mom. We have lots to catch up on."

"You're all over the news, lady." My dad's voice comes onto the line.

"Always someone looking for a story." I hesitate a moment before saying, "My project got approved."

"Ah, honey, that's wonderful news. We're so proud of you," my mom gushes, her voice warm and effervescent, like sunlight filtering through an open window. I can almost see her smiling on the other end. Probably clutching Dad's hand.

"I trust you're celebrating," my dad chimes in, his voice steady. "Things like this don't happen every day." I let his words sink in.

It's more than just words—it always has been. These phrases aren't just familiar; they're sacred. They've been woven into every milestone of my life, from the glittering gold stars of elementary school to the framed degrees hanging on my walls. Each one was met with the same unwavering pride, no matter how big or small. Because to my dad, every achievement wasn't just about what I did—it was a celebration of *who* I am. And in moments like this, hearing their voices wrapped around me like a thick sweater in winter, I remember exactly why that's always mattered.

"Mom, Dad...there's more."

There's a soft rustle on the other end, like they're both leaning in closer to the phone.

"We're listening, baby," my mom says, her voice gentle but tight with worry.

Taking a steadying breath, I go for it. I explain what it's been like to be an executive with Ross Enterprises, detailing the security concerns surrounding my research and the dangerous people trying to get their hands on it. There's a long pause when I finish.

"Ross Enterprises, huh?" Dad finally says, his voice low. "I've always heard good things about them. Serious people."

"They are."

But I can tell his mind is already racing ahead, thinking about the threat.

"You said they haven't caught this ring yet." His tone sharpens, the protective edge I know too well creeping in. "What's the plan?"

"Troy and his team are handling it. I'm under his protection twenty-four seven."

That earns me a sharp inhale from both of them.

"That doesn't sound normal," Dad says, his voice stiffer now.

"It's not." I swallow hard, dreading having this discussion over the phone. But it has to happen. I can't put it off. "It's more than that—"

"Are you trying to say...?" Mom's voice trails off, hesitant, but I know where she's headed.

I cut in before she can finish. "Yes, Mom. Somewhere along the way...we fell in love."

Silence screams over the phone. Then Dad clears his throat, the sound rough in my ear.

"Kenni," he starts, his voice gruffer now. "I think I need to hire more people to keep an eye on things—"

"Dad." I sigh, trying to keep my voice calm. "Troy *is* the best. I'm safe with him."

"She's right, honey," Mom jumps in, her tone softening. "He protected Rick and their daughter, remember? That whole thing in Ireland?"

Dad grumbles something under his breath, but I catch the shift. He's still worried, but he's listening.

"Dad, he would die for me." The words slip out before I can stop them, heavy and raw. "But it's not going to come to that. He's got this under control."

Another beat of silence. This conversation is worse than telling them about my first boyfriend. I cringe at the thought. Finally, Dad sighs, the fight leaving his voice just a little.

"Kenni, baby...I trust you know what you're doing. But your mom and I—." His voice cracks slightly. "We need you to keep us in the loop. Don't think for a second I'm not happy you found someone who loves you. But your safety comes first. Always."

"I know, Dad." My throat is dry, but I push through, knowing my parents love me. "I promise."

"It'll be okay," he says quietly, like he's trying to convince himself as much as me.

"And honey," Mom adds, "we'd love to meet Troy soon. When things settle down."

I smile, even though they can't see it. "I'll arrange it."

Chapter 35

Free-Fall

"Each person deserves a day away in which no problems are confronted, no solutions searched for. Each of us needs to withdraw from the cares which will not withdraw from us."
– Maya Angelou

Troy

A FAINT GLOW FROM my phone vibrating on the nightstand cuts through the darkness. I shift enough to check the screen, careful not to wake Kennedy. She's still asleep beside me, her breathing slow and steady. Six months ago, I never could have imagined she'd be here, in my bed, in my life. And yet she is.

I smile—something I've been doing more since she came into my life.

I grab my phone. *Marcus.*

Slipping out of bed, I throw on a robe and then move down the hall to my office, shutting the door before answering.

"What's up? Don't you have surgery?"

"Naw, man. It's Saturday. I have a great team on staff today." His voice is relaxed, but I know Marcus. He always calls for a reason. "How's our girl?"

Our girl. I should be used to him saying it by now, but the words still land differently. Kennedy *is* ours—to protect. To care for. To love.

"She's good. Walking great." I pause. "Is that why you called?"

"Partly. I wanted to talk about the party."

I exhale. Our birthdays have always been a big deal—born a year and two days apart, we've celebrated together every year. The world sees us as twins. It's a tradition that keeps us close despite our demanding lives. This year, Kennedy is part of it.

"I know you're worried about security," Marcus continues. "We can do a smaller event at the mountain house."

"That'll limit the guest list significantly. I don't want to spoil it for you."

"What do you suggest?"

"The Blumberg building," I say without hesitation. "Josh keeps his place locked down like Fort Knox. I set up a facial recognition system for him a few years ago. It'll meet my security standards."

When Josh first started dating his now-wife, she had a stalker. He had me install a state-of-the-art security system in his office building, which was close to hers. The level of access he has—government-level clearances—is unheard of. Anyone stepping within a mile radius is logged and flagged.

Marcus whistles low. "Sounds solid. Set it up."

"Done. Anything else?"

He pauses a second, and I know what's coming before he says it. "When's the wedding? You know Mom and Dad want grandkids."

My phone buzzes—another incoming call. Saved by the bell.

"Gotta go," I say, cutting the call.

I glance at the screen. *Anita.*

I swipe to answer. "Tell me you have news."

"I do, but you're not gonna like it."

I sit up, my jaw tightening. "Talk."

"I've been monitoring that missing employee phone. Turns out, it wasn't lost—it was stolen."

My pulse ticks up. "How do you know?"

"I traced a digital footprint. The data was accessed remotely." She pauses. "And the computer that did it—it's connected to one of the IP addresses registered to Lisa."

A slow burn ignites in my chest. *We got her.*

"What she was looking for?"

"Confirmation that Kennedy's work is complete."

Damn it.

"She pulled the internal memo about Project Grace," she pauses. "The one sent to key employees."

So now the word is officially out that Kennedy's breakthrough is done. That means the people after her will escalate their activities. I pinch my chin, combing my fingers through my beard, trying to get my thoughts in order.

"Lisa is the key," I say, my voice hardening. "I want eyes on her at all times. And Anita, I want the name of every person connected to Lisa through that IP."

"Understood."

I hesitate then add, "What about Ford?"

"He's not connected to Lisa's activities. From everything I can tell, he's in the dark."

I pinch the bridge of my nose. Lisa got close to him for one reason—to stay close to Kennedy. But she didn't anticipate Kennedy would cut Ford out completely. Now she's operating blind.

"Keep me posted," I say, then end the call.

I exhale slowly, my mind already calculating the next move.

Kennedy is still asleep down the hall. For now, she's safe. But if Lisa's digging, that means someone else is about to make a move.

And I'll be ready.

Following my calls, I return to the bedroom, slip off my robe, and slide beside Kennedy. Propping my head on one hand, I use the other to pull Kennedy closer to me. The warmth of her skin against mine, the scent of her, everything about her activates my body.

"Hey," she says, her voice just above a whisper.

Cupping her face, I brush my thumb across her cheek. "Morning, beautiful."

Her eyes blink as she tries to adjust. "You're up early. Did you work out?"

"No. You were sleeping."

Playfully, she pats my bicep. "In the gym," she corrects me.

"I had a few calls to take. Nothing for you to worry about."

Kennedy searches my eyes, seeking the truth buried beneath the surface—the weight of my choices, the silent battles I fight to keep her safe. I don't let her see it. I lock it away, leaving only one thing visible. Love. Because, in the end, that's what holds us together. That's what keeps us alive.

She reaches between us and grabs my already hardened length, stroking it. Telling with her touch what she wants. "I love you, Troy."

I growl in her ear, feeling the effects of her delicate fingers, wanting to be buried deep within her. Dipping my head, I kiss her, our tongues mingling, hands roaming until I'm ready to explode. Flipping her on her back, I hover over her—one arm on either side of her head, her legs spread...wanting...waiting. She guides my length to her entrance, circling it with her hand situated between us—a technique she uses until she fully adjusts to my size.

I slow my pace. "Does it hurt?"

"No. It's so...good."

"That's it, beautiful." I moan in her ear as she pulls her hand away. *I'm in.* Her body moves in time with mine. Each thrust bringing us closer to becoming one.

"Oh, God, Troy."

She screams my name, a feral call to her forever mate as we free-fall together.

***

I'm fighting a constant battle within—not about being in love with Kennedy, but how to love her. The way I feel when we're alone is dangerous in itself. When we step outside, I'm her bodyguard. My focus sharpens like a blade—protect her at all costs. I can't let my mind wander to the warmth of her touch or the scent that clings to my clothes after she leaves. No. I'm thinking about when I pull my weapon—I can't miss.

Even though we discussed our situation before leaving the mountain, it still comes up occasionally. Her instinct to reach for me and hold my hand when we step outside is undeniable. On the surface, that seems simple—in reality, it can mean the difference between life and death. My compromise—impromptu getaways from the city where I openly love her and give her what she needs...what *I* need.

Today, we're in Mendocino at the Botanical Gardens. Love blooms everywhere—stunning beaches, vibrant flowers, and her smile lights the path ahead. Kennedy squealed, taking in the view of the azure waters of the coastline as we flew in. And on the short drive to the gardens, she held my hand the entire way, filling the car with chatter about the variety of plants we'd see.

This is what she meant when she said she was missing out on life—the simple things. In hindsight, even when I was with Justine, I didn't have this—the happiness filling me when Kennedy hugs me, the excitement in her eyes as we explore the flower-filled landscape—the passion behind each kiss.

"You good?" I gently shake her hand as we enter the gardens.

She nods. "Perfect." She lets go my hand and takes out her phone.

Walking along the flower-filled paths, the air is thick with the mingling scents of salt and lavender. The crunch of gravel beneath our shoes is the only sound besides her occasional gasp of delight when she spots a new bloom. Every few feet, Kennedy dips her head, inhaling deeply, her nose brushing petals before she snaps another picture. Observing her taking breaks from her research in the mountain house garden, I knew she'd enjoy this.

As we continue, Kennedy spots the path to the Mediterranean Garden. Her fingers find mine as we walk the gravel path. My instinct is to pull away, scan the crowd, check every shadow for a threat. But here, it's just us and the wild stretch of blooms. So, I let her hold on, even if a part of me stays on edge, waiting for the other shoe to drop.

"These are stunning." She points to the vibrant fuchsia-colored petals with tiny cream-colored cone-heads in the center resembling artichokes.

"Leucadendron," I say.

She turns to me in wide-eyed surprise. "Most people don't know their African flowers. I suppose I shouldn't be surprised after seeing your mountain garden."

"Some grow naturally on the mountain, others I chose specifically for their ability to thrive in those conditions." She snaps another picture. "You like this one? We can get some to grow."

"These are beautiful," she says, brushing her fingers over the petals. She glances up, that mischievous spark in her eye. "But if I'm picking, I'd go with the King Protea."

I raise a brow. "Yeah."

She grins, stepping closer. "Big. Strong. Hardy. And smells amazing." She tips her head, her breath warm against my neck. "Kind of like you."

Pulling her into me, I dip my head and kiss her. Only this woman could compare me to a South African flower to get me going.

Breaking the kiss, I lick her lips. "What am I going to do with you, beautiful?"

"Buy me some flowers." She laughs, and it's lovely and everything I need at this moment.

While exploring the gardens, I decide it's time for a break. Kennedy wants to keep going, but I'm mindful of her foot, so she gives in to having a garden picnic.

Sitting cross-legged on a blanket in the grass, Kennedy pops a grape in her mouth. "There were a few plants I saw that might make good additions to those at the mountain house," she says in between chewing.

"Beautiful, let me cut those grapes if you insist on eating and talking."

She rolls her eyes, and I already know what she's thinking—that I'm over the top when it comes to her safety. There's no such thing as too much when it involves her.

"The flowers…," she prompts.

"We can plant whatever you want." I take a bite of the turkey wrap I made for our picnic. Kennedy said I was spoiling her when she learned about today's trip. When she told me about all the things she wanted to do that night at the mountain house, I made up my mind then that I'd give it all to her. There's so much more I want to give her, but we have to get past this ordeal.

"Something to pair with the fuchsia, you know—"

My phone buzzes, and so does Kennedy's.

Niall.

Good news. Rose and Niall just welcomed their first child.

"Yeah," she exclaims. I nod, but it's not enough for her. She gets up and sits on my lap. "If you don't give me that smile—" She doesn't get to finish her statement because I cover her mouth with mine.

I break the kiss and say, "Let's send our congratulations."

She smooths her hands down my arms as I type a message.

"Do you want kids, Troy?"

I don't have to think about my response. "With you." I pause as I brush my thumb across her cheek. "But you're gonna have to get off my lap, beautiful—now is not the time to make them." I lift her and set her beside me. My girl has me so hard.

Her laugh warms me. "You really do have it bad for me," she teases.

"I do." I pause a beat. "Let's order King Protea."

She smiles, lighting up my soul. Everything about my woman draws me to her. Therein lies the problem. There are dangerous people after her. They want her mind. Her work. Her life. I need to stay focused. If I'm not careful, I'll lose more than I bargained for.

CHAPTER 36

A Thousand Pair of Jeans

"It is within your power to see that all you have experienced, trials, errors, faults, deceptions, passions, your love and your hope, shall be merged wholly in your aim."
– Friedrich Nietzsche

Kennedy

STARING AT MYSELF IN the full-length mirror, I reflect on how ridiculous I'm being. I can solve the mystery of life but not decide which of my twenty-something pair of jeans to wear. Smoothing my hands down my clothes, I turn, chin over my shoulder, to get a rear view.

I jump, surprised to find Troy leaning against the dresser, legs crossed, eyeing me. He straightens, walks over, hugs me, and says, "I didn't mean to scare you. You look great in those. We should get going."

"It only took me a thousand pairs," I say, pointing to the pile on the chair. "Why can't I wear heels? All those were meant to be worn with heels."

"Give it some time. Now we need to leave. Doc just picked up Sasha. They're headed to the restaurant."

Sasha and Dax hit it off. Unfortunately, their schedules don't sync as well as they do. Today is a rare day when we all get time together. Sasha is on the conference circuit, here only for one day and gone again on Friday. We figured we'd double date since it's my regular restaurant day.

"Since Dax is with Sasha, who's in the lead car?"

"Lucien."

I untangle myself from Troy and slip into a pair of flats. "None of this makes sense to me. I received a clean bill of health, there haven't been any further hacking attempts, yet my security is doubled, and every time we step outside, you transform into something I don't recognize."

The words sound bitter coming from my mouth. He has a job to do. This is what I signed up for the moment I locked eyes with the man standing in Rose's office over six months ago. But no one was after me then.

"It's for your safety."

"Troy Armstrong, what are you not telling me?"

He takes a step, closing the distance between us. He grabs me by the waist, picks me up, and sits me on the dresser. His jaw is clenched, and I brace myself.

"Lisa is part of the group trying to access your work." The words hit me like a physical blow. My breath stutters. My hands shoot to my mouth, as if I can shove the truth back inside. "We tracked the people she's working for."

Lowering my hands, I ask, "Why don't you get them?"

"We can't do anything until she makes another move to get your work."

"Oh, my god. Is Ford in on this?"

"He has no idea."

My mind races through all my interactions with Lisa. She's been in my line of sight for years. "All this time, it was her. That means she has something to do with Dr. Rutledge's disappearance. She would have been so young—"

"A small fish in a big pond. They've been training her for this."

"Why didn't you tell me? How long have you known?"

There's a flicker of hesitation in his eyes. "The day you confronted him," he says.

"The call I overheard."

"That's right."

I want to throw up. I want to scream. I want to pound my fist in frustration. Troy senses my angst and cups my cheek, his thumb tracing slow circles against my skin.

"Take a deep breath," he says, his voice lowering, coaxing. I inhale, but my chest is too tight. "Again," he urges, his forehead nearly touching mine.

"Why?"

"What would you have done if I told you?"

I think for a moment, running all the scenarios in my head. Each one leads back to him. The things he's been telling me all along—let him do his job. "Nothing," I reply, my voice heavy with resignation.

He smooths my curls over my shoulders and asks, "You want me to call and cancel?"

And let fear take hold of me more than it already has? To let Lisa and her cronies win? "No. Let's go."

Troy helps me to my feet, assists me with my coat, and we head out.

Chapter 37

Too Late

"Calmness is the cradle of power."
– Josiah Gilbert Holland

Troy

THEY CALL ME THE Man of Steel. Unbreakable. Untouchable.

Protecting Kennedy should be straightforward. Guard her. Keep her alive. Stop the people hunting her and her groundbreaking research. But nothing about my woman is simple. She's brilliant, headstrong, and impossible to ignore. Right now, she's here, holding my hand as we head to dinner. And all I can think is—I hope I don't have to kill anyone today.

As I step out of the vehicle, I check my surroundings. The four cars lining the block in front of the restaurant belong to us, signaling that Doc is already here. I help Kennedy out of the car, and instinctively, she slides her hands around my waist inside my jacket.

"Baby, we have to go in," I tell her, lowering her hands. She nods and heads toward the door. Lucien takes his position close behind.

My earpiece buzzes and Anita's voice comes across. "Ford is on the move. He's close."

He doesn't live far from the restaurant. "ETA," I call out.

As she says, "Seconds," I hear his voice and catch a glimpse of him.

"Kennedy," he calls.

She stops and turns to me.

"Keep moving," I tell her.

"Kennedy," he insists.

Before he can get near, a team member stops him three stores down the block.

"Get him out of here," I command.

"No. Let me talk to him."

I hold Kennedy's arm, leading her to the restaurant door. When we reach it, she turns to me again.

"You said he wasn't involved. Let me talk to him."

"Search him," I call out to my team.

I don't trust Ford. Not because he's dangerous, but because he's a distraction. A loose end. And loose ends have a way of unraveling everything.

Doc steps out of the restaurant and stands behind Kennedy, having listened to the whole incident through his earphones.

A team member hands Ford over to Lucien, who escorts him toward us.

"Kennedy, why haven't you answered my texts?"

My eyes track Ford's movements, his stance, his breathing. No sudden twitches. No sign of a weapon. But he's agitated, his pulse visible at his throat. My team stays locked in. If he so much as blinks wrong, we'll put him down.

"I blocked you. What do you want? How did you know I'd be here?"

"You always eat here on Thursdays."

"You have to be insane to roll up on me like this." Her eyes dart to various team members. "What is so important?"

Ford's voice cracks. "Kennedy, I didn't know." He hesitates before continuing. "I heard Lisa talking to someone about you. I didn't know she'd been stalking you," he confesses. However, it's apparent he doesn't understand the extent of Lisa's involvement.

Kennedy doesn't even flinch. "That's the problem, Ford. You never knew. You never *saw* me. And now? It's too damn late," she tells him, then touches my arm. "Let's go." She turns and opens the restaurant door. I make sure she's in before turning back to Ford.

"Kennedy. I'm sorry, Kennedy."

His voice is drowned out by the roar of a car engine, the screech of tires, and a loud bang. Reflexively, I pull my gun and aim it at the car speeding down the sidewalk toward me. A shot shatters the windshield. Glass explodes outward, glittering under the streetlights. The driver jerks the wheel—too late. The car slams into parked vehicles with a sickening crunch of metal.

"Incoming," Lucien calls out as another car hops the curb from the direction where Ford entered. The car speeds toward us. A gun points out the window in our direction. Lucien, Doc, and I fire into the vehicle, obliterating the front window as it continues past us down the sidewalk. We continue to fire into the car as it passes until it collides with the other vehicle.

Sirens blare in the background, and within seconds, the street is blocked by police.

"Secure the area," I call out. My team heads toward the vehicles, and I go inside to get my woman.

It takes a millisecond to take a life. A single pull of the trigger. But what matters is who you're willing to kill for—and who you're willing to live for. And Kennedy? I'd burn the world down for her.

CHAPTER 38

It's Not Over 'Til It's Over

"No Plan survives first contact with the enemy."
– Helmuth von Moltke

Troy

THIS WOMAN HAS BECOME my everything, I say to myself, glancing at my mobile screen displaying a video of Kennedy and Sasha huddled in the office next door talking. I run my fingers through my beard, the tension in my shoulders refusing to ease as I sit at the head of the long conference table in our secure briefing room. Dax, Lucien, and the rest of my team are scattered around, some leaning against the walls, others sitting, all of them sharp-eyed and locked in. The air is thick with the weight of what went down.

Dax crosses his arms, his jaw tight. "So Lisa was using Ford to track Kennedy."

Lucien exhales sharply. "She knew exactly where Kennedy would be every Thursday because of him."

I nod, one hand balled in a fist, the other adjusting the screen. "Ford didn't know what she was up to—at least not at first. He came last night to warn Kennedy after overhearing Lisa talking about stealing her work. Claimed he didn't sign up for that shit."

"Yeah? And where's Ford now?" one of my new team members asks, his voice measured but edged.

There's a beat of silence before I answer, my voice flat. "He didn't make it."

No one says anything for a second, but the shift in the room is undeniable. They all get it. Ford was collateral damage. Unintentional or not, he got caught in the crossfire.

Lucien clears his throat. "And Lisa? She sent those men?"

"Yeah," I confirm. "Her uncle is the head of Gene Tech. He's been trying to get his hands on Kennedy's work, planning to sell it on the black market."

"To who? Our government?" someone asks.

"Anyone that will bite," I say, my jaw tightening. "In the wrong hands, Kennedy's research could be worth billions."

"If not more," Lucien mutters. "World domination type shit."

I don't argue. He's not wrong. Kennedy's work isn't just groundbreaking—it's dangerous in the wrong hands. If Gene Tech succeeds in weaponizing it, the consequences could be catastrophic.

Dax leans forward. "And then there's Nate."

I exhale through my nose, shaking my head. He seemed so benign at first. That's how it always is. I'm glad I kept tabs on him. "Yeah. The kid who couldn't get a job in Kennedy's lab because he failed the background check. Turns out the company he recently contracted with was a front—a shell company tied right back to Gene Tech." I tip my head toward Anita. "Great work on that." She nods. She's always humble about her work.

Lucien curses under his breath. "Lisa recruited him."

"Promised him millions," Dax says. "Not hard to figure out why he went for it. There's not much money at his level in academia. Like Lisa, Nate was also a follower of Dr. Rutledge. Kennedy's rising star under his tutelage fueled their scheme. With a talent for biophysics, Lisa's uncle used her to get what he wanted...power to create artificial life."

"But she didn't have Kennedy's talent," I say.

"Neither did Nate," Dax adds.

"So they had to steal it," I say, lifting my phone. "That stolen employee phone was our break."

"How'd we trace it?" someone asks.

"We traced the phone download and transfer IP back to Lisa," Anita says. "Calls between her and Nate confirmed it."

The room falls silent as everyone lets the information sink in. This wasn't just a random attack. It was a long game—carefully calculated. And Lisa? She wasn't just some disgruntled former student. She was in deep, moving pieces on the board while we were still catching up.

I rake a hand down my face. "We shut down last night's attempt. But it won't be the last. We need to go straight to the top at Gene Tech. They want Kennedy's work, and they're not going to stop."

Dax nods. "Then neither do we."

The resolve in the room is solid. This isn't over. Not by a long shot. And as long as Kennedy is in the crosshairs, I'll be right there, making sure no one gets to her. No matter what it takes.

Chapter 39

Goodbyes

"You cannot protect yourself from sadness
without protecting yourself from happiness."
– Jonathan Safran Foer

Kennedy

I'VE SPENT MY LIFE searching for answers—in data, in experiments, in the safety of logic. It's easier that way. Equations don't leave. Hypotheses don't break your heart. But Troy...

He's not an equation I can solve or a variable I can control. He's steady, solid, like he was made to hold me together when everything else falls apart. And that terrifies me. Because I know what it feels like when someone chooses something else—someone else—over you. Ford did. And what's stopping Troy from doing the same? His job, his life...I've seen how easily people walk away when their priorities shift.

Today has me second-guessing everything. Maybe I'm just in my feelings. But when Troy looks at me, it feels different. Like maybe, just maybe, I'm worth staying for. And that's the scariest discovery of all—because if I let myself believe it, and I'm wrong...I don't know if I can survive losing him, too.

Standing in the closet, wrapped in the strength of his arms, breathing him in—I'm exactly where I want to be. Turning in his embrace, I gaze at his reflection in the mirror. His expression is full of love layered with solemnity as he stands in his black suit and tie, watching me. I love this man more than I ever thought possible. And when he says he loves me, I believe him—not just because of his words, but because every action, every protective glance, every quiet sacrifice whispers it louder than any declaration could. He's here, choosing me above all else. Standing by my side during the hardest time in my life. Taking a deep breath, I let that knowledge wrap around my heart like armor, driving out the lingering shadows of doubt. Troy isn't Ford. He won't leave when things get hard. He's shown me that love isn't just spoken—it's proven. And with him, I finally feel safe enough to believe it.

"Can you unzip me?"

He pushes my hair over my shoulders, dips his head, and kisses my neck. His warm fingers brush my cool skin as he slowly glides the zipper down my back.

"You okay?" he whispers.

My black sheath dress slides down my body, pooling around my black stilettos. Wearing only my black silk underwear, I turn around in his arms. "Yeah. I still can't believe he's gone."

I search for grief, but there's nothing. Just a dull acceptance that Ford was never truly mine to mourn. The lies and deceit have me numb.

When the car crashed onto the sidewalk and Troy shut the door, that was the last time I saw Ford. With his gun drawn, Troy's prominent figure shielded my view of the chaos outside. Sasha rushed over to me and we huddled to the side, away from the action.

When Troy walked back into the restaurant, he gently turned me around and examined me, then cupped my cheek, searching my face to make sure I was okay. Then we grabbed Sasha and exited through the rear. I didn't realize that Ford was caught up in the commotion. Days later, I learned that when he ran to escape the first car, he was struck by the second.

Ford's voice echoes in my mind. "Kennedy." An unsuspecting farewell.

"You want to talk about it?"

I shake my head. "I need a drink."

Troy loosens his tie. I reach up and undo the buttons on his shirt. He gently grabs my wrist and kisses my palm. "I got this." I nod and slip out of my underwear into an oversized T-shirt while Troy changes into his sweatpants.

Together, we head to the kitchen. I pour myself a shot of tequila while Troy opts for a glass of water. We bring our drinks with us into the living room, which overlooks San Francisco. Days after returning from the mountain house and realizing someone had accessed my apartment, I moved out and in with Troy. He sits on the couch, and I sit on his lap, facing him.

I throw back the shot. The burn is immediate, sharp. Necessary. Troy sips his water, steady as ever. Observing me. Watching over me. I set my glass on the table and do the same with his. "When those people came rushing down the sidewalk, what were you thinking?"

His jaw tightens, recalling the day. "One target. One shot. Keep her safe."

"You and your team walked away unscathed. Why didn't Ford?"

"I don't have an answer for that, beautiful. Maybe Ford didn't understand the situation."

I trace an invisible line down his cheek, following the sharp cut of his jaw. "Sometimes, when we're out, you get lost in a thought, a feeling, something—I'm not sure what." I vacillate, unsure whether to ask. "You saw something he didn't. What?"

"Baby, what are you asking me?"

"Why didn't Ford move?"

He hesitates as if he doesn't want to say whatever it is. He grips my hips tightly, taking a deep breath before saying, "The distant look you see is focus. In those chaotic moments, I see everything you do, but my brain processes each second with extreme clarity—like a movie reel in slow motion, but it's not."

"That's why your aim is so precise."

"Yes."

"That's why you don't want me touching you in public."

His intense gaze compels me to understand the unspoken. *He doesn't want to say it.* I touch him, giving him permission. "I can't focus when you're near. The moments you describe when I seem detached are when I'm suppressing my feelings, focusing on my surroundings."

"Keeping me safe."

"Always."

"Lucien, Dax—they have it, too."

"They developed it. Same as Mack and the rest of the crew. Kenni, if you're worried about additional attempts—don't. No one can get to you...not through me. You witnessed that first hand. We've identified most of the players. We'll have them all soon."

"And Dr. Rutledge? Any news on what happened to him?"

"Nothing."

Wrapping my arms around his neck, I lay my head on his shoulder. He told me he'd protect me—he did. He said he'd find the culprits—he found them. Now it's time for him to take them down. I know he will. I would have never guessed the big conglomerate Lisa worked for in Seattle was behind this. She wasn't just on their payroll; she was part of it. Her uncle was chairman of the board.

I sigh heavily. Ford is gone. And maybe, in some ways, he was never really here. So I won't cry. I'll just say goodbye.

CHAPTER 40

Breathe Again

"Breathe. Let go. And remind yourself that this very moment is the only one you know you have for sure."
– Oprah Winfrey

Troy

HEADING DOWN THE HALL, I think about how different my life is with Kennedy. She fits so seamlessly into my world. With the heightened security she's been working from home more often—this time it's been her choice. But that's all about to change.

I find Kennedy in the study, hunched over her laptop, fingers gripping her pen so tightly I half expect it to snap. The frustration rolling off her is thick, almost palpable. Sasha is across from her, scrolling through data, lips pressed into a tight line.

I lean against the doorframe, arms crossed. "You planning to kill that pen, Green?"

Kennedy exhales, rubbing her forehead before glancing at me. "I might. The variables aren't lining up, and I'm starting to think it's not just the data—it's me."

Sasha gives me a quick look, then stands. "I'll grab some tea." It's her way of giving us space.

I step forward, waiting until the door clicks shut behind Sasha before pulling out the chair next to Kennedy and sitting down. "We got him."

Kennedy stills. Her fingers loosen around the pen, but she doesn't say anything. Her breathing changes, though. Just slightly. "Lisa?"

"Flipped. Gave up her uncle, Craig, but we didn't need her confession. He screwed himself the second he heard his little kidnapping plan failed."

She finally looks at me, searching my face. "How?"

I smirk. "Like an idiot, he moved money around—tried to cover his tracks. Big transactions flagged all over the place. People he paid off. We followed the trail, and let's just say, he won't be a problem anymore."

I don't go into the depth of accounting forensics or the list of players in and out of the country involved, because it runs deep and wide.

Kennedy exhales slowly. "It's really over?"

Yeah, baby. It's over."

She closes her eyes for a moment before nodding. "Good."

I reach for her hand, running my thumb over her knuckles. "I know it doesn't feel like it yet. You've been on edge for weeks, looking over your shoulder. But you can breathe now."

She shakes her head, letting out a short laugh. "I don't remember how to."

I squeeze her hand. "Guess I have to remind you."

She gives me a look—part exasperation, part something softer. "You always do."

I tug her forward, pressing my forehead to hers. "Damn right."

CHAPTER 41

Girl in the Red Dress

"Your task is not to seek love, but merely to seek and find all the barriers within yourself that you have built against it."
– Rumi

Troy

THIS YEAR, CELEBRATING MY birthday has a whole new meaning. I'm not just celebrating life. I'm celebrating love. I found my other half and the doctor who was searching for the meaning of life gave me life. *Kennedy Green.*

The setting is perfect: a three-hundred-sixty-degree view of San Francisco. Our closest friends and family are scattered around the room, some eating and others dancing. Everyone is having a good time. "Let's Groove Tonight" blares from the sound system. Scanning the room, it's easy to spot her. Kennedy is stunning, dancing with Sasha in the center of the dance floor, wearing her short red strapless dress. That outfit made us late. The moment she stepped out of the closet, flaunting it along with her spiked red heels, I went hard. I took her right there against the bedroom wall—her feet never left the floor. The only thing saving her now is that thirty minutes after our arrival, she changed out of heels into her red jeweled flats. Still, watching her swing her hips.... *Damn.* I need to go get my woman.

"You're looking at her like she's the birthday cake," my brother pokes, pulling me out of my lustful thoughts.

Because she is, I think but don't say. He doesn't need to know I'll have her later. "She's happy. That makes me happy."

"Our girl is all over the news lately. Should I be concerned?"

My eyes shift from the dance floor to him. "You need to work on getting your own girl. But no, she's safe with me."

He smiles smugly. "Once you settle down and start a family, that'll take the pressure off me."

I narrow my eyes at Marcus, who is always meddling. I can't wait for the tides to turn. He was right about one thing, though—letting go of the residual memories left behind by Justine allowed me to breathe again.

Kennedy is my air. She and I are in sync. We've discussed building a life together. I plan to leave the field to focus on developing new security technology. Her latest role leading RE's biotechnology research and development wing allows for more free time and relieves her from the lecture circuit. Together, we can do the things we'd been putting off—building a life with the one you love.

"You really should consider settling down."

My brother shakes his head. "I'll live vicariously through you for now. Speaking of which, I'm going to have a birthday dance with the ladies."

The song changes to *Nasty* by Tinashe as my brother, smooth as ever, works his way to the dance floor.

Dax and Lucien approach me.

"You still look like a killer," Lucien says.

A smirk tugs at my lips. "I am."

The last time we discussed women, none of us were sure we'd ever settle down. I was confident I'd be the last man standing. Then I got the call that changed everything. That seems like a lifetime ago.

Dax pats me on the shoulder. "Anyone who looks at her for longer than two seconds is dead."

Stepping back, Lucien raises his hands as if surrendering. "Well, okay. Damn."

"It's not that bad," I say, tipping my head toward the dance floor. "My brother's still alive." I pause before adding, "For now. I'm going to get my woman. What about you, Doc?" We bump fists and head to the dance floor.

The song shifts again. This time, the DJ slows it down with Kendrick Lamar and SZA's *Luther*.

My brother shakes his head, smiles knowingly, and walks away as I step in and wrap an arm around Kennedy's waist. I smile at her. The warmth of her body against mine, making it hard to focus, is a constant with her.

"Having fun?" I ask.

"Yeah, I haven't partied like this since...I can't remember when," she replies, snuggling into me.

"How's your ankle holding up?"

She wrinkles her nose and replies, "That's another story."

"Kenni."

She tries to play it off. "It's okay." But it's not okay. I take her hand and guide her off the dance floor. She tugs at my hand, and I already know what's coming. "Hold on. What do I get out of leaving the dance floor?" She smirks, making me want to kiss it off.

"To wear heels for more than thirty minutes." She gives me a frown that says, "you gotta do better than that," and I can't help but laugh. "Cake?" I suggest.

"Deal."

My woman.

We grab the cake and make our rounds, chatting with family on the way to a private lounge. Once we're alone, she sits on the couch. I sit beside her, placing her legs across my lap. Removing her flats, I massage her feet while she leans back, enjoying her cake. Soft groans escape her lips, whether from the massage or the cake, it doesn't matter. She's content. She's safe. She's mine.

"Did I tell you happy birthday?"

I smile inside, thinking about all the times she did. "This morning beneath me. In the shower. At breakfast. When I had you for lunch—"

She cuts me off. "Okay, I guess I did a few times. Happy birthday, honey."

"Thanks, beautiful, I love you."

I set the cake on the table, pull her close, and kiss her passionately. It's messy and wet, the kind of kiss I usually give her when we're at home. I've come to realize that home is in her arms.

When I break the kiss, she pants, "I love you too."

Love. I used to think love came with conditions.

Justine had taught me that. She seemed to love me—but only in the way that suited her, in the way that didn't inconvenience her life or defy her father's expectations. She wanted a version of me that didn't exist. A safer Troy. A man who could sit in a suit and play house, who could be predictable, reliable in a way that meant she never had to worry. But that's not who I am. And in the end, she chose security over me.

I've made my peace with it. I tricked myself into believing I wasn't built for love, not in the way people wanted. My job became my life—the rush, the discipline, the risk. I accepted that it would never be enough for someone who needed more.

And then Dr. Kennedy Green came crashing into my world.

I hadn't planned for her, hadn't expected the way she would unravel me with her mind and her stubbornness, the way she'd push back when I tried to keep her at arm's length. She is so damn brilliant, so fiercely dedicated to her work, but she never uses it as a shield. She let herself care. She let herself need me. And she didn't try to change me.

Kennedy sees all of me—the protector, the soldier, the man who has spent years burying his heart beneath steel and discipline. And she doesn't ask me to be anything but hers.

That's the difference.

Justine wanted the idea of love. Kennedy *is* love.

I cup her face and kiss her cheek, inhaling her essence. I love her with every breath—the woman who has upended my world, who has turned my solitude into something unbearable because I crave her presence more than I crave my own space.

My woman. She isn't a choice. She isn't a risk. She is the one thing I know with absolute certainty. And I can't live without her.

I reach for the ring in my pocket, the weight of it grounding me.

For the first time in my life, the future isn't a question. It's a promise.

And I'm was ready to make it.

Chapter 42

He's the One

"The purpose of life is to live it, to taste experience to the utmost, to reach out eagerly and without fear for newer and richer experience."
– Eleanor Roosevelt

Kennedy

The way Troy kisses me, like I'm giving him life, leaves me breathless. Breaking the kiss, he trails his nose along my cheek, making me weak. I'm seconds away from hiking my dress and riding him. It felt like it took forever, but I'm so glad I finally found him.

I've spent my whole life chasing answers—breaking down molecules, mapping out the invisible threads that bind the universe together. But for all my research, all the late nights spent hunched over data, I never expected the biggest discovery of my life wouldn't be on my laptop or in a lab. It's here, in the quiet moments when Troy looks at me like I'm not just a project to be solved but someone worth protecting, worth loving.

Tonight, watching him celebrate with family and friends gives me an even deeper insight into the man behind the steel—the man who captured my heart with a flicker in his eye. Maybe life isn't about equations or control. Maybe it's about the people who stand by you when everything else falls apart—the ones who see past the walls you build and stay anyway. Like all those celebrating with us tonight. I've been searching for meaning in all the wrong places, and it turns out, it's been right here, in the way his hand fits perfectly in mine, steady and sure, grounding me in a way I never knew I needed. The one who cares. The one who sees me. The one who once promised we'd figure this out...together. And we did. He's the one.

Troy.

I press my nose to his. His breath caresses my skin as his desire thickens beneath me. I want to go home. I want him in me. I want to scream his name while I fall apart beneath him. He shifts, reaching into his pocket; I eye him curiously as he pulls out a black leather box.

"Troy?" I cover my mouth, my breath hitching as he opens the box. Light refracts off the surface of the massive diamond, scattering shards of fire that dance across every surface. "It's beautiful."

"Kenni, I had planned to give this to you when we were at home. Then it struck me that wherever I am, as long as you're there, I am home. I told you once that I broke every rule to be with you, and I'd do it all again to see the sparkle in your eye when I hold you and tell you I love you. I meant it when I said you made my life better by simply being there. You brought life to my soul, broke through my tough exterior, reached in, squeezed my heart, and now it beats only for you. You, Kennedy Green, made me whole. From the beginning, my job was to protect you. I always said I would die for you—the truth is, I can't live without you. I love you. Will you marry me?"

With my mouth hanging open and tears streaming down my cheek, I nod vigorously and manage to say, "I will."

Then my man slides the brilliant solitaire diamond ring on my finger before crashing his lips to mine.

I spent my career searching for the meaning of life, never expecting to find something that transcends it. That's exactly what I found in Troy. He is everything and the only thing I need.

Chapter 43

Never Gonna Let You Go

"Love knows not its own depth until the hour of separation."
– Khalil Gibran, *The Prophet*

Kennedy

"Get away from me."

My scream rips through the silence, yanking me out of the nightmare. My eyes snap open, heart pounding against my ribs like it's trying to escape. Darkness presses in from all sides, thick and disorienting.

It's not real.

I repeat the words like a mantra, but the dread clings to me, sticky and suffocating. My breath comes in shallow bursts as the fragments of the dream claw their way back. Ford—his face twisted with anger—was trying to rip the engagement ring off my finger. The ring Troy gave me last night at the party. But Ford's gone. Dead.

Even from the grave, he's still trying to control me.

I squeeze my eyes shut, forcing the images away. The bed shifts beneath me, and the steady warmth of Troy's body beside mine envelops me. His breathing anchors me, pulling me back from the edge. I flex my hand in the darkness, searching for the reassuring weight of the ring—it's not there.

My pulse spikes, recalling the dream. I remember that I took it off before bed, but its absence feels like the moment Troy's hand leaves mine—empty. I need to see it. Touch it. Remind myself that last night was real.

I shift carefully, stretching my arm across Troy's broad chest, reaching for the dresser. But it's too far, and I end up half on top of him. His hand shoots out, strong fingers curling around my wrist.

"What are you doing, beautiful?" His voice is rough with sleep, but there's an edge of concern beneath it.

"My ring," I whisper, the words like dry cornbread stuck in my throat.

He doesn't hesitate. "I got it."

Troy reaches over, and I cling to him as he retrieves the ring. I can't see it, but I feel its weight as he slides it onto my finger, his thumb lingering against my skin.

"There," he whispers, pressing a soft kiss to my fingers. "It's not going anywhere."

The warmth of his touch seeps into me, easing the residual chill of the nightmare. I press my palm against his chest, feeling the steady beat of his heart beneath my hand.

Sensing my mood, he turns to his side, facing me and pulling me close. His hand presses into my hip, conforming my body to his. "Something's bothering you. You want to talk about it?"

No. I don't want to dwell on dead people. I want to move on with my life. Do all the things I've put off for far too long. Most of all, I want my man. I shake my head. "I want you."

That's all it takes. My man dips his head, parts my lips with his tongue, and kisses me with such passion, for a moment, I can't remember which house we're in. When he reaches between us to test if I'm ready for him, I know exactly what he finds, because he doesn't hesitate to lift my leg over his shoulder and fill me. And when he does, I'm in heaven on earth feeling his love.

No, Ford can't touch me anymore. But Troy...Troy is here, and I'm not letting him go.

***

One hour. That's the maximum amount of time Troy will be gone. I wanted to go with him, but he assured me it wouldn't take long. *"Everything is ready for pickup,"* he said before kissing me and heading out the door. That was ten minutes ago.

I walk past the credenza, where crimson sand slips through the slender neck of the hourglass, each grain marking a moment I never thought I'd have. The sunlight spills through the windows, golden and warm like it knows something I don't. I pause, closing my eyes, letting the light settle over me. *He proposed.*

My hand flies to my mouth, trying to stifle the scream bubbling in my chest—but it bursts out anyway, raw and real, echoing through the quiet house. I glance at my hand, the ring catching the morning light, scattering reflections across the walls like tiny fireworks. *My man wants to marry me.*

The thought blooms in my chest, wild and unstoppable.

After I finally calm down, I make a late breakfast—fried egg on toast and creamy slices of avocado laid carefully on top. I smile at myself at how his eating habits have rubbed off on me. The kitchen smells like home, something I never expected this mountain house to be. Plate in hand, I step onto the patio, the crisp air brushing against my skin, grounding me. As I sit I jot down a quick list of things to prep before our families arrive. I can't wait for Mom to see this place. She's going to love the view, the quiet.

My phone buzzes and Tanya's name flashes on the screen.

"Hi, Tanya," I answer, already smiling. "How are you?"

"I was just about to ask you the same thing."

I laugh softly, still elated. "I'm great."

"Congratulations on the engagement." Her voice is warm like she's been holding on to the words, waiting to call. "I just wanted to see if you need me to bring anything."

"No, just you and Maurice. Everything we need is on the way."

She's quiet for a beat before she says softly, "I'm so glad you two found each other."

"So am I. I love Troy."

"You know, sweetie," she continues, her voice thick with something deeper, "the second I saw you, I knew. I've never seen my son look at anyone the way he looks at you."

A lump forms in my throat, unexpected and sweet. "Everything about this feels right." *We are right.*

"Would you mind if I helped with the wedding planning? Only if you and your mom are okay with it, of course."

"Absolutely." I flex my fingers, glancing at my ring again, my heart dancing. "We haven't set a date yet—"

In the background, I hear Maurice call her name. Whatever he's doing causes her to laugh. "That's fine. I just want to help where I can. We have plenty of time to talk about it. I'll see you soon."

We say our goodbyes, and when the call ends, I sit for a moment, the weight of her words lingering. I can tell this means a lot to her. There's a story there—I'm sure of it. And I'll learn it, just like I've learned everything else about Troy. *Piece by piece.*

I love his parents. In so many ways, they remind me of mine—loving, self-made, fiercely protective of their family. But where mine are subtle, his are more...vocal about wanting grandkids. I laugh to myself, picturing family mugs in my future. Marcus has no idea what he started.

Tanya's call pulls me into the past year like a current. I think about everything I've been through—the self-doubt after Ford, the crushing pressure to deliver the work I've been dreaming of my entire life, the ache in my ankle that reminds me daily of how fragile we are. But then I remember the day I walked into Rose's office and my eyes locked with Troy's.

Everything changed.

It's like when Herbie Hancock hit the wrong note, and Miles Davis followed it with the perfect one, turning a mistake into magic. "It's not the note you play that's the wrong note," Miles said. "It's the note you play afterward that makes it right or wrong."

Troy is my *right* note.

He never made me doubt myself. He lifted me when I faltered. When I was injured, he didn't just offer help—he *planned* it, made sure I had everything I needed to heal, to focus, to thrive. He's been the steady rhythm beneath the chaos, the melody that made it all make sense.

I look at the ring again, light flickering across its surface, and my heart swells. I love him.

Troy. Sitting here, taking in the view, I get lost in the thoughts of my man. We tried to get all the loving we could in last night and early this morning, knowing we would have company later today. I feel him still—the soreness between my thighs. The strength in his arms as he hugged me goodbye. The look in his eyes before he left—like he didn't want to leave me. It's all there.

"I love you so much," I call to the wind, hoping my voice will reach him. A small breeze brushes my cheek. Instead of comfort, a chill runs down my spine.

My phone buzzes.

Dax.

I answer immediately. "Dax, don't tell me—you and Sasha, are running late."

"Kennedy, there's been an accident."

CHAPTER 44

Without Words

"Love is composed of a single soul inhabiting two bodies."
– Aristotle

Troy

THE SKY IS CLEAR. Perfect for flying. The sun bounces off the rotor blades as I guide the chopper toward the city. Yeah…it's another beautiful day in California—made even more so by waking up to my beautiful woman. This will be a quick trip—grab some supplies, get back to Kennedy, and plan the party. *Our* party. *Hell*, I still can't believe she said yes. I glance down at my finger where soon I'll be wearing a ring. The weight of that promise settles in my chest. She's mine now. For good.

I barely have time to register the glint of metal in my periphery before it's on me. *Bam!*

The sound is deafening, like a sledgehammer slamming into the side of my craft. The entire helicopter shudders, tilting hard to the left. My instincts kick in. Things seem to move in slow motion. As my hands tighten on the controls, trying to steady her, the instrument panel screams at me—altitude dropping fast. *Shit. Shit.*

I fight against the spin, my heart pounding in my throat. There's no time to think about what the hell hit me. A drone? Something else? Doesn't matter. I've got seconds to put this thing down without dying. I have too much to live for. The ground rushes up too fast, trees blurring

250

past the windshield. I spot a clearing—a narrow strip of dirt between the oaks—and pray it's enough. *Hold on, Troy. Set this baby down. Nice and easy.*

My landing is messy. The skids catch the edge of the clearing, jerking the chopper sideways. Metal groans, glass shatters, and my shoulder slams into the doorframe as I skid to a stop. Silence.

A cloud of dirt swirls around my craft before settling. My pulse roars in my ears louder than the crash. I sit there for a second, dazed, breathing hard, tasting copper in my mouth. I flex my hands—still attached. Good. I glance down and—*fuck*—there's a deep gash on my forearm. Blood runs hot and fast, staining my sleeve crimson. But I'm alive.

Kennedy. The thought slices through the fog, sharper than the pain. *She's alone.* Dealing with this mess will take hours. I need to know she's safe. I fumble for my phone with my good hand, fingers slick with blood. The screen's cracked, but it works. "Call Dax," I say, issuing a voice command.

He answers immediately. "Boss?"

"I need you at the mountain house. Now." My voice is hoarse, tight. "Something happened. A drone hit me mid-flight."

"Jesus. You okay?"

"Need to get stitched. Meet at the hospital. Kennedy first. I don't want her alone. Get her, now."

"Copy that."

I hang up before he can ask more questions. The adrenaline's wearing off, and the pain's settling in like a knife to my nerves. Ripping the rest of my sleeve, I press it against the gash, teeth gritted, and radio for emergency evac. I don't like the idea of being grounded, but I'm no use to Kennedy if I bleed out.

By the time I reach the hospital, my arm is a throbbing mess. A nurse cleans me up and numbs my arm while asking me questions, but my mind's elsewhere—*on her*. I need to see Kennedy to know she's safe. Moments later, Marcus walks in.

"Man, what happened out there?" His voice is steady as he washes and gloves his hands before stitching me up.

"Someone being careless."

"Drone?" In his career, he's seen this a thousand times—different person—different story.

"Likely."

"Tell me someone has eyes on our girl."

Before I get a chance to respond, the door creaks open, and I don't even have to look up to know it's her. Her steps are soft, hesitant, but I'd know that scent—lavender, honey, and something uniquely her—anywhere.

"Troy?"

She rushes to me, eyes wide, worry etched across her face. For a moment, the pain fades, replaced by something warmer, deeper. She's safe. She's here. My chest loosens, the knot of tension unraveling just enough.

I hold out my good arm to her, grabbing her around the waist. "Took a detour." My voice is rough, but seeing her, it's like breathing again. "Miss me?"

"That's not funny." She pats me on my thigh.

"Ouch."

"Oh my god—," she screams. But before she can say more, my brother shakes his head.

"Troy," he warns. "There's nothing wrong with his leg. Aside from this cut, he's fine. He might need ibuprofen once the anesthetic wears off and stiffness sets in from the accident, but he'll be fine."

I pull Kennedy closer, pushing the crash from my mind. It could have been worse. "I didn't mean to scare you." I rest my head against hers. "Looks like we'll be in the city for a few days until I can get the craft replaced."

"Forget about it. We can always host another time. I'm just glad you're safe." She palms my cheek, checking me.

"Kennedy, I assure you, my brother is fine. He's been through much worse." Marcus stands, touches my shoulder, and smirks before saying, "Take it easy tonight. I don't want to have to redo those." He tips his head. "Kennedy, congratulations again. Get this guy to sit still for a couple of days. The nurse will provide you with a package of everything you need to dress that," he says before leaving.

I dip my head and kiss my woman. Her love permeates my soul. All I can think is I'm glad she's here.

Breaking the kiss, I smile at her because I know it's one of her favorite things. "Kenni," my voice is low, just above a whisper. "I don't want to wait."

I don't have to say more. She nods, understanding everything unspoken between us, proving...we are one.

CHAPTER 45

The Ties that Bind

"In family life, love is the oil that eases friction, the cement that binds closer together, and the music that brings harmony."
– Friedrich Nietzsche

Troy

"W E GOTTA GO BACK out there," Kennedy whispers against my lips. Arms wrapped tightly around my neck, she makes no effort to untangle herself from me to rejoin our family on the patio.

I cup her hips, pressing her body into proof of my craving for her. "You should have thought about that before you gave me mouth-to-mouth." A smirk teases on my lips.

"Me?" She brushes her thumb across my lips, removing evidence of our kiss. "I was getting more champagne before you pulled me into you. Not that I'm complaining."

"Just checking to see if you're okay." Stepping back, I smooth her curls over her shoulders and look her up and down. "Yeah, still fine."

"Troy, you have me so ready—"

I jump in before she can finish. "How about you take out the champagne and say you have to come back and help me with something?" She pushes my pecs like that's going to do anything. I bark out a laugh.

"I'm gonna need at least an hour."

I adjust myself. "Come on. There'll be plenty of time for us once everyone leaves tomorrow."

This get-together was meant to happen. We'd delayed our engagement celebration long enough—three weeks. Long enough for my body to start healing, for us to catch our breath after that happened. But mostly, we needed time to find each other again—to remember what life feels like when we're not fighting for it.

My accident hit Kennedy hard. *Hell*, it wrecked both of us. The crash wasn't just bent metal and broken glass; it was a final punch after a year that wouldn't quit. We held up in the penthouse for two weeks after I got out of the hospital—no visitors, no phone calls—just us.

That first night, she curled into me like she was afraid I'd disappear if she let go. *"I just want to feel your heartbeat,"* she whispered. So that's how we slept—her ear pressed against my chest, her hand flat against my pecs like an anchor. My good arm wrapped around her, holding on just as tight.

And fuck, I was hard as a rock the whole damn night. Knowing she was there, feeling her breath against my skin—it wrecked me in a different way. But I didn't dare move. I wasn't about to break the fragile peace she'd found in that moment.

But the next morning? Yeah, Marcus wasn't wrong—I need to be careful. Nearly tore my stitches trying to get too close, too fast.

My woman.

I hold Kennedy's hand and lead her out to the patio.

As soon as we reach the lounge area where our families are seated, she lifts the bottle. "More champagne," she announces.

"We were just about to send Marcus in after you two," Kennedy's mom says.

It's nice to see how quickly our families have bonded. Everything about Kennedy and me feels like it was meant to be.

"I was beginning to think you were getting started on that family mom keeps talking about," Marcus blurts, and I narrow my eyes at him. He knows exactly what he's doing.

But I don't miss a beat. "So, Marcus, what are you waiting for?"

Kennedy sits, stretching her arm over the back of her dad's chair as if she's settling in for the show. She's seen this before.

"Since you mentioned it, why don't you two open your gift?" He points to a pile at the edge of the table. Kennedy searches for one from him.

She holds up a large, flat, square box. "This?" Marcus smiles smugly and nods, and I'm curious to discover what he's up to.

Everyone watches with bated breath as Kennedy tears the white paper with a repeating pattern of linked gold rings, revealing the box. She lifts the top and then pulls out two white T-shirts with black lettering on the front and an image on the back.

"Hold them up," my mom encourages.

She hands me one. I stand and hold it up while Kennedy does the same with the other. Everyone breaks into laughter when we flip them.

My T-shirt says, "In case you're wondering, yes, I have a brother." Kennedy's shirt reads "Yes, he has a brother." And on the back of each is a picture of Marcus. Beneath his image, it says, "The love doctor."

Marcus makes a shooing gesture. "Go on. Put them on. Start marketing for me."

I throw my T-shirt at him, but he ducks, and it misses. He's laughing so hard and loud that we all can't help but join in. I pull Kennedy close to me, and we stare at each other, our smiles so wide that my cheeks hurt.

This is it. This is what I've been chasing. Just like the day I met Kennedy, moments like this will remain with me for a lifetime. Precious moments. "Let me tell you about that time when..." moments. They're the things that bring our family together: laughter, love, and living.

Epilogue

Life Saver

"We should never forget that God granted us the power to reason so that we would do His work here on Earth - so that we would use science to cure disease, and heal the sick, and save lives."
– Barack Obama

Troy

Six months later.

"Just in time."

Kennedy doesn't need to look over her shoulder to know I'm in the kitchen with her. Standing at the counter in powder blue lounge shorts and an oversized tee, she's intensely focused on her latest drink recipe—something citrusy by the scent hovering in the air.

I walk up behind her, cup her hips, pull her into me, and kiss my woman like I wasn't just buried in her two hours ago.

When I break the kiss, she's panting, and I'm ready for another round.

"What am I in time for?"

Her eyes are closed, and her words come out breathy when she says, "Olives."

Still in her haze, I lift her and sit her on the counter. "I don't want any olives. I want you," I say, lifting her shirt and latching my mouth on one of her breasts while palming the other.

Arched back, her hand on my head holding me in place, her breath hitches. "They're not for you. They're...for me." Still in her haze, she barely gets the words out.

I straighten, placing my hands on either side of her on the counter. "Olives," I repeat, locking eyes with her. "You don't eat olives."

She hesitates for a moment, fingers combing through my beard. "I do now."

"Since?"

"Since we decided we were going to start a family."

"Beautiful, are you serious? Are you—?

"Maybe."

A smile spreads across my face. We've been planning for this, and now—wow. I look around the counter. There's no alcohol to be found. She looks at me knowingly and rolls her eyes.

"Kenni, this is the best news." I pull her into me and kiss her hard. When I break the kiss, she bites her lips. "What's that look?" I ask.

"We still need to get confirmation."

"We will."

"And..." Here comes the inner monologue. "Can you promise not to threaten to kill anyone who comes near me?"

I bark out a laugh. "I can't agree to that."

"Just checking," she sings the words.

Lifting her, I set her back on her feet. She hands me a jar of olives to open. After opening it, I hand it back and say, "Kenni, beautiful, you're my world. I'll be with you every step of the way. Appointments, everything. I love you."

My phone buzzes. *Marcus.* I swear, ever since Kennedy and I got married, I've talked to him every week. He wasn't lying when he said he was going to live vicariously through me. I think he secretly wants to settle down; he's just not saying it.

I palm Kennedy's hip. She smiles and says, "I love you, too. Take your call."

Nodding, I answer and walk into the living room.

"Marcus, what's up?" I put in my earphones and stretch my arms across the back of the couch.

"Hey man, how's my family?"

"Kenni and I are doing great. You should be working on your family, too."

"That's what I'm calling about."

"What? You finally found a woman?"

"Not that part. But I just got a big-time medical award. There's a celebration in two months."

"Congratulations. What's that got to do with me? You need security? I can assign Dax or Lucien."

"No. I don't need security. Besides inviting you and Kenni, I was wondering if she could set me up with a friend to be my plus one for the event."

Caught off guard, I laugh so hard that Kenni peeks around the corner at me. "Sorry man, I didn't expect that. You don't want to take any women from the hospital?"

"We've talked about this already. I don't date the staff."

"I'll talk to Kenni, but don't get your hopes up. You really should consider asking someone you know. I'm sure after all these years you've had your eye on someone."

"Man, just let me know what she says."

"Sure. Is that it?"

"Just waiting for my nieces and nephews to arrive."

"Get off the phone."

"Later," he says, and I end the call. If I want any privacy, I might have to help find him a woman. I shake my head at the thought of my brother settling down.

Kennedy walks in with a plate of snacks. She sets them on the coffee table and then sits astride me. "You giving your brother a hard time?" she asks, smoothing her hands along my arms.

"Believe it or not, he wants you to hook him up with somebody. He's getting an award and needs a date."

"For real?"

"Yeah."

"I don't know...everybody in my circle is nerdy like me."

I grip her hips and pull her against me so she feels what she does to me. "You're the sexiest, fieriest, and kindest nerd I know. By nerd, I mean blow-my-mind brilliant."

"Thanks, handsome." She kisses me and then adds, "Your brother's sweet, but he's a prankster. He needs someone who can keep up with him."

"Well, we have a few months before his event."

"Before we were interrupted, I was going to tell you that Sasha and I will be working together again. It's all still confidential, but we're tackling eradicating certain diseases based on the work I completed."

"Saving lives."

"If we can."

She can and she will. *This is it.* Everything is coming together.

Driven by a single incident many years ago, I've spent my entire career protecting people. Keeping them safe. Saving lives when I could. It's the only thing I've ever been good at, the only thing that's ever made sense. But this—*her*—this is different.

Kennedy isn't just another person I've sworn to protect. She's *my* person. The woman I'd die for. The woman I've already risked everything for. And now, because she's still here—because I kept her safe—she's going to save so many more.

It hits me like a punch to the chest. Every mission I've ever taken, every life I've ever shielded, it all led to *this moment*. To *her*.

I pull her close, my hands steady even though my heart is anything but. "Baby, this is so beautiful. I'm so proud of you." The words aren't enough, but they're all I have.

She looks at me, and I see it—the fire, the brilliance, the unstoppable force that is Kennedy Green. She doesn't need me to save her. But I did. And because of that, the world gets to keep her.

And God help anyone who ever tries to take her from me again.

THE END.

Thank you

Thank you for reading *Troy*! If you enjoyed this story, I'd love for you to share your thoughts by leaving a review on Amazon, Goodreads, or your favorite book platform. Your support means the world and helps other readers discover the book?

If you'd like to see more of Troy, you can revisit where it all began in *30 Days in Belfast* or catch him in *Taming a King*. Excerpts from both books are included for you to enjoy.

Thank you again for your support and for being part of this journey!

Excerpts

30 Days In Belfast

Just one distraction could lead to failure—several may spell ruin.

As the daughter of the wealthiest Black man in the country, Rose Ross struggles to make a name for herself as the COO of her father's tech company. She's even forced to let go of a promising relationship to focus on her career, but still cannot seem to escape her father's legacy. Rose fears that if she remains at Rick Ross Enterprises, she will never rise above the vast shadow his name casts.

When her ailing friend reaches out to her for help, Rose doesn't hesitate. She has just thirty days to curate the most important charity art exhibition in Europe and break into a field she is truly passionate about. However, just before she leaves for her flight to Belfast, her father informs her that she has only three weeks to decide whether she will succeed him as CEO.

With her concentration already split between one life-altering decision, Rose is stunned when she meets her friend's handsome and overprotective brothers. Right away, she recognizes an undeniable, yet different, attraction to both.

Her mind in turmoil, Rose's focus is now fractured among love and business. If she cannot make a decision—or if she makes the wrong one—she will lose everything she has worked for and, perhaps, more.

30 Days In Belfast *is a standalone contemporary romance.*

Excerpt

30 Days In Belfast

PROLOGUE

We Have Time

"If you love somebody, let them go, for if they return, they were always yours.
If they don't, they never were."
– Kahlil Gibran, *A Tear and a Smile*

"I'll race ya," Shannon called as she ran past Rose toward the foam remnants of a forgotten wave on the shoreline.

Rose stopped scribing her initials in the sand heart drawing, a covert confession of love to her celebrity crush. She jumped up and headed toward the water. "Wait for me," she shouted to Shannon, who didn't see her. The glare from the sun dancing on the waves mimicking a million miniature mirrors distorted her view. Rose chased a wave and jumped in the water, pushing through the powerful current. When it subsided slightly, she popped up. "Shannon!" she called over the waves, but didn't see her friend. Rose continued to push through the currents, shoving the waves back with her arms, which were growing sore by the minute. With each breath she took, she became more panicked, still unable to spot her friend.

Rose looked toward the shore to see if Shannon had made it back. "Shannon, where—" Rose called out before being sucked under by the current. Before it all became a faded memory.

Fifteen years later, the aftermath was fuzzy in her head. She remembered eventually getting herself to shore. The shock and overwhelming sense of loss she felt when she realized Shannon was not by her side finally came into focus as people crowded around her in the sand. An endless stream of questions rushed through her. The sudden end of a forever friendship stolen by sun, sand, and sneaker waves. Rose felt her face grow warm as memories of Shannon flooded her mind. Her heart started to race. Panic washed over her as she relived the day her friend died. All she wanted to do now was run.

"Rose, talk to me. I know it feels like it came out of left field. Tell me what you're thinking." The sound of Alejandro's voice sitting across the table pulled her out of her head. He was staring at her with a mix of concern and longing in his eyes. Shelved was the swoon-worthy smile that usually greeted her. The smile that made her melt after spending weeks away from her man. He reached his hand across the table.

Rose averted Alejandro's gaze and looked around his London flat, where they had just spent the last three evenings wrapped in each other's arms. Where they had made love for hours until they were both sore, satiated, and spent. Where they had shared rare stolen moments between their busy schedules. She was the one who convinced him to get the flat since he spent so much time traveling between New York and London. He was busy building his career as an international attorney, and Rose was recently promoted to COO. A reward for endless hours helping her father build his business and developing new technologies to innovate the company. Living on the West Coast, paired with the busy travel schedule that came with her new position, meant they spent more time on video calls than in person.

Rose focused her attention on the modern, muted earth tones of the room. Her eyes were drawn to a painting she commissioned: A Black woman with a crown of flowers blooming from her head and partially covering her face. Rose remembered posing for the portrait with her chin turned toward her bare shoulder. "Think about your man," the artist had instructed her.

Now, she was sitting across the table from the man she thought she could build a life with. His words washed across her, pulling her down like the sneaker wave that snatched her childhood friend from her life forever. Stirring within her was the same sense of shock and sudden loss.

Rose sucked in a breath. "You sure about this?" she said, sounding as if negotiating a business deal—placing a wall around her heart and tamping the need to reach across the table to take his hand.

"No. But I do know we're both committed to our work. The time in between when we finally get together keeps growing. I'm torn between you and the job, and I don't want to ask you to bend for me. I respect that you're building your career, too. I want to make it work, but I can't see a way. You just got promoted and want to make a name for yourself away from your father's shadow. That's a tall order, and I'll use all my resources to support you in that effort. But trying to build something more between us is no small feat. Think about it. How many things did you and I have to shift to get these three nights together?"

"Quite a bit," she answered, hesitant to strengthen his argument.

"That's exactly the point. You and I know that you had to rearrange twice as much as me. I won't continue asking you to do that. Your father is my largest client. I know the demand he puts on me. I can only imagine how exponentially higher that is on you. I care about you, but I won't be the one to stifle your success. Let's take a step back and focus. Let's give ourselves a year." Alejandro leaned back in his chair and ran his hands through his hair.

Rose knew he was rethinking his words. But they were out, weighing heavy between them.

Was he right? Should they take a break, allowing time to establish them-selves? Could they walk away and get back when the time was right? Would it ever be right?

The idea of them not being a couple made Rose feel like she did when she lost her best friend. The same emotions flowed through her all over again. She paused to think, unaware of what was keeping her from ending the conversation, putting her foot down, and refusing his suggestion.

Rose closed her eyes, inhaled, and opened them. Alejandro's gaze was still locked on her. "This isn't about something else. Or is it? You—" she started.

Alejandro stood, rounded the table, and pulled Rose to her feet and into a tight embrace. He planted kisses all over her face before touching his forehead to hers.

"Oh, Rose. Don't ever think that. I...I'd be hard-pressed to believe I could be with anyone other than you. You are the center of my universe, but I know I'm not yours. This is me setting you free—giving you time to do what you need to do. To be you without me interfering."

Rose listened intently, her breath becoming synchronized with his.

"I'm not saying it's just about you," he continued. "I also need to figure out why I haven't moved heaven and earth to be by your side. And for that, I'm at fault." Alejandro swallowed, then turned to look out the window. Rose held onto his hand, walked up behind him, and pressed her chin to his back.

"Okay." Rose paused. "We'll give it some time."

30 Days In Belfast

Copyright © 2023 Rita A. Gordon

Excerpt

Taming a King

She was born to rule his heart. He was sworn to protect hers.

In a world where fairy tales are nothing but broken promises, June Ross has learned to trust no one but herself. Scarred by a traumatic childhood event, she's built her life on the ironclad belief that love is a dangerous illusion and guards her heart with walls so high that even she can't see over them. But when a deadly threat from the past resurfaces, she finds herself under the protection of Aedan King, a hardened bodyguard with his own battle-worn past. Trained to take a bullet without flinching, Aedan never expected to be blindsided by the one mission he can't walk away from: breaking through June's defenses and convincing her that true love isn't a fairy tale—it's the most perilous adventure of all. With danger closing in, June must decide whether she's willing to trust someone else to protect her for the first time in her life, or if she'll let fear keep her from the only man willing to risk everything—even his life—for her.

Taming a King is a standalone, bodyguard, contemporary romance.

Excerpt

Taming a King

PROLOGUE

Fairy Tales

"We delight in the beauty of the butterfly, but rarely admit the changes it has gone through to achieve that beauty."
– Maya Angelou

June

I stopped believing in fairytales years ago. Long before my first kiss, I learned there is no such thing as a knight in shining armor. Before my first sexual encounter, I realized real princes don't exist. Years before my first heartbreak, I concluded that I'd never sit beside a king. Staring down the barrel of a gun, I learned that the only person coming to my rescue...was me.

Exhausted, I close my eyes.

The sun streams brightly through the shop windows, warming my face. I'm seduced by the soft lull of diners' voices surrounding me. Briefly, I glance at my watch and then turn to observe the patrons. Smiling faces, chopsticks in hand, conversations between bites—it all feels surreal. Though I'm in a restaurant, there is no scent hovering in the air hinting at the deliciousness awaiting me. That's how it is in Japanese restaurants—clean, calm, aesthetically pleasing, unsurprisingly good.

The warmth from the sun is suddenly gone, replaced by a shadow suspended above me. I turn, expecting familiar faces, but find the devil cloaked in a black hoodie instead. Before I can scream, a heavily tattooed hand clasps my neck and the touch of a cold steel blade converges with my cheek.

"Don't say a word," the deep raspy voice says.

I don't know if he actually says the words or whether they are a figment of my mind, forged from fear. Just as quickly as he appears, he's gone. The sound of a pop followed by the clunk of something collapsing captures my attention. I turn toward the sound; the walls are splattered with what I pray is sauce and the sound of a siren in my head overtakes me. *What's happening?* I can't stop the noise that sounds like the scream of electricity cutting through the silence when you're trying to sleep, only louder.

"No," I scream.

Mom?

Taming a King

Copyright © 2024 Rita A. Gordon

Drink Recipes

Lucious Lemon Drop

Recipe information

Total Time 5 minutes | **Yield** 1 serving

Ingredients

2 oz. Vodka

1.5 oz. Triple sec

1 oz. fresh lemon juice (from 1 medium lemon)

3/4 oz. simple syrup

Ice

Lemon slice or peel (for serving)

Sugar (to rim glass)

Preparation

Wet the rim of a cocktail glass with a lemon slice. Next, dip the glass upside down into a small plate of sugar until the rim is fully coated. In a cocktail shaker, squeeze the juice of one medium lemon. Add vodka, triple sec, simple syrup, and ice. Close the lid and shake until the container feels cold. Open the lid and pour the strained mixture into the glass. Garnish with a fresh twist of lemon peel or a lemon slice. Serve chilled.

Blueberry Bliss

Recipe information
    Total Time 5 minutes | **Yield** 1 serving
    Ingredients
1 oz. Vodka
1/2 oz. fresh lemon juice (from 1 medium lemon)
1/4 oz. simple syrup
Approx. 20 fresh blueberries
Ice
Lemon slice or peel (for serving)
Sugar (to rim glass)
Preparation

Moisten the rim of a cocktail glass with a lemon slice. Next, dip the glass upside down into a small plate of sugar until the rim is fully coated. Slice the blueberries in half, place them into the cocktail shaker, and muddle them. Add vodka, simple syrup, and ice, then shake until the container feels cold. Open the lid and pour the strained mixture into the glass. Garnish with a fresh twist of lemon peel or a lemon slice. Serve chilled.

Pure Pear

Recipe Information

Total Time 5 minutes | **Yield** 1 serving

Ingredients

1 medium-sized pear (soft or over-ripened)

1 oz. Bison Vodka (or Grey Goose or vodka of choice)

1/2 oz. fresh lemon juice (from 1 medium lemon)

3/4 oz. simple syrup

Ice

Lemon slice or peel (for serving)

Sugar (to rim glass)

Preparation

Moisten the rim of a cocktail glass with a slice of lemon. Next, dip the glass upside down into a small plate of sugar until the rim is fully coated. Peel and slice one pear, placing the slices into the cocktail shaker and muddle them. Add vodka, lemon juice, simple syrup, and ice, then shake until the shaker feels cold. Open the lid and pour the strained mixture into the glass. Garnish with a fresh twist of lemon peel or a lemon slice. Serve chilled.

Strawberry Blitzer / Blueberry Blitzer

Recipe Information

Total Time 5 minutes | **Yield** 1 serving

Ingredients

5 Fresh Strawberries (or 20 Blueberries for a Blueberry Blitz)

3 oz. Champagne (for non-alcoholic, substitute with ginger ale)

1/2 oz. fresh lemon juice (from 1 medium lemon)

3/4 oz. simple syrup

Ice

Sprig of fresh rosemary (for serving)

Sugar (to rim glass)

Preparation

Moisten the rim of a cocktail glass with a slice of lemon. Then, dip the glass upside down into a small plate of sugar until the rim is completely coated. Slice fresh strawberries (or blueberries depending on drink), place the slices into the cocktail shaker, and muddle them. Add lemon juice, simple syrup, and ice, then shake until the shaker feels cold. Open the lid and pour the strained mixture into the glass. Top with champagne. Garnish with fresh rosemary. Serve chilled.

Purple Haze

Recipe Information
Total Time 1 minutes | **Yield** 1 serving
Ingredients
3 oz. Champagne (for non-alcoholic, substitute with ginger ale)
1/4 oz. Ube syrup
Lemon slice or peel (for serving)
Sugar (to rim glass)
Preparation
Wet the rim of a cocktail glass with a slice of lemon. Next, turn the glass upside down and dip it into a small plate of sugar until the rim is fully coated. Pour a quarter ounce of ube syrup into the glass and top it off with your favorite champagne. Finish with a fresh lemon twist (peel) or a lemon slice as garnish.

Playlist

The Journey // Brian Culbertson
Bridge Over the Stars // Keiko Matsui
Venice // Chris Boti
'Round Midnight // Miles Davis
Europa // Gato Barbieri
Girl in the Red Dress // Gregg Karukus
luther // Kendrick Lamar & SZA
Pandora: **https://pandora.app.link/rl5a1MsCCQb**
Apple Music: **https://apple.co/3CuHVGA**
ritaagordon.com

Acknowledgments

Writing Troy's story was both a challenge and a revelation. Though purely fictional, the subject matter coincidentally aligns with real-world events in ways I never anticipated, making this book particularly meaningful for me.

A heartfelt thank you to Cassandra—your sharp editing skills and keen insights continue to push me to grow as a writer. I learn something new from you with every project. To Dr. Gould, your expertise and guidance on the medical content were invaluable. Your willingness to share your knowledge helped bring authenticity to this story, and I truly appreciate it. To my readers—your enthusiasm, support, and love for my characters keep me going. Thank you for coming on this journey with me.

And finally, to my big sister. You were the first to see Troy's potential, long before I did. Your patience, encouragement, and belief in this story from the very beginning mean more than I can say. I'm so glad I finally got to bring his story to life. Thank you!

Love you all,

Rita

About The Author

Photo by Abigail Huller

Rita Gordon is an indie author and former corporate baddie who writes Black and interracial romance stories where love triumphs. As an emerging voice in the contemporary romance genre, she brings a fresh perspective to story telling. Inspired by the power of love and the beauty of cultural exploration, her writing captures the essence of human emotions, leaving readers spellbound with each page turn. When she's not busy tackling her TBRs and writing, she creates intricate floral illustrations for her coloring books, combining her love for detail and storytelling, travels the world, drawing inspiration from diverse cultures, and volunteers in her community.

To learn more about the author, visit **ritaagordon.com**.

Connect With Rita

Stay in touch! You can find Rita here:
SUBSCRIBE TO HER NEWSLETTER:
https://www.ritaagordon.com/subscribe-page
FOLLOW RITA ON:
Facebook | Tomebooks: authorritagordon
YouTube: @AuthorRitaGordon
Bluesky: @authorritagordon.bsky.social
Instagram | Pinterest | X: @rgordonshaw
TikTok: @authorritagordon (ritagordonwrites)
Goodreads:
https://www.goodreads.com/author/show/21524163.Rita_A_Gordon
ritaagordon.com